SILENCE

Isaac Jordan Myers, II

Writers Club Press

San Jose New York Lincoln Shanghai

SILENCE

Published by Writers Club Press
an imprint of iUniverse.com, Inc.

For information address:
iUniverse.com, Inc.
620 North 48th Street
Suite 201
Lincoln, NE 68504-3467
www.iuniverse.com

ISBN: 0-595-00527-6

Printed in the United States of America

I dedicate this book to my beloved mother.
I miss you. Thanks for giving me the knowledge of life.
This has made me what I am today.
You will always be with me.

Acknowledgements

I would like to thank my daughter, Shamika, who helped me develop the characters Sarah and Ganeli.

Special thanks to my wife, JoAnn.
Your encouragement has meant so much.

To the rest of my kids, Shivaughn, Jordan and Joseph
Thanks for the quiet moments and sharing your time with the book.

Thanks to the Pizarros, Furays, Carrolls, Balchans, Tracy, Sherry, Benja, Utrice and the rest of my friends and family who supported me through this project.

Thanks to all the professionals who helped me understand their careers: Springfield, Ohio, Police Officers and Realtor David Winebrenner And special thanks to the Staff at Tavern On The Green, New York City.

Thanks to Candie Pemberton for her first edit and helping me put together our book club.

PROLOGUE

It was a late fall evening and Richard Manelli had just arrived at his home in a quiet suburb of Newark, New Jersey. As Manelli pulled into his garage, his car collided with the lawn mower. Ignoring the incident, he rushed into the house, dropped several papers, then headed toward the telephone.

"Hey, John, it's me—Manelli." Manelli tried to catch his breath.

"Manelli, where are you?"

"I just got home. I can talk now."

"Wait a minute, Manelli." John closed the door to his study. "I'm back, and Nick just walked in. Are you alright?"

"Yeah, but I wanted you to know something. I'm going to the police, and I'm not gonna pay Riggins another penny. I'm afraid someone will figure out what's going on," Manelli explained, while he poured himself a drink.

"Manelli, do you know what they're gonna do to you? Do you want to lose your bank and be locked up to boot? We can find another way to get Riggins off our backs; besides, I'm already working on something. One of my men has put together a list."

"What list?" Manelli asked.

"It's a list of all the investment bankers Riggins is bank-rolling. My guy is meeting with Sam Dunn, an upstate New York banker, who Riggins is putting the heat on."

"Upstate?" Manelli asked, baffled.

"Yes, Manelli, upstate; you heard me right! Riggins' scam has become bigger than you can imagine. Sam Dunn is an old friend who used to work on Wall Street with Riggins and me. Riggins has wiped him out financially, and the guy's broke. I had to send him money. He's ready to go to the Feds."

"I can't believe this! As if he hasn't siphoned enough from us New York bankers," Manelli paused as he finished his drink.

"That son-of-a-bitch is ruthless, Manelli. We never should have used our clients' money for his investments; I can't believe that I didn't see this coming."

"I hear you, John, but what are we gonna do?"

"Give me a day or so. When Ron gets back, we'll have enough support to bring that bastard down. I just need a day or two."

"I'm not sure, John. Riggins will never let us go. I've already given him millions, but he still wants more. After his visit to my office today, I….wait a minute, John, I think I heard something, hold on…" Manelli walked into the living room. He immediately noticed that the silk curtains on the front windows were billowing, and a plant was overturned on the floor. He walked toward the window, but had not traveled two feet when his stride was interrupted by a blow to his head.

He went down instantly. His dizziness was marred by the shadow of the intruder, who loomed over him and spoke in a hushed voice, "So, you plan to go to the police?"

"Who the hell are you?" Manelli asked, holding his head.

"I'm your Fairy Godmother, here to carry you away, compliments of Riggins."

"Riggins?" Manelli asked, as his body quivered, ready to piss his pants.

"Yes, you dumb shit! He knows what you're up to. I can't believe you would snitch on him." The intruder kicked Manelli in the gut.

As Manelli writhed and screamed in pain, he was silenced by another blow. Between kicks, he begged, "I'm not…I'll give you money! I'll give you anything…don't hurt me, I'm not going to turn anyone in."

"I don't want your money, you worthless piece of banker shit. Get up!" The intruder grabbed Manelli's hair and lifted him to his feet.

"What are you doing? For God's sake! Please!" Manelli cried out.

"Look into my eyes! Look into my eyes!" the intruder shouted as he wrenched Manelli's neck.

"For God's sake, no!" Manelli screamed as the intruder cocked his gun next to Manelli's head.

"Manelli? Manelli !" John yelled into the unanswered phone.

CHAPTER ONE

Katherine Mills did a celebratory dance around the halls of Harlem High School. Mrs. Cohen, her guidance counselor, had just given her the good news. Katherine had been chosen as the new clerical trainee with Walter and Vein, one of the largest investment firms in New York City. For weeks, Katherine had been crazy with anticipation. She had been a nervous wreck at the interview, stumbling over her words. All that fear turned out to be for nothing; for today the job was hers. She couldn't wait to get home and tell her father, Al, who, after all, was responsible for encouraging her to enter the Harlem High School Vocational Program two years before.

The timing of this good news could not have been more perfect. Katherine and Al needed the additional money. The real estate business had declined for Al. He had not sold a house in months, and he blamed his bad fortune on the Democrats' power in the White House. Nevertheless, in two weeks time Katherine would graduate from high school and begin her exciting career.

Al had sacrificed so much of his life for Katherine; being two parents in one since Katherine's mother, Sarah, died during childbirth. Katherine loved her father as much as any child could love a parent. They lived in a two-bedroom apartment in Upper Manhattan, close to Central Park. The twelfth-floor apartment provided a distant, yet beautiful view of the Park.

As Katherine exited the graffiti-laden subway, she saw her favorite police officer, Glen, standing next to a pay booth. Glen usually worked the afternoon shift and all the girls loved him. He was fresh out of the academy, young, dimpled, blue eyed and all around gorgeous. Glen helped everyone and Katherine felt safe whenever he was around. As she pranced through the turnstile, she headed straight toward him. "Officer Glen, guess what? Guess!"

"Katherine! I haven't seen you this excited since that time you aced your algebra exam."

"Algebra! It's much more exciting that that. I got the job…you know, the one with the investment firm that I've been talking about? The one I thought I blew?"

"That's great, Katherine! That's really great! Welcome to the working world."

"Thanks, but don't think you won't see me anymore. I'll still be riding the train to work, except now I'll be going downtown," she called out, as she happily fled up the stairs.

"Congratulations, Katherine!" Glen shouted after her.

*   *   *

When Katherine reached her apartment building, she hoped that Al would be home. Ignoring the three guys out in front with their ghetto blaster at maximum volume, she dashed inside and waited for the elevator. When she stepped out onto the twelfth floor, the smell of Al's pipe filled the hallway.

She burst into the apartment. "Daddy! Daddy! Guess what? I got the job. I got the job." Katherine's hands were flying in the air as her books fell to the floor. "Can you believe it? I got the job!"

"Kate, what happened today? Which job?" Al interrupted, knowing she had interviewed for several.

"Daddy, I'm going to work for that big investment firm, Walters and Vein. Mrs. Cohen called me into her office today and informed me that I was selected out of fourteen girls at school. She said they were impressed with my typing skills, my maturity and my performance on the pre-employment exam. Can you believe it? That was the interview I thought I'd bombed. Isn't it great? Isn't this what you sent me to vocational school for?" Finally, she paused.

"Yes, Kate, it's wonderful, but I thought you wanted to go to college."

"I still do…but, Daddy, we need the money, and this will be a great start for my career. I can still plan to go to college."

"I don't want you to change your plans because of me, Kate. Believe me, this real estate slump is only temporary, plus I can get other jobs. I want you to go on to college, I've worked hard for that."

Daddy, I will, but this is what I want to do. I'll take a night class or something. Please be happy for me."

Al was proud of his daughter and he knew she was right and she meant all that she said. Katherine always had a way of seeing the big picture. He gave her a congratulatory hug, then he sat back down in his aged brown leather easy chair and gloated, while Katherine called her friends to tell them her good news.

As he listened to Katherine on the phone, Al remembered how she had fought against going to vocational school. Katherine had been angry and scared to leave her friends, especially Melody, her best friend. Melody's parents were divorced and she led a reckless life that included dropping out of school.

Yet, today, Al knew his baby had blossomed into womanhood. She reminded him so much of her mother! Katherine had beautiful caramel-colored skin and long brown hair that she loved to wear in a ponytail style with bangs. Her perfect figure was only a starter for the essence of her beauty. She had a heart of gold and was always willing to give, to help and to comfort others. Al knew his wife would have been very proud of their daughter.

That evening, they went to their favorite restaurant, Tony's, to celebrate. Katherine had her favorite hamburger and fries, while Al had his double cheeseburger and onion rings. As they ate, they enjoyed each other's company; laughing and reminiscing.

CHAPTER TWO

Graduation day was beautiful with not a cloud in the sky. When Katherine awoke, she could smell something good coming from the kitchen. As she looked toward the bedroom door, she saw Al standing there, smiling, with breakfast tray in hand. The pride he felt, in having such an accomplished daughter, was evident.

"Kate, get up. I've fixed your favorite breakfast. I want you to remember this day forever." Al set the beautifully decorated tray in front of her. The fresh flowers colored the room with their essence. In addition to fresh fruit and blueberry pancakes, there was also a small box wrapped in gold and blue paper.

"Daddy, you've really outdone yourself. A girl should graduate everyday! Tomorrow morning, I expect a repeat performance, don't let me down." They both laughed.

Katherine picked up the small box. "Oh, Daddy, you didn't have to buy me a gift."

"Open it," Al responded.

Inside the box, she found a beautiful gold pin shaped like a five-leaf clover. On the stem of the clover, the name 'Al' was engraved and, on the fifth leaf, the name 'Sarah'. Al had had the pin specially made for his wife and had given it to her on their wedding day as a symbol of his undying love.

"Daddy, this is so special! I love you." Katherine said, as tears welled up in her eyes.

"And I love you, Kate. Your mother would be so proud of you. I'm sure she would want you to have this." He struggled to maintain his composure.

By now, Katherine's tears were spilling freely. "Thanks." She embraced Al. "Okay, enough of this mushy stuff, now that both of us are emotional wrecks. Go, Daddy. Get ready. I don't know how the two of us will get through this day. We should have invested in Kleenex. I'm sure their stock will reach an all-time high with our help, after today. Okay! Alright! Go!" Katherine shooed Al away. "I love you," she reminded him.

"I love you, Kate," he responded as he walked out of the bedroom.

While Katherine prepared for her graduation, she kept thinking about the look in Al's eyes when he gave her the pin and about how much he must have loved her mother.

"Kate, are you ready? We don't want to be late." Al shouted as he knocked on her bedroom door.

"My! My! My!" Katherine exclaimed as she opened the door. "Don't you look distinguished in your navy blue suit and red tie? If I didn't know better, I would swear Billie Dee was at my door; minus the salt and pepper hair, of course," Katherine said with a grin. "Daddy, I'll have to fight off all the women trying to hit on you today!"

"Kate, please, let's go. I don't think you have a fighting bone in your body. Hurry up, I don't want to be late, I want a front-row seat for this occasion."

"Daddy, you are too much," she cooed, as she pinned the gold pendent on her graduation gown for all to see, then she and Al headed out the door.

CHAPTER THREE

As the cab pulled up in front of Harlem High School, the crowd was starting to arrive. Al was right about getting there early. "Let's get out. Each moment we sit here means a row further back for my seat," Al said as he nudged Katherine in the side. She got out of the cab and began greeting everyone.

"Hi, Joe!" "Hello, Barbara!" "Hi, Ron, I like your tie." "Hey, Judy, congratulations."

Katherine should have been a politician, Al thought, while gently nudging her forward. When they got inside the school, Katherine stopped and looked around. She thought about how much she would miss this place, and the good times she had had with her friends and teachers. She even thought about Mr. Bain, the janitor, who passed away at the beginning of the school year. He had always been nice to her and looked out for the students.

"Katherine! Katherine." It was Mrs. Cohen rushing toward her. Katherine had never seen her so dressed up. She was wearing a beautiful red two-piece skirt suit, with a collar trimmed in black. She even had her hair up!

"Okay, Daddy, I guess I better get ready to start fighting."

"What are you talking about?"

"Here comes Mrs. Cohen. She's a widow, you know."

"Kate, you're crazy," Al chuckled.

"Congratulations, Mister Mills. I'm sure you are very proud of Katherine and excited about her new job. I will really miss her. You have a very special daughter." The accolades continued as she shook his hand.

"Thank you. Kate will miss you, too. She talks about you often," Al replied. As he shook Mrs. Cohen's hand, he glanced over her shoulder at the people moving into the auditorium.

"Thanks for everything, Mrs. Cohen," Katherine repeated, as she gracefully tried to close the conversation and rescue her father. "I'll keep in touch."

"Katherine, your pin is beautiful!"

"Thanks, Mrs. Cohen, it's a special graduation gift from my father."

"It's really beautiful, Katherine."

"Thanks, Mrs. Cohen. I promise, I'll keep in touch."

The music was starting, so Katherine gave Al a kiss and rushed to join the other graduates in the line. Al hurried to find his long-awaiting seat. 'Pomp and Circumstance' played overhead, as fifty graduates marched down the aisle, single file. Katherine had heard that music many times, but, today, it was playing for her as she marched proudly down the aisle.

Mr. Cline, the principal, stepped up to the podium and spoke for a few minutes. Then he introduced the guest speaker, Mr. John Walters. Walters was a big tall white man with gray hair and a black mustache. He was dressed in a black double-breasted suit. When he spoke, his deep voice resonated like a herd of cattle rumbling beneath the building.

"Congratulations, graduates. My name is John Walters of the Walters and Vein Investment Firm."

"Katherine's eyes lit up. She whispered to everyone around her, "That's my boss! I'll be working for him." She gave Al the thumbs-up sign. He did the same.

Mr. Walters spoke to the graduates about staying focused. He stressed how important it is for them to have a vision of their future. He told them that, if they remained focused on their tasks, anything was possible. He closed with his famous motto: 'Find yourself first, then others will find you'.

When Mr. Walters finished his speech, Mr. Cline returned to the podium and introduced the graduating class. As Katherine stood, she was so nervous she thought she might stumble on the stage or something, but, by the time her name was called, she had collected herself and proudly marched up onto the stage to receive her diploma. As she left the stage, she looked for Al, but he was not in his seat. She briefly panicked as she searched the room, then saw him at the foot of the steps, snapping pictures so fast, you would think he was competing for the 'Pulitzer Award'.

As Katherine strolled by Al, she handed him her diploma. The next thing she knew, his familiar voice yelled out: "That's my girl!" She turned around only to hear Al repeat the phrase as he held the diploma high above his head. The crowd went wild. Every parent in the entire place began mimicking Al as they applauded.

"That's my girl!" a parent yelled out. "That's my boy!" another yelled. It was one of those moments that truly would have made the cover of a magazine.

*   *   *

The ride home was quiet, as they each reflected on the events that day. Katherine rested her head on Al's shoulder. She decided she did not want to go out that evening, she only wanted to be with Al and share a quiet dinner. That night, she made Al's favorite, homemade spaghetti and meatballs. They talked about the graduation and enjoyed each other's company. They cleaned up the kitchen together.

After they finished, Katherine kissed Al goodnight and went to her room. She lay in her bed staring at the pictures of Sarah and Al and the many pictures of herself and Al. She thought about how lucky she was to have such a special father, as she anticipated her first day on the new job.

CHAPTER FOUR

It was Katherine's big day, starting her first job. The long awaited opportunity to work at Walker and Vein, had arrived. When she awoke, she lay in the bed and looked around the room. She could see the light of day as it shone through the cracks in the window shade. Outside her window, the pigeons provided her with early morning music, as they twittered and flapped their wings.

As she reflected on the rumbling voice of Mr. Walters, Katherine began to worry about making a mistake on her first day. But, just as her panic rose, Katherine's fears turned to excitement and she jumped out of bed. Her thoughts focused on the beautiful building and the office where she would be working, imagining how many new and exciting people she would meet. People, from whom she could learn a lot.

She walked toward her closet wondering what she should wear. She pulled out her blue skirt and white blouse but, they reminded her of something kids wore to Catholic school. That was not the thing to wear. She tried on her black dress, but it was too formal. Then she got out her two-piece plaid suit. It was too colorful, she decided. Katherine decided to take her shower, hoping the soothing water would help her pull it all together.

"Kate, are you up?" It was Al. He slowly opened her bedroom door, then could not believe his eyes. Her room looked as if she were planning a rummage sale. There were clothes all over the place. Al walked toward the open closet door while clearing the pile of clothes blocking his path. There was no Katherine. In fact, there was barely anything left on a hanger.

At that moment, Katherine opened the bathroom door. The grin on her face said it all. Al heard her chuckle, as she stood in the doorway wearing her white robe and with a towel wrapped around her head.

"I guess you found something to wear?' Al laughed.

"Oh, Daddy, that's not funny. Most of my clothes don't seem right. I'll have to work another job just to buy clothes for this one."

"I'm sorry for laughing, Kate, but I couldn't help it. After I made it across the room, all bones intact, I was reminded of my first day of work. The difference was that I had even fewer clothes, but you could have hung yourself with all my ties. Remember, it's not the clothes that make the person."

"Daddy, can I take you to work with me?' she gave him a warm kiss on the cheek.

"Kate, enjoy the day. Believe me, you will see a day like this again. I just stopped in to wish you well and give you a little advice. Be yourself, and you will do just great. I'll see you this evening. Oh, my boss called this morning, he has a potential client who's interested in one of the houses I have listed."

"I'm sorry, Daddy, I've been so busy thinking about myself…"

"You should be thinking of yourself, Kate. This is a special day for you."

"But, Daddy, I know you're worried about your job."

"Don't you worry about me. Call me at lunch and let me know how things are going. I'll be anxiously awaiting the news. Remember, I love you," Al smiled.

"Good luck. I love you, too." She said a silent prayer for Al.

   *   *   *

On her way to work, Katherine came upon Officer Glen, who smiled and winked at her. "Katherine, you look very nice. Good luck with your new job, I'm sure you'll do well." She was grateful for the confidence boost and smiled a thank you to Officer Glen.

As she stepped out of the forty-second street train station, Katherine was pleasantly stunned by the aroma of coffee and donuts. The pedestrian traffic was shoulder to shoulder as she made her way to the Walters and Vein building. As she crossed the street, she noticed a large yellow and brown sign, 'Choc-Full-of-Nuts'. That's where the wonderful breakfast smells came from, she thought. Katherine promised herself that she would visit that shop.

She stood directly in front of the Waters and Vein sign. The building was gothic. Katherine became dizzy as she looked up at the countless windows and a huge American flag that hung from the center of the building. Pushing through the revolving door, she was awed by the colors surrounding her. It was more beautiful than she had been told. There were paintings everywhere, rainbows of colors streamed from the stained glass that embellished the entryway, and the marbled emerald-green floor provided a perfect prism. The floors mirrored Katherine's reflection. In the center of the floor, a trail of plush red velvet carpet led toward the elevators. She stood breathless, as the elegance captured her. As she gazed at the collection of impressionist paintings on the wall, one painting seemed to beckon Katherine. It was splashed with musical faces; faces with eyes that enslaved her.

When the elevator doors opened, she could hardly believe her eyes. The elevator was a miniature version of the grand entryway. She stepped inside and the doors closed behind her. Katherine closed her eyes as the elevator rose toward the 29th floor. She pretended she was a princess, riding in her carriage, absorbed by the beauty and electricity of the moment. The doors opened; the carriage ride was finished, and she stepped out onto the royal blue carpet. In front of her was a magnificent floral arrangement on an antique wooden table with a green marble top. The flowers were magnified by the splendor of the canary yellow walls. The corridors were massive and imposing paintings added life to the walls.

The carpet led her to a pair of large glass doors. 'Walters and Vein Investment Office' was richly painted on the glass. On the other side of the doors, she saw a woman sitting behind a desk. Katherine entered.

The woman greeted her: "You must be Katherine. Welcome to Walters and Vein. I'm Mary, the receptionist, and I've been expecting you."

"I'm please to meet you," Katherine replied. "This building is beautiful!" The words tumbled out of Katherine's mouth as she admired Mary's attire. She wore a charcoal gray skirt suit with a baby blue ruffled blouse.

Her voice was welcoming as it projected from her petite body. "It is a nice building, Katherine. I think you'll enjoy working here. You're assigned to work with Michelle. I'll let her know you are here. Please, have a seat, and help yourself to coffee or tea."

Katherine walked over to the coffee and tea station. She had never seen a silver coffee and tea set. She rubbed the top of the silver canister, hoping she would not dull the finish. She wasn't that fond of coffee. She remembered trying it a couple of times with Al, but the taste repulsed her. She decided to have a cup of tea. There were varieties of teas wrapped in packets. She saw a familiar Lipton tea bag and was about to pick it up, when she heard a door open. Mary came in with another woman who was dressed similar to Mary, except that her blouse was white. She was wearing the most beautiful butterfly comb, which accented her blonde hair.

"Hi, my name is Michelle. Welcome to Walters and Vein. I can't tell you how much I've been looking forward to your arrival. We have plenty of work for you, and I've been given the responsibility of orienting you to the job. Don't worry, you'll learn the job easily. Mister Walters assured me of this, and he is never wrong; that's why he screens all the applications before an employee is hired. It's a gut feeling he goes with. I've been here five years, so I can tell you, his record stands at one hundred percent. Katherine…is it okay if I call you Katherine?"

"Yes, that's fine. My father calls me Kate."

"I like Kate also, but I'll call you Katherine for now. I'm going to take you next door to meet Gretchen, then I'll give you a tour of the office. Gretchen will explain all the office policies and benefits. I guess you can see, we have a uniform policy, or dress code, which I prefer to call it."

"I don't think your clothes look like uniforms. They're beautiful."

"We think the clothes are lovely. Mister Walters and Mister Vein wanted everyone to dress professionally, so they decided to purchase the career apparel. They did not want to put the financial burden on the employees. Their motto is, 'The employees who look good, feel good and work harder as they strive for excellence.'"

Michelle escorted Katherine to Gretchen's office. "Have a seat, she will be with you in a second. Katherine, remember to be patient. You'll only have to go through this once. I'll see you in about forty-five minutes." Michelle smiled and walked away.

*   *   *

Meanwhile, at the real estate office, Al was hard at work making follow-up calls to some of his clients. He was having a hard time concentrating because of a tremendous headache that had started hours earlier and refused the many aspirin he had taken. It seemed that Al's stress headaches were becoming more frequent. He was just about to call Mrs. Hinson regarding a lead on a condo, when Bill Carter walked into his office. Carter was the head of the small real estate firm that Al worked for and, on this day, he was not looking very pleased.

"Al, we have to talk," Carter said, closing the door. Al could see that Carter was holding one of the real estate files in his hand, and his usual pleasant expression was absent.

"Have a seat, Bill. How can I help you?"

"I really don't care to, Al. What in the hell are you doing?" Carter flapped the folder in front of Al's face.

"I don't understand. What are you talking about, Bill? Have I done something wrong?"

"Done something wrong! That's an understatement," Bill shouted and slammed the file onto Al's desk.

Al didn't know what to make of Bill's demeanor. He had never seen him so upset. He looked down at the file and saw the name 'Thelma

Graham'. He had sold her a brownstone in downtown New York. It was his most recent sale, although it had been a while.

"Due to your blunder, we lost several thousand dollars in commission on this deal! This was a cash deal. How in the hell could you screw this up? You're my best agent and I've looked to you to teach others around here. But, this…I mean, a mistake like this does not make sense!"

"What did I do?" Al asked, as Bill's pale face grew beet red with anger.

"Al, my accountant just finished reviewing several of our accounts. When he went over this one, he noticed you had calculated the commission fee to be twelve thousand dollars. It should have been twenty-one thousand dollars. How in the hell could you make such a mistake? Your calculations have always been perfect before this."

Al could not believe what he'd heard. "There must be some kind of mistake, Bill," he said, as he sat down to look over the file. By this time, his head felt as if it was about to explode.

"You're damned right, there has been a mistake, a big one!"

"Bill, I don't know what to say. You're right," Al held the file. "It seems I transposed the numbers somehow. I can't believe I did that." He stared at the papers, trying to figure out how this could have happened. "I'm sorry. I'm…" Al was embarrassed and yet he could barely concentrate because of his headache.

"Al, this firm can't afford mistakes like this! We are small and, even if we weren't, mistakes like this are costly! This is not like you; you're my best man. I know business has been slow, but I sense something else is going on with you. You haven't been yourself lately and I'm not sure why. Review the file and meet me in my office at the end of the day," Bill ordered, as he walked out.

Al sat there, holding his head while he stared at Mrs. Graham's file. *How could I make such a mistake?* he asked himself as he recalculated the numbers again.

*   *   *

By this time Katherine had completed her orientation with Gretchen. As she walked into Michelle's office, she had a most peculiar smile on her face and a gleam in her eyes. Michelle looked up from her desk with a similar smile. She knew that Katherine had met Gretchen.

"Gretchen is really something else. The orientation was great, but I was not prepared for the conversation outside of the orientation. You should have given me more warning," Katherine scolded, with a schoolgirl blush on her face.

"Katherine, if you could see the look on your face! Gretchen really knows how to make a new employee's day. She has become a fixture in this firm. For some reason, she tells everyone about her breast implants and the day she got the first squeeze. The story is so graphic: most people's reaction is 'I can't believe she's telling me this'. No one has ever asked her if the story is true. I think they are afraid of the answer. The look on your face confirms your young innocence. Don't worry, you'll do fine in this firm.

"Please come with me. I'll introduce you to the rest of the staff and take you to your desk. Mary will take you for a fitting later." Michelle escorted Katherine into the grand stateroom where several investment clerks worked. After introducing her, she led her to her desk, which gave Katherine an impressive view of downtown New York City. From afar, she could see the Statue of Liberty.

When she was settled into her new space, she remembered she had not called Al. It was around eleven-thirty. The telephone rang several times before Al answered.

"Hello, Kate, how are things going?"

"Daddy, how did you know it was me? You sound kind of down. Is everything okay?"

"There's only a select few who know my private number, Kate. Of course, everything is okay." Al was working hard to disguise his concerns, but Katherine knew him as well as he knew himself.

"Daddy, are you okay?" she asked again.

"Tell me, Katherine, how's your first day going?"

"I know that you're changing the subject, but I'll get it out of you. I want to know how things are going for you! Did the client interested in that house come through?"

Suddenly, the conversation stopped. Katherine felt the news was not good. "Daddy, are you there?"

In a somber voice, Al answered. "Kate, the client did not come through. It happens that way in my business, sometimes." He was telling the truth. He had spoken to Mrs. Hinson and she was not interested in the condo he had found.

"I'm sorry. I know you were hoping this would be a big day for you. I'm sure something better will come along."

"Kate, you sure know how to make a guy feel good. I'm sure you're right. Don't worry, everything will be all right. You'd better get back to work, but I want a play-by-play of your day when you get home. I love you."

"I love you too, Daddy. See you tonight." Katherine hung up the telephone and wondered how much longer Al could take the slump in sales. She thought about the gleam of success and tranquility she used to see in Al's eyes when he sealed a deal. She wondered how long it would be before she would see that spark again. Her thoughts were broken by Michelle's presence.

"Katherine, you seem a million miles away. I came by to ask you to join me for lunch. Is everything okay?"

"Yes," Katherine responded in a monotone voice as she adjusted her thoughts. "Yes, everything is fine. I was just enjoying the view."

"I need to freshen up," Michelle said. "Meet me in the lobby in ten minutes. I'll take you to my favorite lunch spot."

"That sounds great, I could use a good lunch, today." She sat at her desk for a few moments more; her thoughts devoted to Al. She wanted to see the Al she used to know: the dad who joked and loved to have fun with her. Everything seemed so serious lately. The stress of the real estate decline had consumed him.

CHAPTER FIVE

A month had already gone by since Katherine had begun working at Walters and Vein. It seems the job was meant for her. She was a natural at organizing the investors' portfolios. Her enthusiasm and energy overwhelmed the clients. Her coworkers all seemed to enjoy her presence and worked hard to make her feel at home.

Katherine had developed a friendship with Gretchen. There was something about Gretchen's acts of spontaneity that intrigued her, she reminded Katherine of her best friend, Melody. One day, while sitting at her desk reviewing accounts, Katherine heard Gretchen's loud and lofty voice from afar.

She was in a hot and heavy conversation with Michelle. "Girl, if you could have been there last night. I had him eating out of my hand, plus a whole lot more, if you know what I mean."

"Gretchen, someday, someone will have you eating out of their hands, and I hope they don't kiss and tell," Michelle replied.

"Oh, girl, loosen up and enjoy life. If you would let your hair down and your skirt up, maybe someday you'll meet Mister Right. Until then, you have to watch me, maybe you will learn something," Gretchen voiced. As they approached her desk, Katherine noticed that Michelle seemed put off by Gretchen's carefree attitude. The conversation was all Gretchen's. Michelle shook her head in abhorrence as she continued to listen.

"Katherine, she's all yours. I don't think I can take too much more of this conversation," Michelle said, then left the office. Katherine sat there and grinned up at Gretchen, who wore a pleased smirk on her face. Katherine knew Gretchen had gotten under Michelle's skin as planned. Gretchen and Michelle had an I-love-to-hate-you relationship.

"I have to teach Michelle the ABCs of life, she takes everything too seriously.

"Gretchen, you can be a little overwhelming at times. I remember the first time I met you."

"Girl, I wished I had a camera to record your facial expression that day. I knew you would make it here, since you survived your first encounter with me," Gretchen laughed.

"I'm sure you didn't come over here to re-hash our first encounter. What's on your mind?"

"That's what I like about you Katherine, you speak your mind. I hope some of the others around here learn from you. You're right, I have a reason for this visit. I want to invite you to my pajama party this weekend. Now, before you say no, let me assure you, it will be nothing more than that."

"Gretchen, that sounds like fun, but I really need to spend some time with my father. He lost his job a few weeks ago. He's really been down since then. I need to try and cheer him up."

"Girl, bring him to the party, I'll cheer daddy up!"

"Thanks, Gretchen, but I don't think my father could handle your cheering up. I'll have to take a rain check."

"Will you at least go shopping with me this evening to pick out something special?" Gretchen asked.

"I thought you said it was a pajama party?" Katherine questioned while giving Gretchen her 'I knew it' expression.

"It is a pajama party. Don't look at me like that. There are all kinds of pajamas, Katherine." Gretchen said with a twisted smile, as she walked away.

"Gretchen, be careful," Katherine advised, as she watched her leave. Then she began thinking about what she could do to cheer up Al. He seemed lost lately. She desperately wanted to see the old Al, as she searched her distant thoughts. Suddenly from out of nowhere, she began to smell some type of mystical masculine scent. She looked up and saw a heavenly man.

"Hello! A penny for your thoughts?" a deep husky voice spoke.

Before Katherine, stood a stunning young man dressed in a navy blue double-breasted suit. His white skin was smooth and his eyes were a crisp royal blue, so crisp you could see the stars twinkling within them. His dark brown mustache shadowed his lips and his perfect white teeth glistened. Katherine sat muddled by his presence. Her lips hung open silently.

"Hello, my name is Nick Walters. Sorry if I startled you. Welcome to the team. I'm sorry I haven't had the opportunity to welcome you sooner."

Katherine was dazed as she continued to stare at Nick. As she gathered her thoughts, she realized this must be the Nick that all the girls, especially Gretchen, talked about. *I can see why*, she thought. He was handsome. He reminded her of Glen. Yet, there was something else, something more intriguing about him.

"Hello, Ms. Mills, I mean, Katherine. Are you alright?"

"Yes, I'm fine. You startled me…I didn't hear you coming. It is my pleasure to meet you, Mister Walters."

"Please call me Nick. Again, I apologize for not meeting you sooner. I've been away on business. Several of our mutual clients have spoken very highly of you, and I hear you have been doing a great job. I hope you're enjoying it here. Are you?"

"Yes," Katherine replied. She felt like a school girl, thinking her every word was coming out the wrong way. "Everyone has been so nice to me, it seems as though I've been here for years."

"I would very much like to take you to lunch and get to know you better. I need to do something to make up for not having the opportunity to meet you sooner. Are you free for lunch today?" Nick asked.

Before she could answer, Nick spoke. "Think about it. I'll be back later for an answer. If not today, maybe another day." He exited and so did the deep breath Katherine had been holding.

Katherine was mesmerized. She could not believe what had happened. She knew about Nick Walters from the office talk, but she had no idea he was so handsome. Her heart was still pounding from his husky voice. It reminded her of the rumble John Walters created when he spoke at the graduation, but different. Katherine could not believe how foolishly she'd acted. She was so overcome by his presence, she could not respond to his invitation to lunch. She felt witless.

Then she began to think about all the rumors regarding Nick being a womanizer. She realized he probably thought she was naïve and wanted to make her another notch on his belt. The more she thought about it, the more upset she became. *He must think I'm easy...that he can use his charm, and I'll respond by melting in his arms. Well, I'm not. I'll have an answer for him when he returns*, Katherine vowed, fighting with her thoughts. She prepared herself for Nick's return, but, before she knew it, Gretchen was standing at her desk again. She could tell Katherine was miffed about something.

"Girl, you look like you are preparing for war. I'll give you a penny for your thoughts, and a dollar for your attitude. I stopped by to see if I could change your mind about going shopping with me."

"Gretchen, you would not believe what just happened to me. I was sitting at my desk, when Nick Walters appeared from nowhere and asked me to lunch!"

"You mean, 'the' Nick Walters?"

"Yes, 'the' Nick Walters."

"I can't believe what I'm hearing. Forget shopping, describe him to me." Gretchen said, prancing in front of Katherine's desk. Katherine went on to describe him in detail, while Gretchen stood there in disbelief. "Girl, girl, that is him, down to the inch. I'm jealous. I've redone by body to make that man notice me. I even prayed for the opportunity to show him what I could do for him. I'm sure he must have noticed my upper body assets." Gretchen pushed up her boobs and gave Katherine the side view. "If he thinks these are my forte, he needs to know my lower body is my trademark."

"Gretchen! I can't believe you. Here I am talking about myself and all you can think of is what you would like do with the man."

"Oh, girl, lighten up. You can't blame a girl for thinking out loud, or, should I say, praying out loud? I know you said 'yes'?"

"Well, not really. He's going to get back with me later for an answer."

"Katherine, do you know how many women would love to just stand close enough to smell his scent? You have the opportunity to sit with him for lunch! Girlfriend, you better find that man. Get up from this tired desk and find him!"

"Gretchen, I'm not like you. I wish, at times, that I could flirt like you. You should have seen how I clammed up when Nick was introducing himself. He must have thought I was some type of bimbo. I'm sure he won't be back, but, if he does come back, I'm positive my nerves will not allow me to say yes. Someday, I may learn to be a little more playful."

"Katherine, you can sit there and feel sorry for yourself if you want. Believe me, sorry don't pay any bills or warm any beds. Now you think about that."

"You have a one-track mind. Somehow, I knew this conversation was going nowhere. You haven't heard a word I've said."

"Girl, some day you will understand. I have to take this tanned body and go, I've got things to do. Are you sure you don't want to go shopping with me?"

"Gretchen, you're ignoring me."

"Girlfriend, I don't think you heard a single thing I said," Gretchen said as she gave Katherine one of her glancing looks, then walked away.

CHAPTER SIX

Several months had passed and Katherine had never had the opportunity to respond to Nick's invitation. He did not return that day. He called leaving a message that something came up. Katherine assumed he was just being polite. She worked hard at Walters and Vein and continued to excel at her job. She had been assigned several of the larger investment accounts. She was pleased with the way things were going. There was only one aspect of the job that troubled her. That concern normally surfaced when she was working with Michelle. It bothered her that Michelle had a group of investment files that she would not allow Katherine to work on. Normally, when Michelle was working on the files and Katherine walked into her office, she would close the files and lock them in her desk draw. Michelle had been very open, teaching Katherine and showing her everything, so it seemed odd that these files were off limits. Everyone in the office would occasionally make comments regarding the secret files and the fact that Michelle was the only one who had access to them. Katherine once asked about the files and Michelle said they were a special project assigned to her. Katherine never questioned Michelle again. She felt they were probably some top investment accounts that needed special attention and she knew how good Michelle was. She felt that, when the time was right, she would earn the right to work on the top accounts.

One day, while Katherine was browsing at the shopping center during her lunch hour, she felt a presence behind her and noted a familiar scent in the air. When she turned around, she was pleasantly surprised to see it was Nick. It looked like he had been shopping. He had a small bag in his hand. Initially, Katherine did not know what to say, but, fortunately for her, Nick opened the conversation.

"Katherine, I thought that was you. You seem intrigued by something in that jewelry store. I thought it would be a good idea not to interrupt you."

Katherine stood listening, her focus of attention was watching Nick's moving lips and his beautiful white teeth. His deep husky voice was making her quiver. She could not believe what she thought or felt at that moment. She attributed these uncharacteristic thoughts to the influence that Gretchen had on her. She tried to compose herself, hoping the Lord would give her the strength to remain standing, as her knees weakened.

"I apologize for not following up on my lunch offer. After I left you that day, there was an emergency. One thing led to another and, before I knew it, my father had me off on another business trip. Again, I'm sorry. I'll tell you what, let's have lunch today if you're not busy."

Before Katherine could think about a response, the words, "Yes, that sounds good," jumped from her mouth. She could not believe she had accepted a lunch date with Nick Walters. It was as if the answer had formulated before the thought process had been completed. As she walked away with Nick, she turned to look at the four leaf clover pin in the store window. So many thoughts raced through her head.

The clover made her think of many things, especially Al. Since he had been laid off, he seemed different. He no longer laughed and joked around. Most of his time was spent trying to find odd jobs to make a few bucks. She thought about college, wondering if she should consider postponing it for another year or, at least, until Al settled into another job. She even thought about Gretchen and what she would say about her accepting this date with Nick.

"Katherine? Katherine, you seem preoccupied. Is everything okay?" interrupted Nick.

"Everything is fine, I was just thinking about my father. I'm sure you do the same thing at times."

"You're right. I think about my parents a lot, at times. They think we are so preoccupied with our lives, that we forget about theirs. That is far from the truth. Is everything okay with your dad?" He felt Katherine wanted to talk about something.

"Things seem to be as well as can be expected, for now," Katherine remarked in a distant voice as they continued to walk down the street.

Nick did not press Katherine to talk about what was on her mind, although he felt something was bothering her. He felt when she was ready to talk about it, she would. He stopped in front of a little restaurant called Sporatto.

"Ah, this is the place. Shall we?" he said as he opened the door. The aroma was out of this world. The dimly-lit candles provided a soft setting. It was just what Katherine and Nick needed that day.

"Nick, how did you know I liked Italian food?"

"Katherine, just give me time." Nick said with a devilish smirk. Katherine did not know how to take his comments.

The hostess seated them. Katherine thanked Nick for the lunch offer as they were escorted to their table. The two of them had a wonderful lunch that day. They talked about a little bit of everything. She could not believe how relaxed she felt around him. It was as if she'd known him for years. He appeared to be a true gentleman. She finally understood why the women at work called him a womanizer: any woman would be charmed by him. However, Katherine sensed that, beneath this hunk of a man, was an innocence, an innocence that she found alluring.

   *   *   *

When Katherine got home that evening, she was so thrilled about her day, she couldn't wait to tell Al. She was even more excited because Nick had invited her on another date. She rushed into the apartment full of cheer, suddenly halted by what she saw. Al was home, sprawled across his easy chair. In front of him was a bottle of Jack Daniel's, and the room reeked with the odor of alcohol. She was shocked! She had never seen Al like this before. She knew he was having a hard time, but he was a strong man, and she'd felt he would get through this rough period. Never had she imagined that he would allow himself to be a quitter. This was unlike Al.

Katherine walked towards Al with tears in her eyes. She could not accept what had happened. She even blamed herself because she had been so involved with her work, she did not see the warning signs. She could not understand why Al did not talk to her. They were always able to talk about things.

"Daddy? Daddy, are you okay?" Al just moaned as he turned his head in the opposite direction, the scent of alcohol flaring from his mouth. Katherine was taken aback, she did not know what to do. The sadness she felt emptied her of every other emotion. She rubbed Al's head softly and placed a blanket over him.

She walked into her bedroom, but before she closed the door, she looked at the chair in which Al was sleeping. She could see one of his legs hanging over the chair and she thought about the many times Al set her on his lap and talked to her in that chair. She closed the door, emotionally puzzled. She looked around at the many pictures of them together and thought about all the happy times they shared.

One picture stood out. It was the picture of the two of them on her graduation day. Al looked handsome, happy and proud. Katherine looked at the picture of herself that day. She thought about how she felt then, wishing she could turn back the hands of time and recapture those feelings. She looked at the gold five leaf clover pin on her graduation robe. She thought about the look in Al's eyes when he gave it to her and about her mother. She wished her mother were there to help her.

That night Katherine cried herself to sleep. For the first time, she felt she had no one. It had always been she and Al. There were no secrets; they talked about everything. Katherine could not understand why Al was acting so different. She knew he loved his job and he missed working. But, Al was always the one to say 'if something doesn't work out, try something else'. He would be the last person to throw in the towel.

Katherine decided not to discuss that evening with Al. She knew it would only make him feel worse if he knew she was aware of his drunkenness. She prayed this would be a one time event, although her heart knew better.

She got up early the next morning and straightened up the room. She threw away the empty bottle of alcohol, and left Al a sweet note telling him how much she loved him. Al was sound asleep with a cherubic smile on his face. Katherine smiled as she thought the angels must be talking to him. She hoped they were saying, 'Get it together Al'. Katherine kissed him on his cheek, then she left. As she got on the elevator, she asked God to watch over Al. "He's a good man, and I need him," she murmured.

CHAPTER SEVEN

The Christmas holiday season approached. It had been several weeks since Nick and Katherine had their first lunch, and the two of them had become quite close. They went everywhere together. Katherine seemed to enjoy her time with Nick. She used these good times to block out the feelings she suppressed regarding Al. He had withdrawn into himself and the drinking continued. Although nothing totally got her mind off of Al, she pretended that it did.

One day after completing a phone conversation with a client, she was surprised to see Gretchen standing at her desk. She had not seen Gretchen in a while. "Girl, I thought you dropped off this earth, or might I say, landed a big deal. Have you gone and done it? You know what I mean, Katherine, don't look at me like that! The word is out. You and Mister Nick are an item. All the girls are jealous. I mean all, do you get my drift?" Katherine did not know how to respond.

"Girl, don't give me that look. It's me, Gretchen. You can tell me if you have done the nasty with Nick."

"I can't believe you asked me that, Gretchen!"

"Girl, get off of it. If you haven't, you must be out of your mind. If I had the opportunity, I would eat the sheets that man slept on, plus a whole lot more."

Katherine shook her head in disbelief. "Gretchen, you haven't changed. I hope someday, Mister Right comes into your life. I'm looking forward to that day."

"Girl, they haven't made the man that can handle all of me. I've decided that I'll have fun until I get tired. Then, I guess, I'll settle down with a man that can satisfy fifty-percent of my needs. Don't try to change the subject, I came here to talk about you. Now tell me what is happening with you and Nick? Tell me, how does it feel to date a man ten years your senior?"

"Oh please, Gretchen, don't act as if you haven't dated older men. It's not the age, it's the depth of the relationship that's important."

"Well, listen to Miss Mature," Gretchen said as she put her hands on her hips. "My, have we changed! So you admit there is a relationship. I knew it! I knew it! Katherine, we will have to finish this discussion over lunch real soon. I actually came by to invite you to my New Year's party. Do you have plans?"

"I would love to, but unfortunately, I do. Nick invited me to his parents' house. I'll take a rain check, if that's okay?"

"Girl, what I wouldn't give to be in your shoes. Hot damn! Girlfriend, you're having New Year's dinner at the Walters'? I wish I could be a fly on the wall for that party. I hear their house is fabulous. To be there for New Year's and have Mister 'Hunk of Love' at your side, is truly to die for. Girl, I want you to call me with all the details. I mean all!" Gretchen said, as she gave Katherine a list of instructions on how to handle herself around the royal family.

Katherine was polite and listened, with a faint smile on her face. She knew it would not do her any good to say anything. Katherine's phone rang.

"Girl, I got to go. Remember what I said."

Katherine waved Gretchen off as she picked up the phone.

It was Nick. "Katherine, I'm calling…I'm calling to let you know our New Year's plans have changed."

"Nick, you mean we're not going to be together for New Year's? Has something happened? Are you going out of the country again?"

"No, no, it's not that, Katherine. I plan to spend New Years with you but, it will not be at my parents' house. I'll give you a call later, and explain it all to you."

Katherine sat there, puzzled. She thought maybe Nick and his father had another fight. Nick told her the two of them were not getting along lately, they were arguing about everything. Then she thought, maybe Nick was too embarrassed to bring her around his parents. She really did not know what to think.

As Nick hung up the phone, he sat there wondering how could he tell Katherine that his parents, especially his father, did not want to meet her. Nick and his father had just finished an awful argument about Katherine. John told Nick that Katherine was a gold-digger and that she had negative class, and, if he was smart, he would see through her facade and let the little trollop go. John held his thoughts regarding Katherine being Black. He did not want to overly inflame Nick that evening.

It was not until that moment, that Nick actually realized how fond he had become of Katherine. He defended her, telling John that Katherine was the most beautiful woman he had ever met, and that her beauty was inside and out. He assured John that, if he allowed himself to get to know her, he would see her differently.

John did not care. He would not entertain Katherine in his home. Nick was mad as hell, knowing he could never tell Katherine what his father thought of her. He decided he would do what was best for him and plan an unforgettable New Year's Eve with Katherine. He decided to take her to his favorite place, the Tavern On The Green Restaurant in Central Park. He called the restaurant to make reservations for their New Year's Eve bash.

John stood in the foyer listening to Nick make plans to be with Katherine. As John listened, he realized he had to do something to sever this relationship, but exactly what he would do was uncertain. John stood behind the stairs and watched Nick leave the house. Then, he rushed to the telephone. "Bobbie, I need you to come over. There's something I need to talk to you about. I'm at home. Don't forget, you owe me a favor." John said.

Bobbie was an old friend of John's. They had worked together on several business deals, both legal and illegal. John knew he could count on Bobbie to help him come up with a plan. He was not about to see this uptown girl, without downtown class, woo his son. To him, the relationship did not make sense. He had to end it.

It wasn't long before Bobbie arrived at the Walters' estate. John opened the door. In front of him stood a massive man, six-foot four inches tall. His body was so muscular, the outline of his biceps was visible through his dark overcoat. His hat shadowed his stone face. Bobbie was a thug. John knew this and he planned to use those skills, if necessary, as he invited Bobbie inside.

"Hello, John, what can I do for you? You seemed to be troubled by something. What's going on?" Bobbie asked.

"Thanks for coming over, Bobbie. You and I have been friends for a long time and we've done a lot of business together," John said, as he placed his hand on Bobbie's shoulder. "I really need your help. You see, Nick seems to be taken by a young lady who works at my firm. At first I thought she was just another one of Nick's playmates, but I now realize that this relationship has become more serious. He talks about her more than any woman he has met. He spends all his free time with her. I **must** end this relationship. Nick is blinded by this woman, and he can't conceive she is after him for his money. I know the type; I had to dump several like her before I met his mother."

"John, are you sure about this young lady and Nickki? The last time I spoke to you, you told me Nickki was very preoccupied with the business."

"He used to be, Bobbie. He seems different now, and he's less interested in taking trips to handle our big accounts. He told me, just the other night, that he would like to handle more of the business in town. I have built this business around him, and I refuse to let this little Black gold-digger ruin that!"

Bobbie listened. He was not surprised that Nick's playmate was Black, knowing Nick had dated Black women in the past. What surprised him was how much this particular relationship was affecting John.

"John, what can I do to help? You name it."

"Today, I just need a close friend to talk to. I think I can handle this myself."

"What do you plan to do?"

"Bobbie, I plan to terminate the little gold-digging wench. If that doesn't work, well…I will probably have to call upon you for a bigger favor."

"John, do you think that will resolve the relationship? I can see this blowing up in your face. Nickki will know you're behind all of this. I don't know, I really think you should think this through carefully."

It was obvious to Bobbie, that John was really disturbed by all of this, even more so than usual. He watched John as he paced the floor, looking at the picture of him and Nick on the mantel. What Bobbie feared most was what John did not say. He had seen him like this before. He knew that what John wanted, he usually got, no matter what.

"Bobbie, I can make things happen in a way so no one will know I had anything to do with it. Believe me, I know what I'm doing. Yes, Bobbie, there is something you can do. I know this little trollop lives with her father up in Manhattan. I want you to find out everything you can about the two of them. If I need a trump card, I'm sure you will find it."

"I'll do what I can, John, but remember, be careful. This could backfire in your face."

"Thanks for coming over, Bobbie. Thanks for the warning, but I know what I am doing. I'll keep in touch. Remember, I'm counting on you, so don't let me down."

Bobbie left the house as John began to work on getting Katherine out of the firm. He decided to call upon the accounts which Katherine was working on. Many of those clients owed him big favors. Just as he had summoned Bobbie, he felt it was time to gather others. John spent most of that afternoon on the telephone. His plan was to ask each client to become dissatisfied with her service. The clients would threaten to pull their business if something wasn't done. This would be the perfect excuse to fire her. John realized this would take time, but he felt that, this way, Nick would not suspect that he was behind this scene.

Totally oblivious to any of this, Katherine continued to go about her daily routine. In a short period of time, she had become the top investment secretary. Although her job consisted mainly of organizing the accounts and keeping clients updated on their investments, she had done her work well, and the clients loved talking to her. However, this young lady from the big city was about to get her first true taste of the business of corporate America. That evening, Katherine shared a quiet diner at home with Al. Al was no longer his usual self. He was tired all the time, and Katherine was worried about him. She wanted desperately to tell Al about Nick, but she realized the time was not right.

CHAPTER EIGHT

It was New Year's Eve and Katherine was excited. She awoke early that morning and fixed a big breakfast for Al and herself. She was happy the office was closed and decided she would spend the day with Al, then the evening with Nick.

It seemed a little like old times with Al. He smiled more and he even talked a little more that day. He wanted to know where she was going that evening. Katherine was initially taken aback by the question. It seemed like such a long time since Al had asked her about her life. She thought for a moment, *maybe this would be a good time to tell him about Nick*, but it was only a fleeting thought. Katherine realized Al was only trying to get her to worry less about him. She knew exactly what he was up to.

"Kate sweetheart, you haven't told me where you're going this evening. I saw that beautiful dress you bought."

"Daddy, you don't miss a beat!" Katherine had to think of something quick. She was not going to tell Al that Nick bought the dress. *Gretchen, that's it!* she thought. *I'll tell him I'm going out with Gretchen.* As she talked about her evening, Al seemed to be pleased. He wanted nothing more than her happiness.

It was finally time to go. Katherine had been preparing for this moment all day. When she walked out of her bedroom in her red dress, Al was overcome with emotion. The dress was an off-the-shoulder number, fitted to the waist, then it ballooned to the floor. It was red lace with the edges trimmed in black satin. Her red satin shawl and red patent leather shoes completed the ensemble.

Al could not believe his eyes. Katherine looked as if she had stepped out of a fairy tale. "My beautiful Kate. I wish your mother were here to see you." Al said with tears in his eyes.

Katherine's mascara ran, as tears rolled down her cheeks. She loved Al, but the tall, strong and cheerful man she once knew had become a weakened, fragile man with diminished hope. Al was beginning to lose weight and the worry lines on his face were more apparent. This picture of Al hurt Katherine deeply. She walked over and gave him a hug and whispered, " I love you," in his ear as tears covered both of their faces.

Al looked into Katherine's eyes and wiped away the tears as he spoke. "My Kate, everything will be alright. I don't want you to worry. I want you to have a wonderful evening. Now go and fix yourself up. You know, we haven't had a moment like this since your graduation." Katherine did not say anything, although she felt Al was trying to say something.

Leaving the apartment was not easy. She asked Al if he wanted her to stay with him. Al insisted she go out and have a good time. Before she left, she wished Al a Happy New Year. As she shut the door she saw Al sitting in his easy chair. She stood on the other side of the closed apartment door in the empty hall of the building, her back against the door. She knew that, if she did not take a step forward at that moment, she would not be able to leave. Never in her life had she experienced so much love and indecision.

Finally, she decided to meet Nick as planned. She needed someone to lift her spirits. The elevator moved like molasses. When the door opened, she forced herself to step out of the elevator, then leave the building, her gaze drawn to an impressive white stretch limousine parked in front.

Standing next to the car door was Nick. In one hand he had a dozen long-stemmed red roses. His other hand stretched out towards her. It was as if God knew this evening had to be perfect from start to finish.

As she approached the limo, she began to feel like the belle of the ball. This moment was hers and hers alone. She was the Princess of New

York, Nick was the Prince, and their carriage awaited. The plush seats made her feel as if she were sitting on a bed of pillows. Nick leaned down to kiss her as he handed her the roses.

"How gorgeous you look, Miss Mills."

"How handsome you look, Mister Walters." And he did, in his black tux and tails. His cardinal bow tie matched Katherine's dress perfectly.

"Thank you, my lady," Nick said, bowing as he delivered the royal treatment to a young woman so deserving. Katherine was special to him. He felt a love like never before. To Nick it was almost embarrassing, he felt so boyish.

For the first time in her life, Katherine knew what it felt like to be Cinderella, going to the ball with the man she loved at her side. "Thank you for the dress," Katherine softly spoke, as she looked into Nick's captivating eyes. Katherine's knight in shining armor had come to rescue her, and she decided she would not let anything spoil the moment or evening.

As the limo driver pulled away, Nick pulled Katherine close to him. He gave her a soft kiss on the lips and held her in his arms. Katherine grabbed Nick's firm hand, and felt the warmth of his touch, as her heart smoldered in rapture.

They rode through Central Park, enjoying the serenity of their adoration for each other inside the car as the noise, lights and glitter of New Year's Eve provided the outer bliss. Finally, the limo pulled up in front of a dazzling glass-lit restaurant. Katherine had never seen anything like it before. The blizzard of lights in the trees was mesmerizing.

While Katherine basked in wonderment, Nick stepped out from the limo. She flashed him a sensuous smile and he reached out for her hand, then escorted her into the restaurant. Katherine felt as if she had stepped into another world when she walked through the ornate glass and wood doors. It was like walking into a glass menagerie. The foyer was filled with huge ornaments hanging from the ceiling, in an array of colors beyond belief. The music, the lights and the glitter were almost too heavenly to be true. It was definitely a welcome fit for a princess.

They were escorted to the Crystal Room, walking along a corridor filled with luminous stained glass. When Katherine stepped into the Crystal Room, the images in her mind froze, as she gazed upon the jewel-tone chandeliers that gleamed like diamonds and the Christmas tree that dazzled in the center of the room. The staff and patrons had a glow about them. The place was magical. There were waiters and waitresses maneuvering in and out of the aisle with such grace, it was like a ballet. The women had on the most gorgeous evening gowns. The men were tailored beyond elegance, but none were as dashing as Nick.

Nick seemed to know everyone there. As he escorted her around the room to introduce her, everyone was very pleasant. Katherine noticed that Nick seemed rather excited about something. He had focused on a crowd of people gathered in the center of the room. There was a short, half-bald man in the center of the crowd. Everyone was greeting him.

He looked very distinguished in his black tuxedo with tails. His white hair, what was left of it, was perfectly combed, and he held his head high while reaching out to shake hands. There were several people standing around waiting to talk to him. The crowd did not bother Nick as he moved through them without hesitation. Within seconds, they were standing in front of this man and the beautiful woman in a white-sequined dressed who was holding his hand.

"Mr. Brown, how are you? I want you to meet a mutual friend of ours. This is Miss Katherine Mills." Nick said.

Katherine could not believe it! Nick was introducing her to Clifford Brown! She knew the name. Mr. Brown was the owner of one of the largest chain of restaurants on the East Coast, and he had invested millions with Walters and Vein. Katherine knew his background very well, as she was responsible for organizing the records for his accounts. She had spoken with him several times on the telephone, and he was always so nice to her.

"Mister Brown, it is a pleasure to meet you," Katherine said, as she reached out to shake his hand.

"Hello, Miss," Brown said, shaking her hand in a rather cold manner, his face unsmiling. Katherine wondered if he had heard Nick's introduction, although he looked directly at him when he spoke. She thought maybe he hadn't, so Katherine decided to reintroduce herself.

"Mister Brown, I'm Katherine Mills. It is my pleasure to meet you." Again the reception was polite without warmth. This time Katherine was sure he had heard. Her feelings were crushed, and she was embarrassed. She felt everyone around her was watching, although, in reality, no one except she and Nick detected the unusual behavior. The others were wrapped up in their merriment as they waited their turn. Katherine had no idea what was going on. She had spoken to Mr. Brown just two days ago on the telephone, and he had been very pleasant. Why was he being cold to her now? She wanted to run someplace and hide.

Nick knew Brown wanted to meet Katherine. He had spoken so very highly of her just a few weeks ago. He'd even asked Nick to introduce Katherine to him if he ever got the chance. "Mister Brown, is something wrong? I don't understand what is going on here." Nick knew Brown could be rather pompous at times, but his reaction to Katherine did not make sense.

"Nick, please excuse me. I'll talk to you later." Brown said, as he walked off. His pleasantry resurfaced as he and the beautiful woman made their way through the entourage.

Katherine was devastated. She had never been treated so coldly. She tried to think of something she might have done wrong, but nothing came to mind. Her relationship with Mr. Brown had always been so personable.

Nick was infuriated. He started to go after him as he muttered under his breath, "That son-of-a-bitch!"

Katherine grabbed him by the arm and asked that he please let the situation go. She did not want Nick to make a scene on her behalf. She knew how important it was for him to stay out of trouble. He had the family name to protect.

"That son-of-a-bitch. He won't get away with treating you like that."
Nick said, pissed.

"Please calm down, Nick. I think we'd better leave. Maybe it wasn't a
good idea to come here."

"You're right, Katherine! Let's get the hell out of here. I don't want to
catch myself in the same room with that bastard. He hasn't heard the
last of me. I'll call for the limo," Nick gestured for the maitre'd.

"Nick, would you mind if we walked? I don't feel like riding just yet."

"Anything you want, Katherine. I'm sorry I brought you here. I had
no idea something like this would happen. If I—" Before Nick could
continue, Katherine placed her hand over his mouth.

"Being with you this evening has been a dream come true. I don't
want you to apologize for anything. I would do it all again if it meant
being with you, Nick."

As they began to walk away, Nick clutched Katherine into his arms,
and without hesitation the words, "I love you, Miss Mills," came out.
Katherine began to cry as they embraced in a passionate kiss. Her emotions were uncontrollable. She never felt so loved or protected except
when she was with Al, but the love and protection were different. She held
onto Nick, thinking about the look in Nick's eyes as he spoke those words.
It was a look she had seen before. Nick's eyes warmed her heart similar to
Al's when he would tell her he loved her. When the kiss came to a close,
she caressed Nick's cheeks. His eyes glistened in the moonlight.

"I love you too, Mister Walters." Before they knew it, they were deep
into another passionate kiss. They walked away from the Tavern. Nick was
about to bring up the incident again, but Katherine would not let him. She
told him it was their night and nothing would spoil the evening.

While walking around Times Square, trying to decide where they
should eat, Nick spotted a small tattoo parlor. "I have a great idea. I
want to do something special to remember this evening. Katherine, I'm
going to get your name tattooed all over my body."

"Don't be silly, Nick," she replied.

"Katherine, don't try to stop me. I mean it. I'm going to get a tattoo tonight," he said as he quickened his pace toward the parlor. Inside, they noticed that the parlor was empty except for a little old man who worked there. His body, at least what they could see, was covered with tattoos.

"How can I help you this evening?" he asked.

"We are here, or I should say, I am here to get a tattoo. You see, I told this young lady that I love her this evening, and I want a tattoo to remember this night forever."

"Sit down, sir. I think you want something truly special. Let me get my book of love tattoos. I'm sure we'll find something," the man said as he retreated into the back room. Katherine looked at Nick as if he'd lost his mind. She could not believe he was going through with this.

The man returned with a large book. The outside of the book had the words, 'LOVE TATTOOS' in large print. Nick began to thumb through the pages and pictures. None seem to grab his attention. Finally, he asked Katherine to pick a tattoo. He told her he wanted something with her name on it.

Katherine browsed through the book. As Nick watched her, he noticed the beautiful five-leaf clover Katherine had pinned to her dress. He also noticed the pin had something engraved on it. "Katherine, tell me about that pin on your dress. Now that I think of it, you have an attraction to clovers. I remember you were looking at one the first time we went to lunch." Katherine moved closer so Nick could read the engraving. The name 'Sarah' was written on the fifth leaf and 'Al' was written on the stem. "Sarah? Isn't that your mother's name? And, Al, that's your father's name! Katherine, tell me more about this pin."

Katherine told Nick that the pin was a token of love given to her mother from Al on their wedding day and that Al had ordered the fifth leaf put on the pin as a symbol of undying love. She told Nick about the day Al gave her the pin. It was then that Nick decided what type of tattoo he wanted. He asked the tattoo artist to draw a five-leaf clover on his right forearm. He wanted Katherine's name on the fifth leaf and his on the stem. Katherine was touched.

The artist drew the tattoo on Nick's forearm. Katherine watched and held Nick's hand as the tattoo was being engraved. As she watched her handsome hunk going through this painful process, she knew that his feelings were real and definitely not one-sided.

When the artist finished, they stared at the tattoo. Katherine's name flowed across the fifth leaf, and Nick's was perfectly placed on the stem. It was a perfect replica. Only this time, it symbolized the joining of different hearts. Katherine was unable to believe that someone other than Al loved her this much.

They left the parlor after Nick thanked the man and paid him. In the same manner, the man thanked Nick, shaking his hand several times, and Katherine knew Nick had given him a big tip. The two of them stepped outside, their minds focused only on thoughts of each other.

Katherine, unable to repress what she was feeling, spoke first. "Nick, I want to be with you tonight. I want to feel you close to me. I'm feeling something I've never felt before. I want you. Please, I need you." She clutched Nick's arm as she rested her head against his chest.

At first, Nick did not know what to say. He could tell by the look in Katherine's eyes that she was serious. "Katherine, are you sure? I don't want to rush into anything. You know I love you. You have given me a fulfillment that I'd only hoped for. I would love to spend the night making love to you, but I want it to be when you are ready."

Katherine's eyes met Nick's. Her mind was flushed with the thoughts of them in a naked embrace; feeling Nick's muscles enclose her body. "Nick, I have never been more ready. If I should never be loved again or feel this way again, I want to be totally fulfilled this evening. I want to give you the most precious thing I have, myself."

Nick felt the same. His instinct told him the time was right. He needed Katherine also. They went to the Waldorf and booked an elegant room.. It was an evening of intense desire as Nick and Katherine made love. She had given herself to him without regrets. She had never felt such a burning desire, a desire intensified by the height of making love that evening as Nick's rippling muscles enslaved her.

For Nick, it was a commitment to a woman he truly loved, a moment heightened by the enclosure of Katherine's warm body as their souls were joined.

CHAPTER NINE

It was Monday morning and Katherine was back at work. Only today she felt different. There was a warm calm feeling that seemed to envelope her. Her face was radiant as she sat at her desk looking out the window at the blue sky, but seeing the visions of herself and Nick in a naked embrace. The only thought that clouded Katherine's memories of that evening was the fact that this event happened before she married. It was not supposed to be this way. It was totally against her Catholic upbringing. Katherine knew she would continue to wrestle with these thoughts, but, what elated her today, was the fact that Nick's and her love had bonded.

"Hello? Hello, girlfriend," said Gretchen, as she interrupted Katherine's thoughts. "Are you with us? I've seen that look before and I know what it means. I was waiting for you to call me, but I can see you must have been totally preoccupied. Girl, I want details. I want all the details. I want to hear every little inch of details, or should I say every big inch?"

Gretchen stood waiting for Katherine to respond, while Katherine tried to figure out how to change the subject. Yet, she knew how persistent Gretchen could be. As much as she wanted to 'shout to the world' about her and Nick's evening, this was not the person, place or time to discuss her feelings, Gretchen was known to have loose lips.

Katherine decided she would ask Gretchen a few questions, hoping she could elude her. "Tell me about your New Year's party. Give me details!" Katherine said, smiling.

"Girl, don't even try to change the subject. I want to know—was he as good in bed as he is good looking? Girl, do you know how many women would kill for an evening with Nick Walters, myself included? You're sitting here like fresh cheerios floating in milk. I want details, girlfriend! You owe it to me. After all, who showed you how to play hard to get? Wasn't it me, or have you forgotten?" Gretchen asked.

Before Katherine could respond, Michelle walked into the room. Katherine breathed a sigh of relief. Gretchen stood there looking at Michelle with a woman's scorn. Her entire demeanor changed as she glared.

"Katherine, I need to see you in my office. There is something I need to discuss with you," Michelle said as she ignored Gretchen's presence.

"I guess I'd better leave. Three is truly a crowd," Gretchen said, walking behind Michelle as she continued to scowl.

"Katherine, I will meet you in my office. I prefer total privacy." Michelle said as she looked at Gretchen.

"And by the way, Gretchen," Michelle said. " I think it would be a good idea for you to get back to work. Rumor has it your department is unsure of where you actually work most of the time." On that note Michelle left the room.

"That bitch! That no good bitch! If I didn't value my job, I would put my foot in her ass. She's nothing but a little—" Gretchen said, miffed.

Katherine interrupted her. "Gretchen, what in the world is going on? I have never seen the two of you act this way toward each other. Something has happened."

Gretchen sat on the edge of Katherine's desk. Initially she just mumbled words to herself. "I can't believe that bitch! I just can't believe her!" Gretchen said, shaking her whole body as she sat there with her arms folded.

"Gretchen, what in the world is going on?"

"Katherine, I invited Michelle to my New Year's Eve party. I felt sorry for her since her divorce. Miss Thang got to the party almost two hours late. She walks in wearing this slinking white gown, showing major cleavage. Now, that did not surprise me, but when she turned around, the back of the dress was cut to the crack of her butt. That surprised me. She flirted with all the men. That bitch even had the nerve to flirt with my man. I told her right on the spot, "Girlfriend, it ain't that type of party."

Katherine finally understood why Gretchen was so upset. It was always Gretchen who stopped the show when she walked into a room. Katherine didn't say anything, she just listened, and Gretchen kept on talking. She knew Gretchen needed to get this off her chest.

"Katherine, I have to go. I don't want to make you late for your meeting with Miss Thang. Just remember, that innocent little woman role she plays around here is nothing more than bullshit. I got her number, and believe me, I plan to dial it. You know what I mean?"

Gretchen walked toward the door and stopped just before she opened it. "Girlfriend, don't think you got off that easy. I want to have lunch with you today. I want to know what happened. I want details. You have the look on your face that I put on men's faces after an evening with me. Girl, I'll see you later," Gretchen said, laughing.

Katherine smiled as she watched Gretchen walk out, saying to herself, "That woman is crazy, truly crazy."

*　　　　　　　*　　　　　　　*

Meanwhile, Nick had arrived at his family's estate to meet with his father. He had initially scheduled the meeting at his father's office, but John felt it would be best to discuss things at home. He knew what the meeting was going to be about. Nick entered John's study, where John was eagerly awaiting him. He hoped Nick was there to tell him the relationship was over with Katherine.

"Dad, I need to talk to you about Clifford Brown." Nick said, breathless.

"What about Clifford?" John asked, pretending he knew nothing of the incident. He listened as Nick continued to talk.

"Brown was rude to Katherine when I introduced her to him. He might as well have ignored her. He was cold. I could not believe my eyes. A few weeks ago he told me how much he wanted to meet Katherine.

He was pleased with the way she handled his account and how prompt and thorough she was and how much he enjoyed talking to her on the telephone. Katherine was devastated. If it was not for her, I would have…" Nick held his words. He could feel himself getting enraged again. "I don't really know what I would have done. I assure you it would not have been pretty."

"Nick, I have always tried to tell you about the type of woman that is best for you. Women like Katherine and her background are all wrong. I imagine Clifford saw right through her act. I'm insulted that you chose to take her around our close clients."

"Dad, I can't believe you! Here I am discussing an issue that troubles me, and all you can think about is yourself, your clients and your friends. I can't believe what is happening here! I knew I should have handled this myself. I thought I had a father who would understand, or at least listen. You have no idea what love is. That's why mom is never home. You think she likes to fly around the world just for fun. No…it's to get away from you!"

"Let me tell you something!" John moved towards Nick. "You have no right to speak to me that way! I have made you the man you are today! I have given you everything! Do you for one moment think I want to see some little Black trash destroy everything we have worked for? The audacity of you to even speak of your mother and my relationship in that manner! That little gold-digging bitch has blinded you to all reality!"

"Now I see. It's because Katherine is Black that you hate her! That's your problem! Your prejudice will not destroy this relationship! I love Katherine and there is nothing you can do to change that! And, yes, you are right, we have worked hard together. But unlike you, I am not driven by money! You would kill for it. I would rather give it away! We are different, very different! Someday, you will recognize that!" Nick said, as he stormed out of the front door. He knew he'd had the last words, but he also knew his father was a very determined man. A man who would stop at nothing to get what he wanted.

John watched Nick get into his car. Nick drove down the drive so fast that his tires screeched as he almost hit the iron gates. John picked up the telephone. He knew he had to do something. If never before, he realized Nick's relationship with Katherine had to be halted. It was obvious…Nick was blinded by this little jezebel.

"Bobbie, where in the hell have you been? I hope you have what I need on that Katherine slut. I think it's time to put plan D in action. You know…like disappear. I'm at home. I'll wait here for you." John hung up the telephone, enraged.

      *   *   *

In the meantime, Katherine entered Michelle's office. "Please have a seat, Katherine," Michelle gestured toward the chair in front of her desk. "I hope I didn't interrupt company business between you and Gretchen?"

Katherine did not respond. She was not going to allow herself to be dragged into Gretchen's and Michelle's battle. What concerned her more, was why Michelle was acting in such an unusually cold manner toward her. She had never seen her act so businesslike, except for her first day at Walters and Vein. And even then, she had not been so cold and unfriendly. Katherine knew something was wrong as she sat back in the chair waiting for Michelle to reveal what the problem was. Michelle's facial expression was flat. Not a smile or flicker of warmth could be seen. She remained stone-faced as she began to flip through a file that was on her desk.

The suspense was killing Katherine. "Have I done something, Michelle?" she asked.

"Funny you should ask." Michelle said, as she closed the file in front of her. "Katherine, I've received several complaints lately from some of our investors. Several of them have expressed a displeasure in your work. It seems to them you have been less than attentive to their accounts. You have not been following up with them as you used to and your paper work seems less organized. My observation is that you may be a little too preoccupied. Is this a correct assumption?" Michelle stared at Katherine. She could see that her comments had taken Katherine by surprise.

Katherine sat up on the edge of the chair. She could not believe what she had heard. At first, she thought it would be appropriate to discuss the incident regarding Clifford Brown, thinking this was the root of the problem, but she quickly realized there was something deeper. She knew she had done a good job. No one, to her knowledge, had complained about her work. Then it hit her, maybe Michelle was trying to fire her in a nice way. Maybe she had done something wrong and no one had told her, or maybe…so many thoughts began to flow…

Oh my God! I can't lose my job, she thought as the reality of the moment confronted her. Her thoughts settled upon Al, and she realized the pressure he would feel if she lost her job. Katherine did not know what to say. She opened her mouth to speak, but nothing came out.

"Katherine, do you understand what I've said to you? I have personally noticed that you seem a little more absorbed lately in things other than your work."

Finally Katherine spoke. "Michelle, I have worked very hard for my clients. I feel I have done a good job. I assure you, I will do everything I can to satisfy this firm. Please allow me the opportunity to show you." Katherine pleaded.

"I'm not here to drop the ax on you right now, Katherine. I've warned you and I'll be watching you very closely. I mean very closely. I advise you to remain focused on your job," Michelle said, knowing she had put the fear of God in Katherine. She knew how much Katherine needed the job. She also knew she had executed John Walters' plan as directed. Michelle even felt sorry for Katherine, but she could not show her emotion. After all she had to protect her job. To Michelle, this was more important than the friendship she and Katherine had developed.

A brief sense of relief came over Katherine, although she still did not fully understand what had happened. For the moment, she had a job and she had to do everything in her power to keep it. "Thank you, Michelle. I promise I will continue to do the best job I can to represent this firm. If there is something that I am doing wrong, I would appreciate it if you would tell me. I don't want this to affect our friendship," Katherine said as she was about to leave the room.

"Katherine, remember what you are here for." Michelle's final words.

Katherine left shaken. She thought maybe she had been a little more sidetracked lately. She was smart enough to realize that most of her thoughts were centered around Nick. But, she also knew she worked hard and, to her knowledge, the clients seemed very satisfied with her work. She knew something was going on with Mr. Clifford Brown. The pieces did not fit together.

Katherine walked back to her office, relieved because she still had her job. Yet the feeling of uneasiness paralleled her thoughts as she continued to try to understand Michelle's message.

That evening, Nick was to pick her up after work. The plan was for dinner at her place. She had finally told Al about Nick. Matter of fact, Al actually approached her. When Katherine came home on New Year's day, she was beaming. The look in her eyes reminded Al of the look he had seen in Sarah's eyes. When Al asked Katherine if she had met someone, she could not help but tell him the truth.

Katherine was relieved that she had finally told Al, and Al congratulated her and appeared to be happy for her. Katherine wanted the evening to be very special. The two most important men in her life were about to meet. She could not wait. When she returned to her desk, she thought about Nick. Deep within her heart, she could feel that things around her and within her were changing. What bothered her most was that she felt confused. Nick and Al both needed her and she needed them.

CHAPTER TEN

Michelle was at her desk calling John Walters. "Mister Walters, I met with Katherine. I have done everything you requested. I think she realizes she has to make a decision. For her sake, I hope it will be the one to please you."

"Michelle, I hope you're right. You have never let me down in the past. I'm counting on you." John hung up the phone. All of his plans were in motion. He sat back in his chair and waited for Bobbie, as he thought about the timing of putting everything together.

It was an evening Katherine had long awaited. As she left the office, she saw Nick's blue Porsche parked in front of the building. She didn't see Nick, but she sensed his presence. Before she knew it they were lip to lip. His scent surrounded her. In his hand he had the most beautiful long stem pink rose! Katherine did not know who taught him his charm, but she sure liked his style. He was truly her Mister Feel Good.

Nick escorted Katherine to the car and opened the door. He laid the rose in her lap as she sat down. When Nick got in, Katherine gave him a kiss and said 'thank you'. They drove away, both deep in thought. Nick thought about his conversation with John, and wished that he could get him to see that Katherine was different and that she truly loved him. He knew that, if he had to choose between the two of them, it would be Katherine standing at his side.

Katherine wondered how she had gotten herself into all of this. She knew she loved Nick unselfishly and was truly happy, yet she was scared. She wanted to tell him about her conversation with Michelle, but she did not want to upset him, especially after she saw how he reacted toward Mr. Brown.

Nick pulled up in front of Tiffany's Jewelers and parked the car. Katherine did not say anything. "Katherine, I have a surprise for you. Don't say a word." Nick got out and escorted Katherine inside. She saw a picture with musical faces as she entered. This time she knew the artist.

The place was dazzling, as Katherine gazed upon all the beautiful jewelry. Nick led her to an area where a woman awaited his arrival.

"Hello, Mr. Walters. You 're right on time, just like you said you would be."

"I try to be, Barbara. This is Miss Katherine Mills, the young lady I told you about," Nick said proudly.

"Yes, Mr. Walters, I can see why she's so special to you. The two of you look like you were meant for each other."

"Barbara, remind me to pay you later for saying that," Nick said with a grin.

"Is there something going on here I should know about?" Katherine asked as she waited for Nick's response.

"I guess," Nick responded. "Have a seat, Katherine, now close your eyes and don't open them until I tell you."

"Nick, what are you up to?" Katherine asked, curious.

"Katherine, your questions will be answered in a minute. Now close your eyes."

She sat down in the plush chair, closed her eyes and waited. Within seconds, she felt something being placed around her neck.

"Open your eyes," Nick said, as he awaited her response. Katherine could not believe what she saw. Nick stood in front of her, holding a mirror. Hanging around her neck, was a beautiful five-leaf clover diamond necklace. The diamonds sparkled beyond belief. Katherine had never seen anything so beautiful.

"Nick...Nick...it's beautiful." Katherine cried, overwhelmed. Barbara had tears in her eyes as she looked on.

"Alright, let's move on. I hate to see a woman cry," Nick said, trying to break the intensity of the moment. "Katherine, I hope you like it. You deserve so much more."

"Nick, I love it, but not as much as I love you."

"Time to leave, thing are getting steamy," Barbara said, as she walked behind the counter.

"Thanks, Barbara. You did a great job. I love the necklace."

"You're welcome, Mister Walters. I'll be here when you are ready to add some weight to Katherine's hand."

Nick and Katherine beamed as they walked toward the door, Katherine floating in ecstasy over her gift, while Nick was thinking about Barbara's comment. Katherine must have thanked Nick a thousand times for the gift as he prepared to meet Al.

Katherine directed Nick to Sergettie's Restaurant. It was Al's favorite Italian restaurant. Katherine ordered Al's favorite food to go, then she and Nick headed toward the apartment.

CHAPTER ELEVEN

Bobbie arrived at the Walters estate. He carried with him a yellow envelope. John opened the door, eyes blazing as he fired his anger at Bobbie.

"Where in the hell have you been? I've waited all afternoon for you! You told me you would be right over!" he said, as Bobbie entered. John slammed the door shut. As he headed into his study, Bobbie followed. Bobbie had seen him like this before. He knew that, eventually, John would calm down, so he decided to ride out the barrage. John slammed the door to his study as he continued his attack.

"Do you know what that is? A telephone!" John demanded, shaking his phone at Bobbie. "A simple phone call to say, I will be late, I'm stuck in traffic or I don't give a shit, would have been nice!"

Bobbie did not want John to continue. He knew John could become uncontrollable and the conversation would go nowhere. "John, take it easy, I apologize. Believe me, I would have done all the above. Of course, I would not tell you I don't give a shit. After I spoke to you, I received a phone call regarding Katherine's old man. You see, I sent two of my best men out to get all the details on that family. One of them spent most of his time following the old man around. It seems Katherine's old man is about to kick the bucket. You know what I mean, like deadsville."

"What the hell does that have to do with me? I want to get rid of the daughter, not the father!" John said, banging his big fist on the desk and wondering why Bobbie bothered to tell him this.

"Before you say anything else, John, listen. I was informed by my men that the old man has a brain tumor. They followed him down to Sinai hospital. After he left, they slipped a few bucks to the ward clerk and she let them see his records. It appears he has about six to twelve months to live. Its probably going to get pretty ugly near the end, from what I've been told. He doesn't have any insurance. The girl will be unable to take care of him. I think we should offer her some money to take care of her father and, in return, she would leave Nickki. I see this as an offer she would not refuse, especially if she loves her old man as much as she tells everyone she does."

"What makes you think that little gold-digging bitch wouldn't ask Nick for the money?" John asked.

"She might be a gold digger, John, but she is in love with Nickki and, from what you are telling me, Nickki is in love with her."

"That's bullshit! I don't want to hear it!. She doesn't love him! Nick is pussy-whipped. I don't know what in the hell he's thinking anymore!" John yelled.

"Believe me, John, my source knows her well and I believe her." Bobbie said.

"Your source! Who in the hell is your source?" John asked, puzzled.

"You know...Gretchen, the transplant you hired at the office."

"Sure I know her. I think you mean implant. How did she become your source? John asked.

"Transplant, implant, whatever. It seems our Gretchen has befriended this Katherine. Over the past few weeks, I've been spending my evenings with Gretchen. You know there isn't much she wouldn't do for money or sex, John. I'm sure you still have your time with her."

"That's beside the point," John said. "What did she tell you?"

"It seems this Katherine has been quite taken by Nickki. From what Gretchen said, she sincerely cares for him, not his money, John."

John sat down as he listened.. It was obvious Bobbie's comments had captured his thoughts. Bobbie could tell John was listening. It was the hands behind the head that gave this away.

"Bobbie, what do you suggest I do? I can't believe this little peasant could truly be in love with my son, or he with her. I will be damned, before I let this relationship proceed."

"John, I know this is a hard pill for you to swallow, but Gretchen felt even Ray Charles could see Katherine was in love with Nickki and Nickki in love with her."

"Forget the bullshit, Bobbie. What do you suggest I do? I brought you here for answers."

"Let's force her to break it off with Nickki. I know just what to do, John, trust me"

"This better work. If not, I will have the little bitch annihilated," John said, sweeping everything from his desk onto the floor.

"That would not be a good idea, John. Nickki would never forgive you. Remember, he knows what you are capable of doing. We have to let Katherine deal the cards. It's the only way. If for one moment Nickki felt you had something to do with this, it would destroy your relationship. Then, you would have to leave all those millions to me," Bobbie said with the most peculiar look on his face.

"Cut the bullshit, Bobbie. Tell me what you have in mind. It better be good. More importantly, it better work," John said, pissed.

CHAPTER TWELVE

Nick and Katherine pulled up in front of the apartment building. There was a crowd gathered, including Officer Glen. Nick parked the car. The two of them rushed over to see what was going on. From afar, they could hear a woman crying and yelling. The voice sounded familiar to Katherine. It was Mrs. Gonzales. She and her husband owned the grocery store on the corner.

"Officer Glen, what happened?" Katherine asked, as she tried to catch her breath.

"Katherine, someone tried to rob the store. I just happened to be walking by. The robbers saw me and they fled. Mr. Gonzales was shot in the shoulder."

"Is he going to be okay?" Katherine asked.

"I expect he'll be fine, Glen responded. The bullet did not hit any vital area. I think he's in shock. We're waiting for the ambulance to get here."

"Thank God," said Katherine as she looked towards Mr. Gonzales, who was sitting up against the storefront, holding his shoulder with a blood soaked rag.

Mrs. Gonzales was hysterical. She was saying something in Spanish that Katherine did not understand. "*A donde esta los medicos? A donda esta los medicos ovando necesitan?*"

"Officer Glen, I'm glad you were here," Katherine said as Nick cleared his throat, hinting for an introduction.

"I'm sorry! Officer Glen, this is a dear friend of mine, Nick Walters."

"Pleased to meet you Nick," said Glen, as he reached out to shake Nick's hand. "Katherine is a very special lady around here. We're proud of her."

"Thank you," Nick responded. " I think she is very special, also, and she speaks highly of you."

Katherine allowed the two of them time to talk, while she checked on Mr. and Mrs. Gonzales. Mrs. Gonzales hugged Katherine, and Katherine assured her that everything would be alright and to call her if she needed anything. Feeling that everything was under control, Katherine and Nick went into the building.

When they got inside, Nick could not help but comment about Officer Glen. "You seemed a little taken by him. You had that schoolgirl look in your eyes every time you looked at him."

"Mister Nick Walters! Do I detect some jealousy in that voice?"

"Of course not, I just made a simple observation."

" I used to have a crush on Officer Glen…I think all the girls did. For me, that ended when I met this hunk of a man with the most beautiful blue eyes. Officer Glen still makes me feel very safe. Nick, I haven't seen this side of you, but I find it rather charming." Nick set the bag of food down, pulled Katherine close to him and gave her a sultry kiss that seemed to last forever.

"Mister Nick Walters, I love you. You don't ever have to worry about another man. My heart is yours, and yours to keep. Now don't say anything. Let's go meet my dad. The food is probably still piping hot, from all the heat we're sending off."

Nick smiled. "Katherine Mills, don't ever change. I love the way you make me feel." He picked up the bag and they got on the elevator.

"Daddy, I'm home." Katherine yelled. She could tell that Nick was a little nervous as he squeezed her hand tighter. Katherine called out to Al again. She noticed Al's newspaper and glasses were in the easy chair. There was a cup of coffee on the table next to the chair. She picked up the cup, it was still warm. Katherine relaxed, thinking Al was probably in his room and could not hear her.

"I'm sure he'll be out in a moment," Katherine said, as she welcomed Nick to her humble abode. "Have a seat, Nick. I'll be back in a moment.

I need to freshen up. My father should be making an appearance at any second. Just tell him you are here to sweep his daughter away. That comment will get the two of you started on the right track."

"Sure," Nick responded. His facial expression said it all.

"I'm just kidding! Dad's really a pussycat, don't worry. Make yourself at home." Katherine walked into her bedroom.

Upon entering the room, she detected a foul odor. She could not figure out what it was or where it was coming from. As she walked toward her bathroom door, the scent became stronger. She pushed on the door, but it would not open. She pushed harder and the door opened enough for Katherine to see Al's feet and legs. He was lying on the floor.

Katherine let out a horrendous scream. Nick ran into the room. Katherine kept screaming and crying. As Nick moved closer, he saw Al's body through the partially opened door. He immediately proceeded to push on the door.

"It's my dad! Nick, I couldn't open the door! Please help him! Please!" Katherine cried out in shock.

Nick pushed on the door with all his strength. Abruptly the door opened. Al was lying in a pool of vomit and his skin was as white as a ghost's.

"Daddy! Daddy!" Katherine screamed as she rushed to his side. When she lifted his head, she could see he was still breathing, but he did not respond.

"Please, call for help," she sobbed, holding Al in her arms. "Oh, daddy! I love you! Please be okay! I need you! I love you. I love you." Katherine held Al, as she waited for help, devastated.

"Katherine, I'm here to help. I heard over the radio that something had happened up here." It was Officer Glen. "The ambulance just arrived to pick up Mr. Gonzales. They'll take your father, too. Nick is directing them. Don't worry, everything will be alright."

"Officer Glen, please help him! Please help him! Tell me he will be alright! I love him! I need him." Katherine cried, stroking Al's pale face and sobbing, as she pleaded for help.

Al was still breathing, but it appeared he did not have much time. Katherine watched the paramedics place Al on the stretcher. His right arm fell limp, dangling off the stretcher. Katherine turned to Nick, and her head sank onto his chest as she wept.

CHAPTER THIRTEEN

Their arrival at Sinai Hospital was like a scene out of a movie. When Katherine stepped out of the ambulance, there were people everywhere. Officer Glen, along with the ambulance attendants, had radioed ahead regarding Mr. Gonzales and Al. By far, Al's condition was definitely the more serious, although Mr. Gonzales had lost a fair amount of blood and Mrs. Gonzales was a nervous wreck.

On the way to the hospital, Al had several seizures. Fortunately, the paramedics were able to stabilize him. Al's body was limp, his skin was so pale, you would think he didn't have an ounce of blood in him. The stench was dizzying as the oxygen mask covered his face. It was difficult for Katherine to watch as they rolled him to the emergency room. The man who was always her rock of Gibraltar, lay helplessly on a gurney like a piece of meat waiting to be slaughtered.

"It's all my fault, Nick. I should have been there for him. I knew he was devastated over the loss of his job. He tried to be strong, but I'm sure that was just for me. I worried about him because he was losing weight and not eating right. Every time I brought up the subject, he would say, 'Don't worry. I'm okay. I'm okay.'" Katherine went on.

"Katherine, it's not your fault. Everything will be okay," Nick said, hugging Katherine.

Several hours had passed since their arrival. The nurses kept Katherine updated on Al's condition, which remained critical. Katherine slowly began to regain her composure as she and Nick sat in the family waiting area. This seemed so foreign to Katherine. She had never spent any time in a hospital before. The people were all very nice, and everyone in the room seemed worried. She knew they were all feeling the same as she was.

Looking down the corridor, Katherine noticed a man in a long white coat coming toward her. Her heart pounded as she watched the doctor approach. She clutched Nick's hand so tight, it was turning white. The doctor's face was unreadable as he approached her, with one hand in his pocket and the other carrying a yellow folder of some type. He had on a funny-looking blue hat. It matched the covers on his shoes. Katherine wanted to run, but not a muscle in her body would allow her to move.

"Miss Mills," the doctor called out as he looked in her direction.

"Doctor, this is Miss Katherine Mills," Nick spoke out. "Do you have an update on her father's condition?"

"Yes, I do. Are you a member of the family?"

"Well, you can say that. I'm Katherine's fiancé, Nick Walters."

"If you don't mind, I would like to speak to the two of you in private. If you would please follow me…There is a room across the hall where we can talk."

"I know it! I know it, he's dead! That's why he wants to talk to me in private! He's dead!" Katherine cried out as she placed her hands over her face.

"Katherine, we don't know anything for sure. Lets hope for the best. I'm here with you." Nick helped her to her feet as they followed the doctor into a room. The room was small and cold. There were no pictures on the walls, and there were just a couple of chairs and a table. Katherine sat down, as she clutched Nick's hand. She could not look the doctor in the face. She stared at the folder he placed on the table. The name, Al R. Mills was written at the top. The R stood for Richard, Al's father's name.

"Miss Mills, my name is Doctor Singh. I'm a neurosurgeon, and I've been taking care of your father for several months?"

"What do you mean, several months? My father has not been sick. I don't understand."

Nick, also was perplexed, as he waited for the doctor to continue speaking. He didn't recall Katherine saying anything about Al being sick, although he knew she was concerned about his drinking.

"Miss Mills, your father has been ill for quite a while, at least six to seven months. He did not want anyone to know. As a matter of fact, when he first came to see us, it was because he was having very bad headaches. The headaches had started to affect his job performance. We initially treated him with pain medication, but that did not help.

Finally, my associate ordered a brain scan. A tumor was detected…a large inoperable tumor."

"I don't believe this! My father has never complained of headaches. I've never seen him take medicine. I don't understand. Tell me what is going on. Is he alright? What do you mean by inoperable? I need to know."

"He will be okay for now, although he is in very serious condition. He had several seizures and he has aspirated."

"What do you mean by aspirate? Please talk to me so I can understand. You haven't answered my question about the tumor being inoperable. Please!" Katherine begged.

"I apologize, Miss Mills. I'm trying to help you understand. Sometimes it is difficult, so please bear with me. Inoperable means that the tumor is too large to remove. If we try to remove it, it would probably kill your father. I'm sorry." Dr. Singh paused, giving Katherine a few seconds to collect her thoughts.

"Aspiration means fluid went into his lungs. This will probably lead to infection so we have started antibiotics. Several measures have been taken to try and prevent this from happening again.

"To answer your other question, he will most likely get better and you will be able to take him home. However, we will have to be extremely careful, because this may happen again. What is most important for you to understand," he continued, "is that your father is a very sick man. I would expect he has approximately six to eight months to live. He will need a lot of care, and we will do everything in our power to help you. I'm sorry. I wish I didn't have to tell you this, but I feel it is important that you understand everything."

"Is there anything that can be done? Has he gotten a second opinion? What type of things should I watch out for?" Katherine asked as she tried to understand.

"Yes, he has received a second opinion. The diagnosis and prognosis were confirmed."

"Doctor Singh, please explain this to me. I don't understand what you are saying."

"Again, Miss Mills, I'm sorry. His brain tumor has been confirmed by another specialist, and the location of the tumor has been reviewed. There is not a life-saving way that it can be removed. All we can hope for is to shrink it, possibly slow the growth and treat your father's symptoms. To further answer your questions, you need to know that, at times, your father may not be able to say your name, although he knows who you are. You need to look over the things that he writes. He may sometimes get words or numbers mixed up or turned around. Just give him lots of love and support. Let him know you're there for him. Try not to worry about all the things that may go wrong.

"I'm so sorry, Miss Mills." Doctor Singh said as he grabbed Katherine's hand. "My staff and I will do everything we can to help the two of you. Here's my card. Call me if you should have any further questions."

Katherine leaned back in her chair, heaving a long sigh. She could not believe the news she had received. She thought about Al having difficulty on the job, and realized that this must have been the cause. The drinking—the sudden change in his behavior—it was all beginning to make sense to some degree, although she knew she was reaching for answers. The hardest question she asked herself was, why had Al not told her?

Nick placed his arm around her. Doctor Singh gave her hand a soft squeeze, as he stood up. "Hang in there, Katherine, I will talk to you later. We'll be sending your father up to one of our units in about an hour. You'll be able to see him then. I'll send one of the nurses to get you, and I'll talk with you again at that time."

"Thank you," Katherine whispered, her eyes fixed on Doctor Singh's.

Dr. Singh left the room. Nick and Katherine sat in a quiet embrace, Katherine resting her head on Nick's shoulder. So many thoughts were going through both their heads; thoughts that needed to be organized and prioritized before they could share them with each other.

Nick looked around the cold picture-less room. He could smell the perfume from Katherine's hair as he held her. For the first time in his life, he had a reason to think about the loss of someone near and dear to him. He began to think about what he would feel, if he were receiving this type of news about his father or mother. He knew it would trouble him, but it bothered him because he was unable to tell how much.

Nick knew that Katherine's feelings were genuine. The emotional upheaval proved her love. This disturbed him, because he had never been close to either of his parents. Nannies took care of him when he was young. His father had insisted he go to boarding school. His mother traveled to avoid being around his tyrant father. When he finally finished school and came home to live, it was all business. John Walters had become so obsessed with Nick learning the business, he forgot to let Nick know he had a father. As for his mother, she continued to travel. Nick never knew what she truly thought about him. Holding Katherine, he thought: *What if something happened to me? Who would care? Who would miss me?* He knew the answer rested in his arms.

CHAPTER FOURTEEN

Several days passed and Al was coming home. He was moved from the critical care unit to the medicine floor. Katherine tried to mentally prepare herself for his homecoming. She had spent most of her time at the hospital by Al's side. It was difficult for Al to tell her the truth about his health, but, one evening, he finally did so. Al told Katherine he had hoped that all of this was a bad dream. He thought he would eventually wake up and it would be over and he would have his health back. He told her there were so many times that he had wanted to tell her, but he just couldn't. He explained to Katherine that he knew she was happy. It was obvious, well before she told him about Nick, and he did not want to spoil that for her. That evening, the two of them wept as they realized what was forthcoming in their lives. They had shared so many precious moments together, but none was as precious as that evening.

When Katherine arrived home that evening, she sat in Al's easy chair and reminisced. She could not imagine what life would be like without him. He was her father, mother and friend. She worried about how she would provide his healthcare and his home care, as Al's medical insurance had expired. They had been unable to keep paying the high premiums. Katherine was sure Al did everything he could to maintain his insurance. She thought back to the days when he had struggled to keep his part time job that did not work out. It must have been due to the brain tumor, she thought.

Her thoughts were interrupted by someone knocking at her door. She knew Nick was at work; She had just finished talking to him a few hours ago. She walked towards the door, thinking it was probably Mrs. Gonzales stopping by to ask how Al was doing and to update her on Mr. Gonzales, who was scheduled to be discharged tomorrow.

Looking through the peep-hole, she asked, "Who is it?" All she could see was darkness. Whoever was out there, was standing very close to the door, or they were wearing something very dark. Katherine was unable to tell who was on the other side.

"I'm here from Walters and Vein," a man's voice spoke out.

She opened the door, startled. In front of her stood Bobbie. For a fleeting moment, she was speechless. It was obvious he was not from the FTD florist. He carried a large briefcase as though he was about to take a trip.

It was Bobbie, and he was not alone. Two of his henchmen waited downstairs in the car. The other two waited by the elevator, out of Katherine's sight, in case Bobbie needed help. This was Bobbie's first visit to Upper Manhattan, and he did not know what to expect. Today, he would implement the plan he and John Walters had concocted. John felt the timing was perfect, and Bobbie was there that evening to deliver the goods.

"Are you Miss Mills? Miss Katherine Mills?" Bobbie asked. He had more pictures of her than a photo studio, as his men had followed her every move for weeks.

Katherine, unsettled at first, thought that maybe she should lie and say she was the housekeeper. But she knew that wouldn't work. She replied nervously, "Yes, that's me. I mean…I'm she…whatever." Her voice cracked.

Bobbie sensed the anxiety he created and he loved it. He did his best work when people were afraid of him. "John Walters sent me."

"Are you talking about Nick Walters? I don't understand."

"No, I'm talking about John Walters."

"John Walters. You mean John Walters from Walters and Vein? I don't understand."

"May I come in and talk to you?" Bobbie asked.

Katherine did not move. She continued to question him. "Do you mean **the** John Walters?" Something must have happened to Nick. For what other reason would John Walter send someone to her house?

"Has something happened to Nick?" She had to know.

"Nickki, I mean Nick, is okay," Bobbie replied.

Katherine was really puzzled now. Within the last few minutes, she had gone through feelings of fear, anxiety, astonishment and now relief. She still did not know why Bobbie was visiting her. "Please come in, I'm sorry if I seem a little weird today. It seems so many things have been going on lately," she explained, as Bobbie walked in carrying the briefcase.

"You have a very nice apartment Miss Mills."

"Thank you, please have a seat. Would you like something to drink?"

"No thanks, I appreciate the offer. Forgive me, I forgot to introduce myself. My name is Bobbie, and I work for, or I might say, work **with** John Walters."

"Do you work at the downtown office?" Katherine asked, making small talk.

Bobbie chose not to answer. "Miss Mills, Mr. John Walters is very concerned about your financial status, and he would like to help. That is the main reason I'm here."

"That is very generous of Mr. Walters. I really appreciate his thoughtfulness, but I cannot accept. My father told me never to borrow money that I can't pay back."

"Miss Mills, the money does not have to be paid back. It is yours. There is enough money here to help with your father's medical bills plus a whole lot more." Bobbie placed the briefcase on the coffee table and opened it. Katherine could not believe what she saw. The briefcase was filled with hundred dollar bills; thousands of hundred dollar bills, all neatly stacked.

Perplexed, Katherine looked at Bobbie. She did not understand why Mr. Walters was being so generous. As much as she knew the money would help, she could not bring herself to accept it.

"I don't understand. Do you mean that Mister Walters would give me this money for nothing?" Then it hit Katherine. "I can't take it. I don't want Nick to spend his money this way. Thank you for coming. I really appreciate the gesture, and I will thank Nick when I see him."

"Miss Mills!" Bobbie said in a stern voice. "Nick Walters knows nothing about this, but you are very astute. There is something, however, that John Walters wants from you." Katherine clung to Bobbie's every word.

"He wants you to break off the relationship with his son."

Infuriated by Bobbie's comment, Katherine stood up and looked down at the stranger. Bobbie did not move, as his stare became even more piercing.

"Mister Bobbie, or whatever your name is, I think you should leave, and please take your money with you! I can't be bought," Katherine said as she pushed the briefcase toward him. "It all makes sense now. John Walters doesn't think I'm good enough for his son. He thinks I'm some poor girl after his money. Now, I know why I never got an invitation to the Walters'…I was not good enough for them. They must picture me as the Black woman from the wrong side of the tracks trying to woo their son. I can't believe the audacity of that man…that family!" Katherine said, appalled.

"John Walters never had the guts to meet me. He's probably sitting on his throne at the office thinking, 'poor Katherine, what an embarrassment to my family! I can't believe my son cares for that woman'. Well, he can't change that! It must be eating him alive, knowing that Nick loves me. That's why you're here! Well just leave…get out and take—"

Before she could finish, Bobbie was towering over her. "Wait a minute, you little low-life Black bitch!" Bobbie said, inching toward Katherine. She backed up toward the kitchen table, terrified. She tried to scream, but nothing came out. Her heart was beating faster as the sweat of fear made its presence. Bobbie pushed her against the table, and she stumbled backwards, clutching at the table to prevent herself from falling.

"I've tried the nice approach, now it's time to give you the big picture, bitch!

Listen to me, you little slut," Bobbie said, as he grabbed Katherine's collar. "You don't understand. If you don't break up this relationship and leave New York, Nick will be disinherited. Do you understand what I'm saying? Disinherited! He will have nothing. All of the hard work he has put into the business will have been for nothing. He will no longer be the heir to the Walters millions. Do you think he could be happy being with you, if that happened? He would never forgive you, no matter how hard he tried or how much he loved you. Every time he looked at you, it would be a look of resentment. He would despise you. Could you live with that, bitch? You better wise up and do it now! Take the money and help your poor dying old man go in peace. At least, you can do that for him. If you don't break up the relationship, Mister Walters will get rid of your little ass! I hear you're smart. You'd better put your brains to work!" Bobbie yelled, as he lifted Katherine and threw her against the wall.

Katherine fell, defenseless, her eyes as big as Christmas ornaments. She had never been beaten in her life. She prayed; her eyes fixed on Bobbie's knees as he stood before her.

Bobbie walked over to the coffee table and pulled a yellow envelope out of the briefcase. He threw it towards Katherine. "Inside, you will find instructions regarding what you should say to Nickki when you end this farce. Remember, if you tell him anything about this, he will be disinherited, and I will do away with you. You won't get the opportunity to see your old man cold. I'm leaving the money. When your father is discharged from the hospital, I expect you to leave town, and never set eyes on Nickki again. If you do, I will make sure you don't live to regret it. I'm sure you're smart enough to know what that means! You will also find some of your father's medical records in the envelope. Don't bother to make any contacts once you leave."

Bobbie walked out. Katherine, emptied by what had just transpired, looked at the yellow envelope nestled next to her and, with one big kick, sailed it to the other side of the room. She knew her fate rested between the folds of that envelope.

CHAPTER FIFTEEN

It was the evening prior to Al's discharge from the hospital. Katherine sat on the side of her bed, reliving her encounter with Bobbie. She couldn't get the thoughts of that evening out of her mind. She had become somewhat of a recluse since the incident, only leaving the house to see Al. She avoided any personal encounter with Nick. Even their telephone conversations were limited. She told Nick she was busy planning for Al's homecoming, and Nick loved her enough to give her the space she needed.

Katherine had extended her time-off from the job. She feared ever walking back into that building. What she really feared was running into John Walters, now that she knew how much he hated her.

She read and reread the details in the yellow envelope. The plot was for Katherine to tell Nick that she had decided to end the relationship because of her father. She would tell him she realized that it would never work. They even had the nerve to include when she should cry, as she spoke to Nick, in order to seem more convincing.

The one thing Bobbie had said, that Katherine kept hearing over and over again, was that Nick would resent and despise her if he were disinherited. She did not want to be responsible for Nick losing his inheritance. She knew how hard he had worked to help build the business and how much he looked forward to becoming the chief executive officer someday. In her hand, she clutched the five-leaf clover pin that Al had given her. She knew the time she and Al had left was limited. The more she thought about it, the tighter she clutched the pin and the clearer her decision became. She had to choose between the two men she loved. To some, this decision would be a gift from God, but Katherine felt it was God's way of punishing her. Katherine knew that seeing Nick for the last time would be difficult. She did not know if she could go through with the plan as directed, but she could not leave without telling Nick something…it would break his heart.

She decided to leave New York City and take Al to a place where he could live out the rest of his days in peace. She wanted to leave the money behind, but she knew they could not survive without it. She looked at the briefcase setting on the floor. "John Walters! I hate you! I hate you!" she screamed, as she pounded her fist against the bed.

Leaving the man she loved, for the father she loved and adored. How ironic! The thought etched itself in her mind. *Someday, someday you will get yours, John Walters',* Katherine vowed, as she buried her head under her pillow. Never had it been so clear in her mind what had to be done.

She decided to call Nick as she reluctantly reach for the telephone.

"Hello?" John Walters answered, and Katherine dropped the phone, terrified. She felt as if John Walters was standing in front of her.

"Katherine! Katherine!" John shouted. He knew it was Katherine. He had expected she would be calling that evening. Bobbie had made it clear to John that Katherine would follow the plans. His men continued to keep a close watch on her. They were well aware of Al's impending discharge from the hospital, and so was John Walters.

"Katherine, pick up the telephone! I know it's you! Pick it up!" John shouted.

She stared at the phone as John's voice seemed to echo from every corner of her bedroom. As she reached for the telephone, her hand began to shake as the sweat from her armpits ran down her side. Slowly she picked up the telephone. She did not say a word. John Walters could hear her breathing.

"Katherine, you'd better not let me down. I don't play games. Everything Bobbie said, he meant. Do you understand? Do you hear me?"

"Yes," Katherine replied timidly. She was mentally exhausted.

John heard Nick coming down the grand stairs. He was getting ready to walk out of the front door when John called him over to the telephone.

"Nick, you have a telephone call. It's Katherine."

Nick was surprised by John's nice manner. He hoped that maybe the old man was beginning to soften. Nick gave him a rather peculiar look, as he reached for the phone.

"Hello, Katherine, how's Al doing? It's good to hear your voice. I miss you. Are you okay?"

" I'm fine, Nick." Tears filled every line of her face. "Nick, I want to see you tonight. I need to see you tonight."

"Katherine, those are the best words I've heard in a couple of weeks. How about if I pick you up at your place and we go for a ride?"

"I'd like that. That would be nice," Katherine replied.

"Katherine, are you alright? You sound a little down."

"I'm fine. I just miss you. I'm okay."

"Give me about a hour, and I'll be there. I need to stop and get some gas. See ya, pretty lady."

"See ya," Katherine said softly as she hung up the phone. She had no idea where she would find the strength to pull this off, and she asked God to forgive her.

John Walters stood in the background watching Nick. "See ya," he muttered to himself as he watched Nick dash out the door. He knew Nick would be different when he returned, but he felt that, in time, Nick would get over the little slut. To have Katherine out of his son's life, was the only thing he cared about. As John peered through the window watching Nick drive off, the words, 'Good riddance to bad rubbish', parted from his lips. He walked into his study and poured himself a brandy, as he sat back in his chair envisioning how the little peasant would perform her script.

CHAPTER SIXTEEN

It did not take long for Nick to reach Katherine's apartment, and she was waiting in front of the building. It seemed that the apartment that once brought her great peace, love, and warmth, had now become something else. All she could think about, was the night Bobbie entered her life, and how violated and helpless she felt.

Katherine watched Nick get out of the car. She was unable to move. She wished she could stand there forever.

"Sweet lady, it is so good to see you. I've been thinking about you a lot. You won't believe how good it made me feel when you called." Nick kissed her. Katherine felt the heat rush through her body, as if a volcano was about to erupt. A fire raged inside her as Nick's embrace made her heart stop.

How will I tell him? How can I do this? Dear God, I love him. Please help me. Show me another way...I would do anything to keep him..., she thought as she continued to kiss Nick. She knew there was no other way. Even if he gave up everything for her, she knew it would not be enough to satisfy John Walters. He wanted her out of Nick's life, dead or alive, and she knew that Bobbie had meant every word he said. Katherine could not bear the thought of Al dying alone, wondering what had happened to his daughter when he needed her most. That would be a fate worse than death. She could not see beyond the clouds, so she knew what she had to do. It would be best for all involved. Slowly pulling away from Nick, she looked up into his beautiful blue eyes. His look was so intense, she felt she could see into his soul. Nick's soul was speaking to her as the silence surrounded them. *I love you, Katherine Mills. I love you.* His lips did not move. It was the voice of his soul, and that voice was loud. Both of them stood silently, breathing only to stay alive for each other.

The encounter lasted for several moments, but for Katherine, it seemed like years. She did not want the moment to end, she awakened to the reality of the situation when Nick spoke.

"Katherine, where would you like to go? Are you hungry? You seem a little tired tonight. Is everything okay?"

"Everything is fine, Nick, just fine. Let's just go for a ride. I want to see the lights of the city, and to take a good look at New York tonight," she said as they got into the car. She cursed the devil for what he was forcing her to do as she leaned against Nick's shoulder, looking up at all the beautiful city lights as they drove along the streets of the city. Katherine became so engrossed in her own orbit, that she did not even pay any attention to where Nick was going. Suddenly the car came to a stop, and they were in front of the Waldorf Hotel. She looked at Nick as he turned to look at her.

"Katherine, I need to be with you tonight. I need to feel the warmth of our bodies together. I need you. I want you. I love you."

She began to cry. To be here with him again was a dream come true. She needed to feel the naked warmth of his body and hold him in her arms like she never held him before, to feel the warmth of his breath as it blew through the fine hairs on her neck.

She knew this was not the script written for her by Bobbie or John Walters, but she did not care. She would play it her way. She would decide the final dress rehearsal. Katherine had prepared a letter. She knew she would never be able to tell Nick to his face that she was leaving. She could not live with the pain she would see on his face. Katherine wanted Nick's pain to be felt by John Walters. *Let him live with this. The bastard deserves it!* she thought.

They made love until their bodies ached from the weakness. It was as if both of them knew this would be the last time. She allowed every muscle in her body to be possessed by Nick as he took control of every inch of her. When Nick fell asleep, his body wrapped around Katherine, she was unable to sleep. As she watched Nick sleeping, she could only think about what she was about to do. She knew there would never be anyone to take his place in her heart.

Nick was at peace. He had a soft smile on his face that highlighted one of his dimples. His perfectly groomed mustache provided a light shadow over his soft lips. His muscular arm lay softly over the spread. Katherine looked at the five-leaf clover tattoo on his forearm. She leaned over and place her face softly against it. "I'll always love you Nick Walters. I'll always love you," she whispered, before she quietly inched her way out of the bed and got dressed. From her purse, she pulled out a white envelope and set it on the bed, next to Nick. She gazed at him one last time, her heart shattered and tears falling like a broken faucet, then she closed the door behind her. As she ran down the corridor, she vowed that this would never happen to her again. Some day, John Walters would feel the same pain he had caused her, and more...

CHAPTER SEVENTEEN

Katherine rushed home to gather the few belongings that she had packed for herself and Al. She had to move fast, before Nick was able to catch up with her. If he did, she knew she would not be able to leave him again, and her worst nightmare would come true. She quickened her pace, as she grabbed her green duffel bag from her closet. She'd decided to use this bag to carry the money. She could not bear the thought of taking the black briefcase; it would be like having Bobbie and John Walters there with her. It was enough she had to carry the dirty money at all!

There…I'm ready, Katherine thought to herself, as she looked at the three bags. She finished stuffing the money in the duffel bag. There was a bag of clothes for her, and one for Al as Katherine looked around the apartment. She had everything she needed. She closed the door behind her and rushed to the elevator, her thoughts fixed on Nick. She kept envisioning him waking up, reading the letter and coming after her. She knew he would not understand. She had to get to the hospital, as time was beginning to run out.

Katherine flagged down a yellow cab. "Please, I need to get to Sinai Hospital," she said, as she threw the bags into the back seat of the cab. Exhausted, she looked around her, still feeling that Nick might appear.

"Is everything alright, Miss?" the cabbie asked

"Yes, I'm just in a hurry." Katherine responded.

The driver clocked his meter and drove off. Katherine saw Officer Glen directing traffic, but he could not see her. *He finally made it,* she thought. Officer Glen was no longer working underground. He was above ground for all to see. *And, so deserving,* Katherine thought, as she kept her eyes fixed on him until he faded away in the distance.

She remembered all the times Glen had made her and the other girls feel so safe. For a fleeting moment, she thought about running to Glen for help, but she knew this would not work. John Walters was too powerful and too ruthless.

Katherine had decided to take Al to a small town called Alberville, in upstate New York. She'd heard about Alberville from Gretchen. It was a place that Gretchen and her family had visited when she was a child. According to Gretchen, few people knew about this small quiet town. Even Gretchen had stopped visiting the place, after her parents died in a plane crash while coming home from a getaway weekend in Alberville. Gretchen told Katherine that she could never visit the place again after the accident, but it was the most beautiful place on this side of heaven. The visual impact of Alberville had remained steadfast in Katherine's mind ever since Gretchen had told her about it. Not knowing anyone or having any other family, Katherine didn't know much about any other place. She was a New Yorker through and through, but Alberville seemed like the ideal place to take Al. If it was, indeed, the most beautiful place this side of heaven, Al deserved to spend his final days there.

The cab pulled up in front of the hospital, and Katherine jumped out. "Please wait, I'll only be a few minutes. I have to get my father."

"No problem Miss. My time is your time. It's your money. I'll be here."

"Thank you," she said, as she closed the door. She rushed into the hospital, then stopped suddenly. She remembered that she had left the money in the cab, so she rushed outside. The driver was waiting patiently as he read his paper. Katherine breathed a sigh of relief as she opened the car door.

"That was quick, Miss. Where's your father?" the cabbie inquired.

"I haven't seen him yet. I forgot something he needed," Katherine said, realizing she couldn't tell the driver she had a bag of money, even though he appeared to be an honest man. Trust no one, she thought, as she reached into the back seat and grabbed the green duffel bag. The idea that people are nice if you are nice to them is no longer true. This was a lesson learned from the best: John Walters and his crony, Bobbie. "It's his clothes," Katherine explained, looking at the driver as if she were stealing from herself.

"Miss, you will have to leave something behind or pay me now. I've been burnt from customers in the past, playing that 'I'll be back' routine."

"I'm not taking all my things; just this bag. Please, I need your service more than you could imagine. Please trust me." Katherine pleaded.

The driver looked at Katherine, but did not say a word. Katherine knew she had to do something. She reached into her pocket and pulled out a one hundred-dollar bill. "Take this, it's more than enough. Please wait, I'll be right back."

"I'll wait. Like I said before...my time is your time. It's your money," the cabbie said, stuffing the money into his shirt pocket. He opened his newspaper and started reading again, as if nothing had happened.

Katherine rushed into the hospital By the time she reached Al's room, she looked a mess. The collar of her coat was partially turned in. Her hair was half frazzled, as if she had gotten tangled up in a blow dryer. The anxiety was killing her. She had to keep moving. Time was running out, and she knew it.

Al was dressed and anxiously awaiting her arrival. Although it was very early, he was ready to go home. Katherine stood in the doorway of Al's room, and watched the nurse help him button his coat. It broke Katherine's heart to see Al so weak and helpless. He had lost several pounds since his hospitalization. His clothes were loose and they hung from his once-toned frame. They appeared huge. Katherine watched as the nurse placed four extra notches in Al's belt to keep his pants up, then helped him to the wheelchair.

She ran over and gave Al a big hug, then kissed him on the cheek. She could see, as she looked into his beautiful brown eyes, that there was a lot of fight left in him, and she planned to be there for the battle.

Al noticed the green duffel bag that Katherine was holding so close. It seemed strange to him that she would be carrying such a large bag. The last time Al had seen that bag, was the day they moved into the apartment.

"Kate, is there something in that green bag for me?" Al took the fatherly approach. He knew Katherine hated to be asked a lot of questions. She always loved to be the one who asked the questions.

For a moment, Katherine had forgotten about the bag. Her thoughts were fixed on Al. Her mind was traveling through the years, reliving all the beautiful moments they had shared. In addition, she was rehearsing in her mind how she would tell Al that they were leaving New York and why.

Al sensed that Katherine was not her usual self. She seemed distant, as he repeated the question. "Kate, is there something in that green bag for me?"

"Yes. Yes. I'm fine." Katherine responded.

"I asked, did you have something in the green bag for me?" Al repeated.

Katherine looked at the bag. She knew she needed to get them out of there, and quickly

"What time is it?" she asked.

"It's about seven o'clock, Miss Mills," the nurse answered.

"We have to go, daddy. I'll tell you all about the green bag later. There is a surprise in there for you, a very special surprise. Katherine lifted the duffel bag and tossed the strap over her shoulder, as she held the door open. The nurse pushed the wheelchair through the door.

Al looked at Katherine and at the bag as he was wheeled by. He could tell by the look on Katherine's face, that she was pre-occupied with something…something Al felt he would soon find out. He decided not to press the issue any further. He knew Katherine would tell him what was on her mind when the time was right.

As she watched Al being pushed away, Katherine knew he suspected something wasn't right. The only time Al would let a question go unanswered, was when he knew something was bothering Katherine, and Katherine knew Al was right, for her thoughts were fixed on Nick.

＊   ＊   ＊

Meanwhile, Nick had awakened and reached over to give Katherine a good morning hug. He immediately realized she was not in the bed, so he sat up and looked around the room. Nick smiled, thinking Katherine was probably in the bathroom, as the door was closed. He turned back the covers to get out of bed, then noticed the white envelope next to his hand. Nick picked up the envelope. His name was written on the outside, nothing else. He sat on the edge of the bed and opened the envelope. Inside was a single white sheet of paper with words written on both sides. At the top of the letter was a picture of a five leaf clover that Katherine had drawn. On the stem, she had written "*Katherine*" and on the fifth leaf was written "*Nick*". He began to read the letter as he slowly lowered his body to the floor, his back resting against the bed.

"*Dear Nick,*

By the time you read this letter, I'll be out of your life forever. I wanted to say all the things that I have put in this letter to you personally, but I knew I could not. It would only take one look into those beautiful eyes of yours and I would be speechless. Since my father has been ill, I have given our relationship a lot of thought. At first, I felt guilty that I had not realized that he was so sick. I attribute this to the fact that I had fallen in love with the man of my dreams. I was so involved and in love, that nothing else really mattered in my life.

"*It was true, there were many times that I had forgotten that my father even existed. Especially when I was in your strong arms. Over the last few weeks, I have spent a lot of time alone, by my choice, of course. This time has given me a chance to reflect on my life and what is most important to me. By far, you are there, my love, at the top of the list. For you, that is great, but, for me, it can't be, for as much as I love you, I know my father needs me more than anything and anyone in this world. He has given me more love in my twenty years of life than most daughters get in a lifetime. I realize the time has come for me to give him everything I can during his last days on this earth. Nick, to keep you in my life would prevent this from happening. The passion and love I feel for you is overwhelming. It occupies my every thought. Nick, please forgive me. Please forget about me. I want you to find a woman who will bring you much happiness, but I am not the one. I'm leaving, and I do not plan to return after my father's death. I would be unable to pick up where we left off.*

"What I'm saying, Nick, is that every time I would look at you, I would think about my father. It would remind me of how I allowed love to blind me. So blind, that my father suffered for months…months that I spent in your arms. So blinded by love that nothing else mattered.

"You will always be in my heart. Your love will be with me forever. Please don't try to find me.

Your Clover,

Katherine"

Nick was devastated. This was the last thing he expected, and he could not understand why it had happened. He knew that he had done everything he could to support Katherine. When she needed space to be with Al, he gave it to her. Nick could not believe this was happening to him. As he re-read the letter, he kept hoping that this was a bad dream and soon he would awaken.

For the first time in his life, Nick had met a woman that he truly loved and he felt she loved him. Nick had never loved any woman the way he loved Katherine. She reminded him of everything that was pure, gentle and beautiful. Her honesty, innocence, maturity and unselfish love, were all the things he had never found in other women. He had never questioned if she wanted him for himself, or for his money. The answer was obvious. This was something that Nick had never experienced, even from his own mother and father.

Nick knew that his parents wanted him to be the son they needed in their life, but they had never cared about the things that he loved. As long as he was doing the things that pleased them, they were happy. Nick continued to sit on the floor motionless as he reread the letter. In his heart, he believed that he would never see Katherine again, but he knew that he could not live with himself if he did not try to find her.

If I could just hold you one more time in my arms, I would tell you how much I loved you. I would give you as much space as you needed. I would wait for you forever, Nick said to himself as he gathered his thoughts. He would wait for her, and he wanted her to know that she could come back to him...without guilt, and without remorse.

Nick knew he had to try and find Katherine. He dressed and rushed out of the door.

CHAPTER EIGHTEEN

"Port Authority, please!" Katherine signaled to the cab driver after Al and she got in. Al tried to figure out what was going on, but he was puzzled. He had no idea what Katherine was up to. He could see the two pieces of luggage sitting on the seat between them, and he even noticed that Katherine seemed to be holding the duffel bag tighter as she clutched it between her legs.

The Port Authority building. Why the Port Authority building? Where are we going and what is on Katherine's mind? These thoughts rushed through Al's mind as he prepared to question Katherine. He knew that Katherine loved to surprise him, but, today, he was not up for it. He just wanted to go home and rest in his easy chair.

Katherine looked at her father, and knew he was about to begin an inquisition. She began to prepare herself. She had not totally formulated what she was going to tell or not tell him. She hoped the right words would come and, more importantly, that Al would believe her.

"Kate are we going some place? The Port Authority…I don't understand." Al could wait no longer. He wanted an explanation.

Katherine knew the time had come. Al needed to know something, and the last thing she wanted to do was upset him. Al's pale and frail body beckoned for an answer and Katherine knew it. She looked into Al's eyes, eyes that, by now, had become dark and sunken, although the luster of warmth and hope remained. His eyes asked for the truth, while Katherine searched for an answer.

Finally, Katherine spoke. "Daddy, I have a big surprise for you. You know my boss, Mister Walters…the man who spoke at my graduation?"

"Yes, I remember him." Al listened attentively. Katherine's thoughts had not fully come together, as she groped for the right words. All of a sudden, everything seemed so quiet. Even the busy New York streets were silent. Katherine felt as if they had been placed into a sound-proof booth, and were trapped. What Katherine could not see, was the cabdriver. He had turned off his radio and was leaning against the Plexiglas window, trying to hear Katherine's answer.

She continued, hoping the thoughts and words would all come together and make enough sense to satisfy Al with her answer. "You see, Daddy, he found out about your illness. He came to me and wanted to do everything he could to help. He knew of a place where you could seek the best medical care, a beautiful place. He suggested that I take you there for a few weeks. Mister Walters has paid for everything, including your medical care. I could not say no to him, Daddy. I wanted to do everything I could for you. The thought of losing you…"

Katherine loved Al and she really wanted the best for him. She knew she could never tell him the truth about everything, as it would kill him. Katherine also knew she needed Al to understand. She did not want to fight with him, and the thought of upsetting him was unbearable.

"That was very nice of Mister Walters, but don't you think you should have discussed this with me?" Al realized that Katherine was really hurting as he reached over and grabbed her hand. He wanted an answer, but he also wanted her to know he loved her.

"Yes, Daddy, I should have, but I was afraid that you would say no. I know what a proud man you are. If I—" Katherine replied, broken-hearted. Everything seemed to be coming to a head. Here she was, lying to Al. The thought of Nick and what she had done to him was killing her. She never wanted to hurt him; she loved him. She envisioned him opening the letter and knew how heartsick he would be. Katherine thought about how she would have felt if Nick had done the same thing to her. She thought of her brush with death, and relived that horrible feeling of impending doom, as Bobbie had pushed her around the apartment. She had felt all alone, with no one to turn to or help her.

Damn them! Damn them! They have destroyed my life, Katherine thought as her sorrow intensified.

Al could not take it. He could not watch Katherine hurt this way. He felt it was all because of his illness, and he knew he had to do something to calm Katherine down. Her pain was breaking his heart.

"Kate, don't cry." Al brushed away the tears.

"I think this is a great idea, and I don't want you to worry about a thing. I'm not upset with you. Don't cry, sweetheart, it will be alright. Tell me, where are we going?" Al asked as Katherine calmed down.

As she looked up at Al,. Katherine could see the tears in his eyes. She knew he was also hurting—hurting not only because of what was happening to him, but hurting more so on this day because he felt her pain. Katherine did not want to cause Al any unnecessary pain.

"Daddy, we're going to a beautiful little town called Alberville, New York. It's located upstate, and I 'm told it is the most beautiful place on this side of heaven. There are beautiful woods, mountains and running streams. The air is fresh and clean, and the streets are clean and beautiful. I'm told there are tree-lined sidewalks. We will be within a half-hour of the medical center, so you'll get the best medical care."

Katherine could tell that Al felt better about this idea. Even if he didn't, he definitely made her feel better. The tears in his eyes were gone and he had his usual 'Kate-I-love-you' smile on his face. She knew that this would be a big step for Al. What she had not figured out was how she would get him to stay there. Al had never lived outside New York. There were so many things he loved about their apartment: his easy chair, the distant view of Central Park and the treasured pictures of Sarah that he displayed everywhere.

This would not be an easy task. She could only hope that everything Gretchen said about Alberville was true, since Gretchen had not been there for quite some time. Katherine felt anxious and she worried about all the things that might go wrong.

Where would they live? Were good doctors there? What would she do if the doctors and hospital were no longer there? What would she do if Al got sick on the trip? Was this the right choice? Were there any options?

She had to be strong. She did not want Al to sense her apprehension. After all, she really did not have a choice. Going to the police was an option she thought about, but she was not convinced they could protect her. The only thing she wanted was for Al to be happy, healthy and assured that she was there and would always be there for him.

The cab arrived at the Port Authority. She planned for them to take a bus to Alberville. Although neither one of them had flown, they shared a fear of flying. Katherine paid the cabdriver and helped Al out of the cab, then they strolled into the Port Authority building.

CHAPTER NINETEEN

Nick reached Katherine's apartment. He tried to call several times on his car phone, but there was no answer. He hoped Katherine was at home, avoiding his call, and that he would be able to catch her and convince her that what she was about to do was wrong.

He knocked on the door anxiously, hoping she would answer. When she did not he began to pound on the door. "Katherine, are you in there? It's me, Nick. Please, open the door!" The door swung open—in Katherine's haste, she hadn't locked it. He stood in the doorway and looked around. Everything seemed to be in place.

Maybe it's not to late, he thought. *Maybe I made it in time.* But, as he walked toward Katherine's bedroom, he saw a different scene. Dresser drawers were left open and isolated garments were hanging out of them. The closet door was open and there were several articles of clothing on the floor. It appeared that someone had left in a hurry, and Nick knew that someone was Katherine.

He walked toward Katherine's bathroom. The last time he had been there was the night they found Al on the floor as he let the fleeting thoughts of that evening resurface. He could see that the countertop was bare and the cabinet under the sink was open.

Nick left Katherine's room and rushed into Al's bedroom. The room was in the same condition as Katherine's, with clothes scattered all over. He could tell that a few pictures had been removed from the wall, by the outline of the frames in the dust. Nick knew Katherine had been there and gone. Even with this in mind, he felt he could catch her. He had to. If he did not try, he would never be able to live with himself. He loved Katherine and he wanted her to know that. He decided that, if he was able to catch up with her, he would ask her to marry him.

The hospital...she's probably there with Al, Nick thought, as he rushed out of the apartment. He didn't want to waste a minute of time. He jumped into his car, and headed for the hospital, then quickly picked up the car phone, hoping to call ahead and delay Katherine. Driving and dialing, driving and dialing; Nick was on a mission.

"AT&T, how can I help you.? an operator asked.

"I need the phone number for Sinai Hospital, patient information. Please hurry!" Within seconds, Nick had the number and dialed it.

"Hello, Sinai Hospital, patient information. How can I help you?"

"Please, connect me to the room of Al Mills, and hurry!" said Nick. Suddenly, the sound of screeching tires were all around him, getting louder and closer by the second. Screeching...Screeching...Screeching. Nick looked up. "Oh my God!" "Oh my God!" he yelled out. He had run a red light. As he looked to his left, he could see a car about to make contact. Reacting quickly, he turned to the right, spinning out of control. He clutched the steering wheel and prayed. Abruptly, his car stopped without incident. Nick could hear horns blowing. His car faced the oncoming traffic, but he was alive; as he sat breathless.

"Hello...Hello...is anyone there? Hello, is anyone there?" a voice ringing out from the phone that fallen to the floor during the commotion. Nick reached over to pick it up, breathing a sigh of relief as he stared into the oncoming traffic.

By now, traffic was at a standstill. "You crazy bastard!" one man yelled as he leaned out of his car and gave Nick the middle finger. Nick chose to ignore what was happening outside his car, but he knew the gentlemen was right. He was crazy—crazy in love. He wanted Katherine, and that was all he could think about, outside of being glad that he was alive.

"Yes, would you please connect me to Mister Mills' room? That's Al Mills," Nick said, trying to settle down and catch his breath.

"I'm sorry, sir, Mister Mills has been discharged." the ward clerk replied.

"Can you tell me how long ago he left?"

"A couple of hours ago, sir."

"Did they say where they were going?"

"I have no idea, sir. Usually our patients go home."

It was too late, and Nick knew it. Katherine was gone and he had no idea where he could find her. He set the phone on the seat, but he could still hear the voice on the other end.

"Sir, sir, are you there? Sir, are you there?" The voice seemed to become more distant as Nick began to lapse into a feeling of despair.

By now the horns were blowing out of control, but, inside Nick's car, there was silence—a silence that surrounded him with a feeling of hopelessness and loneliness. Nick's world had shattered all around him. Every muscle and bone in his body could feel the reality and pain. It could not end this way, Nick thought, he had to find her.

For the first time in his life he had been happy. He was finally, truly happy. Now it was over. Katherine was gone. "Someday…some…day, some…day," he said to himself as he hammered his fist against the steering wheel. The horns, the people and the drivers around him continued to express their anger, but none of this phased him. To Nick, they did not exist.

As he drove past the angry onlookers, he thought this had to be some type of horrific dream. It was as if time stood still around him, and everything happened in slow motion. Nick knew there was no one that he could turn to; no one who would realize the magnitude of the love that he had lost. He wanted to wake up now; right now!

"Katherine, Katherine, I need you, I love you,." Nick cried out, as tears salted his cheeks.

CHAPTER TWENTY

As the bus crossed the George Washington Bridge, Katherine looked out the window. For the first time in many weeks, she felt safe. This truly was going to be a new beginning. From afar, she could see the Walters and Vein building and her thoughts fixed on Nick.

As the view of the building faded, Katherine's emptiness increased along with her hatred for John Walters. Not only did he take away the man she loved, he sent her and Al into a world they had never explored. *How could a person be so malicious? What would drive a person to do this? Does John Walters hate me that much?* she asked herself. She could not envision someone willing to hurt their own flesh and blood, just to fulfill their own selfish need.

"Nick, I never meant to hurt you. I love you." Katherine whispered as she tried to erase the thoughts of that selfish son-of-a-bitch who had destroyed her life and the lives of those she loved.

Looking into the window, Katherine saw the reflection of Al's face as he sat beside her. He was asleep and he looked at peace. She grabbed his hand as she wiped the tears away from her face. "I'm so sorry for what I have done to you, daddy. I never meant for it to happen this way. I hope, some day you will forgive me. I wish I could tell you the truth. I'm so sorry." Katherine said, while trying to control her emotions as she gazed at Al's pale, withered face. With his sunken cheeks and droopy chin, he seemed only a shell of the man he used to be.

The thought of Al's impending death consumed her. Before she knew it, she was sobbing. "Oh Daddy, Oh Daddy, I'm sorry. I'm sorry. I love you so much." Katherine sobbed uncontrollably, so much so, that Al awakened, along with many of the people on the bus.

"Kate, Kate, don't cry, everything will be alright. I know you love me and I love you. I don't want to see you hurt this way."

"Here, dear, take this," the woman sitting in front of Katherine said, as she passed her a packet of tissues.

"Thank you," Katherine replied, as she blew her nose, then leaned her head against Al.

"I don't want to lose you, Daddy. I need you. It has always been you and me."

"Kate, everything will be alright. Don't you worry. Let's think about this great trip we are taking together. Let's think of it as a vacation in paradise. Just the two of us. This will be the best vacation we've ever had. I love you, Kate."

"Daddy, I love you." Katherine placed her arms around Al as she pressed her head tighter against him.

She soon fell asleep on her 'knight in shining armor's' shoulder. The comfort of Al's words, the warmth of his breath flowing down upon her, the fact that he was still there with her, and the soothing echoes of the wind seeping through the windows provided a serenity from the heavens that consoled her as the bus moved toward Alberville.

CHAPTER TWENTY-ONE

"Ladies and Gentleman, we are now entering Alberville. We have about ten minutes before we reach the bus depot," the driver announced. They had finally arrived in Alberville. Although it was only four hours away from New York City, Katherine felt as if they had been on the bus for days, as she absorbed the view.

Alberville was beautiful, Katherine thought, as she looked out the bus window. There wasn't a skyscraper in sight. There were beautiful rolling hills, enormous trees with specks of snow on the branches. The trees were beautiful even without their leaves. So many different shapes to them, Katherine thought, as she watched a squirrel jump from a tree. There were small and large homes, perfectly nestled among the trees, some so hidden you could only see their roof tops. The air was clean and clear, unlike the smog that hung over New York City.

Katherine smiled as she watched the squirrel jump to another tree. The view was like something out of a fairy tale. She had thought that places like this only existed on television. Al was in total awe, and he did not say a word. Katherine turned around to ask him what he thought. Before she could even get the words out, Al replied, "Kate, this place is beautiful, simply beautiful." The glow on Al's face said it all.

As the bus pulled into downtown Alberville, Katherine was unable to believe her eyes. This was downtown, she thought! What a contrast to the downtown she came from. There were small stores lined up next to each other. All of them had "Welcome to Alberville" signs in their windows. There was one store that caught Katherine's attention. It was an ice-cream parlor. The sign read, 'Joe's Ice Cream Parlor'. There was a radiant red awning that draped the shop. What attracted Katherine's attention was the man and little girl sitting inside eating ice cream. Her eyes fixed on the man wiping the little girl's chin as the ice cream dripped from her mouth. It reminded her of the times she and Al had spent together when she was a little girl. *If I could only turn back the hands of time,* Katherine thought, as the bus drove past the parlor.

It was winter, but the warmth of the landscape made Katherine feel the heat of a summer's day. Nothing made her feel better than the look she saw in Al's eyes as he took in the surroundings. It was the same look you might see in a child's eyes on Christmas day.

The bus pulled into the depot and came to a halt. Katherine sat back in her seat. She looked around her and watched the people gather their things. The nice lady who had given her the tissues, place a lovely red scarf with bright yellow flowers around her head. She could see several family members standing outside the bus, waiting to greet their loved ones. There was a young couple holding hands as they waited for someone on the bus. This made her think of Nick and all the times he had held her close to him.

Katherine watched Al put on his gray overcoat and black short-brim hat. He seemed eager to get off the bus. It was as if being in Alberville, had given him strength. They decided they would stay at Lula's Bed and Breakfast. The nice lady who sat in front of them had given them the tip. She'd said it was the best place in town. It made you feel right at home and the food was great. That was all they needed to hear. They needed to feel at home. Katherine knew there would not be any turning back, as this was to be a new beginning—a beginning that she and Al would face together. It was going to take them back to the way things use to be: the two of them caring and looking out for each other.

As Katherine stepped off the bus, Al was in front of her, reaching out for her hand. She placed her hand in his, then planted both feet firmly on the ground of Alberville. Katherine looked into Al's eyes, searching for forgiveness. Al looked into her eyes, ending her search.

"It's you and me, daddy. Just you and me."

"It's always been that way, Kate. You and me."

Watching their luggage being removed from the lower compartment of the bus, Katherine finally felt she had made the right choice. "I'm home. I'm really home," she whispered, as she stood there holding Al's hand.

CHAPTER TWENTY-TWO

The weeks passed easily, and Katherine never had to worry about dissuading Al from wanting to return to New York City. Al's health failed quite rapidly since their arrival. Katherine was able to find a cozy little home nestled in the woods that Al loved. It was a lovely two-bedroom, two-story home that looked like a dollhouse. The couple who had lived there before them had done a nice job with the decorating. Al's favorite place was the screened-in porch. He loved to go out there and watch the birds and the squirrels.

As for medical care, Gretchen had been right. There was good medical care nearby, and Katherine was able to find a good doctor for Al. His name was Dr. Jones. After he reviewed Al's medical records and examined him thoroughly, he concurred with Dr. Singh. Al's brain tumor was inoperable and it was growing very fast.

Al eventually become so weak and frail, he was bedridden. During his last hospitalization at Alberville Medical Hospital, he decided that he no longer wanted to continue the chemotherapy and radiation therapy. He could not take the way it made him feel, and he wanted to go home. When Al spoke of home these days, he meant their home in Alberville. He never spoke of New York City. Katherine did not know if this was because he truly enjoyed Alberville, or because he was having such a difficult time with his speech and memory.

Al had been heavily sedated, as the doctors were having a very difficult time trying to control his seizures. At times, it broke Katherine's heart to look at him. His face and his legs had become very swollen and, if not for his eyes and his heart of gold, you would think he was a different person. Dr. Jones told Katherine this was due to the high dose of steroids they were giving him. He needed this to help control the swelling on his brain.

Dr. Jones was helpful. After Al decided he no longer wanted anything done, Dr. Jones arranged for Al to be placed in the Alberville Hospice program—a program designed for terminally ill patients who had six months or less to live. Hospices not only helped the patients, they helped the families cope with the dying process—a support that Katherine truly needed.

Through Hospice, Al was assigned a nurse name Beth. She was wonderful. Beth would come to the house about three to four times a week to help him. She would talk to him, feed him, bathe him and even read the Bible and sing to him.

Beth was a rubenesque black woman around forty-five years old. Her skin was silky brown, and she looked much younger than her age. Her hair was black with streaks of gray. She always walked around with a smile on her face, and she never complained. She never made Al feel as though he was a burden. She was there to provide comfort and support, and she did this without question.

Beth loved to sing. Al's favorite types of songs were hymns and Negro spirituals. One day Al asked her to sing, and she sang so loudly, Katherine thought the Lord was about to come through the roof. Beth was a unique lady. She came to know Al well. Sometimes Al was so out of it, he appeared comatose, just lying in bed without response. Katherine would walk into the bedroom and find Beth singing away. Katherine knew Al did not ask her to sing, but Beth did so anyway. She would just say, "I could sense he needed to hear a song." She was wonderful!

Katherine was holding up well, although she was feeling very tired. She had not left Al's side, except for those times when Beth would give her a break. The money that John Walter had given her was definitely taking care of the expenses. Occasionally, Katherine found herself thinking about Nick. It seemed, these days, she had reconciled herself to the fact they would never cross paths again, but these thoughts were transient, since Katherine had become totally committed to devoting all her energy and time to Al.

CHAPTER TWENTY-THREE

One day, while standing at the stove preparing soup for Al, Katherine could see Beth as she looked out the kitchen window. Beth was in her usual chipper mood, singing and smiling as she approached the house. "Come in, Beth. I'm in the kitchen," Katherine said as Beth entered and removed her shoes. This had become a ritual. Beth would always remove her shoes and put on her bedroom slippers, the minute she walked through the door. She would then go to Al's room and see if he needed anything. Katherine continued to cook as she waited for Beth to enter the kitchen.

"Katherine, Al seems to be resting today. Has he awakened for you?" That was Beth's way of saying Al looked the same. She always tried to make the day seem brighter.

"No Beth. I hope I'll be able to feed him some soup or something."

"Don't you worry about that. I'll take care of the feeding. Are you alright, Katherine? You don't look very good today. I think you need to take a little more time for yourself. I'll be coming daily now."

"I'm alright. I'm just tired, Beth. I don't know what I'm going to do without my dad. He's everything to me," Katherine walked toward the chair to sit down.

"Katherine! Katherine!" Katherine had fainted and hit the floor. Beth rushed over to her. "Katherine! Katherine!" Beth shook her face as she felt her pulse.

"What happened?" Katherine whispered as she tried to lift her head. "The room is spinning, Beth. I'm so tired. I'm so tired. What happened, Beth?"

"Katherine, do you know where you are?" Beth asked as she placed her hand behind Katherine's head. "Let me help you to a chair.

Katherine, I'm going to get a cold wash cloth to place on your head. I'll call for help. You're suffering from exhaustion. You need to get some rest. Don't move."

"I'm so tired," Katherine echoed as she laid on the sofa.

*   *   *

"Hello? Hello? is anybody in there?" It was one of the paramedics. Beth rushed to the door.

"Hurry, please hurry!" Beth said. "I want you to take this young lady to the hospital. She fainted, I think she's physically exhausted. Her father is terminally ill and she has been caring for him around the clock. I'll stay here with him. I'm the hospice nurse. I checked her blood pressure, it seems to be okay. Her pulse was rather rapid, around one hundred and twenty."

"Ma'am, did she hit her head when she fell?"

"No. I mean, I don't think so. It happened so quickly," Beth answered.

"Bob, bring in the stretcher," the paramedic yelled to his partner as he began to examine Katherine.

"Miss, are you alright?"

By this time, Katherine was starting to come around. Everything still seemed rather foggy to her as she tried to lift her head. "I'm feeling…okay."

"Katherine, don't try to get up. I'm going to have these gentlemen take you to the hospital. You need to rest. Don't worry, I'll stay here with Al," Beth gestured to the men to hurry up.

The paramedics placed Katherine on the stretcher and whisked her off to Alberville Hospital emergency room. By the time they got there, she had come around. She felt tired and embarrassed by what had happened. The doctors insisted they run a few tests and give her IV fluids, since she appeared to be somewhat dehydrated. Katherine was too tired to fight with them.

"Hello, Miss Mills, I'm Doctor Zerega. How are you feeling?"

"Much better. I'm just tired." Katherine was lying in the bed with her hands over her head and eyes trying to block out the bright lights.

"Miss Mills, everything will be okay. You have enough of a reason to be tired. I hear you have been working very hard taking care of your terminally ill father. I really commend you for your efforts."

"Thank you, Doctor. When can I go home?"

"Miss Mills, we would like to keep you for a few more hours and continue the IV fluids," the doctor paused for a moment. "We would also like to do an ultrasound on you to make sure everything is okay with your baby."

"Baby!" Katherine tried to sit up in the bed, but she was too tired. "What do you mean baby?" Katherine was shocked by the news. " I don't understand, I…"

At that moment, the doctor realized that Katherine did not know she was pregnant. "Miss Mills, I'm sorry, I thought you knew. We ran a pregnancy test on you. That is routine procedure in this case. Your test was positive. With everything that has happened today, we needed to make sure that everything is okay with the baby. Sometimes cases like this turn out to be more serious.

"What I'm saying, Miss Mills, is that, if the pregnancy is in jeopardy, it would not be wise for us to let you go home. I know all of this has come as a shock to you, but, believe me, we are looking out for your well-being. I have requested a special pregnancy test that will give me some idea of how far along you are. I hope this is good news. I'll have one of the nurses sit with you."

Katherine was devastated as she covered her face in disbelief. She'd had no idea, had never thought for a second that she could be pregnant. "I don't believe this. I don't believe this," Katherine cried out.

Katherine was taken home via the courtesy van. Dr. Zerega informed her that everything seemed to be okay with the pregnancy. He told her it appeared she was approximately twelve to fourteen weeks pregnant, and advised her to get plenty of rest. He gave her a prescription for pre-natal vitamins, as well as the names of several obstetricians.

"Thank you." Katherine said to the driver of the courtesy van as he escorted her to her front door. When she walked through the door, Beth was there waiting for her. She ran over to Beth and collapsed into her arms.

"I can't. I can't," was all Katherine could say as Beth held her.

"Everything will be alright, Katherine. Everything will be alright. It will be alright, my precious, it will be alright. Don't you worry, I will be here for you," Beth said as she continued to comfort Katherine." It was breaking Beth's heart to see Katherine like this.

Beth escorted Katherine to her bedroom and helped her get into something comfortable. As she turned back the covers and helped her into the bed, she began to sing…

Katherine seemed to get comfort from the song. And as Beth sang, she could see the calm on Katherine's face as the tear flowed down hers. Beth sat at Katherine's bedside for a long time that evening and prayed. Beth knew that something other than Al's illness had been troubling Katherine. She believed that, when the timing was right, Katherine would confide in her.

CHAPTER TWENTY-FOUR

The next morning Katherine awoke to the smell of fresh bacon and biscuits. Beth was hard at work in the kitchen trying to entice the taste buds of the hungry. At first, Katherine could not get out of bed. She just lay there hoping she was awakening from a bad dream. But she only had to look at her wrist. The identification band from the hospital was still there. She was pregnant with Nick's baby.

How could this be happening to me? What have I done to deserve this? What will I do? How will I tell Nick? I can't go through with this pregnancy. I can't tell him. Katherine's thoughts meshed in her confused state.

"I hate you, John Walters. This is all your fault. You have taken away the man I love. How could you? How could you? I hate you. Oh, Daddy, I need you so much. I really need you," Katherine called out as the tears melted into her pillow.

"Breakfast is ready! Katherine, breakfast is ready." It was Beth, chipper as usual.

"I'll be there in a few minutes, Beth!" Katherine responded, as she wiped her face. She did not want Beth to see her like this. She knew Beth had her hands full with Al.

"Well, Katherine, it sure is good to see you up and about this morning. I was really worried about you. Are you feeling better?"

"I feel better," Katherine replied, as she sat down at the table and watched Beth fix her plate.

"How is Daddy doing, Beth? I think I'll go and check on him before I eat."

"He's doing about the same. I want you to eat first, Katherine. After that scare you gave me yesterday, I need to make sure you eat and get your strength back. Don't you worry, just eat."

Katherine was too tired to argue with Beth. She knew Beth was right. She thought about Dr. Zerega telling her that she was pregnant. She could not get those words out of her head. This was not the way Katherine wanted the start of motherhood to be. She had always envisioned how happy she would be to know she was to become a mother with a strong man who loved her at her side to share in the joy. She had even imagined the look in Al's eyes the day she would tell him he was going to be a grandfather! Everything was wrong. There was no man who loved her at her side, and she would never see that look in Al's eyes. Life was so unjust, so unfair, Katherine thought, as she tried to come to some understanding.

"Katherine, is everything okay?" Beth asked. She detected that Katherine wasn't her usual talkative self.

Katherine felt she had to tell someone what was going on, as she thought about how she would respond to Beth's question. She knew she could not handle this alone and that she could confide in Beth.

"Beth, you're the only one I can talk to…" Katherine's heart was pounding and her skin was clammy as she searched for the words. Beth could sense that Katherine was having a hard time telling her something.

"Beth, I'm…, I'm pregnant!" Katherine said, ashamed…as she unveiled the secret of her lost virginity. She felt she had done something wrong and this was God's way of punishing her. She now understood why she had always been taught to wait until she was married before she had sex. The guilt and pain wrenched her insides. She sat there and waited for Beth to respond.

"Katherine, now I know why your heart is so troubled. I knew there was something going on when you returned yesterday. Oh, my dear Katherine, we will get through this together. I'll help you in any way I can."

Tears of shame flowed freely from Katherine's eyes as she looked at Beth. What a wonderful woman God had brought into Al's and her life! It was as if Beth had rehearsed this moment. Her words were motherly.

"Beth, I don't know what to do. This is the worst time for something like this to be happening in my life. I always thought this would be a happy time. I never…"

"Katherine, the man upstairs knows what we can handle and what we can't. I know this is a difficult time for you, but you must look to the Lord to help you. He has all the answers. Let your prayers be known. It will all work out. Now, I want you to eat."

Emotionally drained, Katherine picked up her fork as she tried to follow Beth's lead. Her fork felt as if it weighed a ton as she lifted it towards her mouth. When Katherine left the breakfast table that morning, flooded by the barrage of decisions swirling around in her head, she left feeling somewhat different. She felt she had been given another challenge, a challenge she was prepared to deal with. She knew her decision whether or not to keep this baby would be something that would shape the rest or her life. A decision she decided that day would await the trust of the God given strength that Beth had helped her see.

CHAPTER TWENTY-FIVE

It was three o'clock in the morning when Beth entered Katherine's bedroom. The time was growing near for Al, and Beth knew Katherine would want to be at his side. As she walked toward Katherine's bed, her thoughts and concerns were burdened by what she had to do. This young woman had been through so much, and now the time had come for a moment that would truly change her life forever. Although this was what Beth was trained to do, this morning seemed very different for her. She wanted to protect Katherine, not see her suffer, but Beth knew that, no matter how much she wanted to protect Katherine, this was something she had to do.

"Katherine, wake up. Katherine, wake up," she said softly as she shook Katherine.

"What, Beth? Beth?" Katherine sat up. The light from the moon shining through her window cast a light on Beth's warm face. Katherine did not say a word. She knew the time had come.

"Katherine, we need to be with Al, I don't think he has much time," Beth held Katherine's hands as she pulled her close to embrace her. Hand in hand, they walked into Al's bedroom. The dimly-lit table lamp provided a soft light. From the doorway, Katherine could hear Al struggling for his every breath—long deep breaths, with short sighs. Beth reluctantly released Katherine's hand.

Katherine walked over to the bed and sat next to Al. She held his cool hand as she watched him fight for his final breaths of life. His face swollen and pale, shadowed by the few strands of hair that remained on his head.

"Daddy. Daddy. Don't leave me. I love you so much, so very much. I'm here with you. Don't worry, you're not alone," Katherine cried out as she lifted Al's hand and rubbed it against her face. "I love you. I love you."

"Daddy, I have a surprise for you. I want you to take this to heaven and share with Mom. You're going to be a grandfather. I will not be alone." It was at that moment that Katherine knew she could not take the life away that lived inside of her. She needed this baby. It represented Al's lineage and Nick's love. Katherine laid her head on Al's chest. She could feel his heart pounding and the warmth leaving his body as she longed to feel his arms embrace her. "Daddy, I love you. I love…"

Suddenly the breathing stopped. Katherine continued to lay her head against Al's chest. She knew he was gone. When Katherine lifted her head, she looked at Al's face, his eyes half open, fixed toward the ceiling.

"Daddy, I will always love you. I'll never forget you. I'll make you proud of me." The tears she shed were of joy and sadness.

Beth placed her hand on Katherine's shoulders. "Katherine, let's go to your room. He's in God's hands. He knows you love him and I know he loved you. Let's go. You need to rest. I'll take care of everything."

Katherine slowly stood up as she continued to fix her eyes on Al's face. She reached down and placed her hand over his eyes and closed them, then leaned over and kissed him. Katherine and Beth embraced as the two of them stood there crying in each other's arms.

"Don't worry Katherine, I will make sure all your arrangements are carried out. Don't you worry, I want you to get some rest."

"Beth, you have been wonderful. Thank you. Thank you. I miss him already."

"I know you do. I know you do. You must always remember he loved you and he was very proud of you. Now, I want you to get some rest. You have to take care of yourself," Beth said as she escorted Katherine to her room.

Beth kissed Katherine on the forehead and turned off the night light, as Katherine struggled with her grief. "Get some rest, Katherine." Beth continued to echo these words as she closed the bedroom door behind her.

Katherine lay there and looked around the room, her thoughts fixed on Al. She reflected on her childhood and all the fun they had had together. She thought about her graduation day and how excited and proud Al was of her. She reached into the drawer of her nightstand and pulled out the five-leaf clover pendent, then placed it next to her heart.

"I'll always love you, Daddy," her words gently spoken as she reflected on the years through her pain and tears.

CHAPTER TWENTY-SIX

As promised, Beth had taken care of everything. The funeral was beautiful. The service was held at a small chapel in Alberville and Al was buried behind the church. All the hospice nurses attended, along with the doctors who had taken care of Al. One of the most touching moments was when Beth sang Al's favorite song. There wasn't a dry eye in the house, not even the doctors. Beth really belted it from her heart that day.

Everyone was so nice to Katherine and they did everything they could to let her know she was not alone. Beth went home with Katherine after the service. She wanted to be with her and to help her pack up Al's things. Katherine wanted to do this right away. She felt it would be very difficult to do when she was by herself, although Beth had promised she would be there any time Katherine needed her.

"Katherine, I'm so proud of you. You're a very strong young woman," Beth said as the two of them walked through the front door of the house.

"Beth, I have to be. My daddy would want me to be, especially with the baby. I have to take care of his grandchild. I know he was looking forward to being a grandfather someday. I'm sure he'll rejoice in heaven the day this baby is born. You know, Beth," Katherine said, laying her black scarf on the sofa, "I've picked out a name for the baby."

"Really? That's great, Katherine. Tell me."

"I've decided that, if I have a girl, I'll name her Sarah after my mother. If it's a boy, I'll name him Al."

"Your father would love that, Katherine. He would really love that. Nothing would please him more."

"Beth, I can't tell you how much it has meant to me to have someone like you in my life. Daddy and I would not have gotten through this without you. You're a true inspiration, the best friend anyone could ever have, and I love you." Katherine gave Beth a warm hug.

"Thank you, Katherine. I was just trying to do my job."

"You have done more than a job, Beth. You're special, really special. You will always be family to me, as long as I live. Beth, I would like you to be the Godmother of my baby."

Beth was moved by Katherine's request. She became so choked up, tears glistened in her eyes as she stood there looking at Katherine.

"I would love to, Katherine. That would be an honor. Now you have me feeling like a grandmother," Beth said, as she wiped the tears away from her eyes.

"That's probably because you truly are," Katherine responded as the two of them embraced.

"Alright, Katherine, we have work to do." They headed towards Al's bedroom.

"Katherine, I have something to tell you," Beth continued, as the two of them were just about to enter Al's bedroom.

"What is it, Beth?" Katherine asked, feeling Beth was having a hard time telling her something.

"Katherine, your father left a letter in his nightstand that he wanted me to give you after he was buried. Beth held Katherine's hands. "He made me promise not to give it to you until then. I'm—"

"A letter?" Katherine asked, puzzled.

"Yes, A letter. He wrote it before his heath totally failed. He said it was something special for you."

Katherine looked at Beth. She could tell this was hard for her. "Beth, where did you say this letter is?"

"It's in the nightstand next to the bed, Katherine."

The two of them walked into the bedroom. Beth walked toward the closet as she watched Katherine walk over to the nightstand. In the top drawer was a white envelope with her name written on it.

Katherine sat on the bed, holding the envelope in her hand. She could tell by the handwriting, it was Al's. Nervously, she opened the envelope. Inside there was a two-page letter. It was dated two weeks after their arrival in Alberville. Katherine rubbed the letter as she read the first line, "*Dear Kate.*" Then she smelled it and, finally, she began to read it.

"*Dear Kate,*

I want to first say I love you very much. You have been my life and if I had to live it all over again, I would not change a thing. By the time you read this letter, I will be watching over you from heaven, my precious daughter. Writing this letter today was not easy, because it brought to light the finality of my existence. I know I am dying and I don't have long to be with you. I wanted to write this letter today, before I become too weak to write or remember all the things I want to say to you.

My precious, my beautiful daughter, I know your heart is troubled by a burden you are carrying inside. I can see it in your eyes when I look at you. I know it is because of this burden, we are here in Alberville. I chose not to discuss this with you. I knew it would cause you pain. Pain I could not have you re-live, because I love you too much. Besides the insight into your troubled heart, I too was happy to leave the city and come to such a beautiful and peaceful place. It brought me comfort to know you were in a safer environment and I wouldn't have to worry as much about something happening to you. For that reason I hope you choose to stay in this beautiful place. Kate, just like you carried your burden, I, for a long time carried one. My illness developed months before you found out. It was one of the reasons I lost my job. I did not want you to worry so I pretended I was strong until my strength ran out.

"*So you see, I too, tried to protect the one I love, from pain and worry also. The most important thing for you to remember is that I love you with every breath that I breathe. You have given me more happiness in my lifetime than any father could ever hope for. From that first day I held you in my arms, I fell in love. Those beautiful brown eyes captured my heart.*

Today, that love has grown into something that words can't express. My darling Kate, I want you to be strong. You must know that I will be alright. I will always be there watching over you, both your mother and I. God has blessed you with wisdom, beauty and a heart so precious. Don't ever let anyone hurt you and change that. I'll always love you. Thanks for being a wonderful daughter. My life has truly been made complete by your presence.

Love Always, Daddy."

"He knew! He knew," Katherine cried out as she clutched the letter next to her chest. "My daddy knew," she continued.

Beth watched as she allowed Katherine her moment of solitude. Beth knew the letter had meaning beyond anything she could comprehend. They were a father's last words to his beloved daughter and Beth did not want to do anything to interrupt that moment.

"Daddy, how I wish I could hold you again. To tell you how much I love you and need you. If I could only see your smiling face, smell your presence, or watch you sleep. What I would give for one more moment with you. I'm so sorry you had to suffer alone in the beginning. I didn't know. I didn't know. Please forgive me. I love you, Daddy," Katherine said, as she clutched the letter tighter as if she was holding Al.

Beth could not take it anymore. She sat beside Katherine and placed her arms around her. "Katherine, everything will be alright. Give it time. I'll be there for you. Your father will always watch over you. He loved you." Beth held Katherine, and Katherine rested her head on Beth's bosom.

As she lay in Beth's arms, Katherine thought about Nick and how much she must have hurt him. She wished it was his arms she was in at that moment. But she knew this would never happen. It was too much to risk.

Katherine and Beth continued to sit on Al's bed as they settled into their personal thoughts. It was the future Katherine began to think about. The baby, the life he or she would have, and her promise to Al. She would make him proud of her. Beth thought of the love Katherine and Al shared, and understood the strength that Al had instilled in Katherine—a strength Katherine would need to guide and protect her as she began to prepare herself for the challenges ahead.

CHAPTER TWENTY- SEVEN

Twelve years later…

The years had been kind to Katherine, at least most of the years. She had a beautiful daughter named Sarah. She worked as a library assistant, and she continued to live in Alberville in the same little house that she purchased for Al. As for relationships, Katherine continued to fail. Two years after Al died, she met and married an accountant named Timothy Oberman. The relationship started off well, and he grew to be the ideal gentlemen for her. Katherine didn't know if she fell in love with him because he reminded her of Nick, or because she wanted Sarah to have a father. But whatever the true reason, the marriage did not work. It lasted five short years. They just seemed to grow apart. Their lives were centered around Sarah, not each other, and they parted on good terms. Tim had become Sarah's father, the only father she knew. Katherine maintained her married name. She was now Katherine Oberman.

Beth moved to South Carolina, after she was offered a job to direct a hospice program, but she kept in touch. She sent cards every holiday and demanded that Katherine send her pictures of Sarah. She wanted her Godchild to know that she loved her. Every holiday, Sarah would run to the mailbox looking for a card or gift from Beth. It never failed, something would always come. This was Katherine's way of knowing Beth was okay.

Nick never found Katherine, and Katherine never tried to contact Nick. She thought of him often, as she watched Sarah grow up. Sarah reminded her so much of him. She had his dark hair and adventurous personality. She stood just under five feet tall and weighed about one hundred and two pounds.

Sarah was always curious. She was smart as a whip and did not have a problem showing it. So much so that Katherine constantly fussed with Sarah to get her to understand things. Sarah's attitude was usually 'her way or no way'. Some of this rebellion, Katherine attributed to the divorce and Sarah's closeness to Tim. Some of it was pure genetics. Sarah's personality seemed to mimic that of Nick's.

Many times, Katherine watched her and thought back to some of the things Nick shared with her about his childhood. It was amazing! Nick Walters had truly left a part of himself for Katherine.

Sarah also had a precious side to her. Some days she would be so sweet and nice, Katherine wondered what she was up to. Her most precious moments came when she was involved in collecting leaves. This was Sarah's true hobby and love. She loved to collect leaves and place them on the walls in her bedroom, in books and throughout the house. Sarah would always tell Katherine that leaves made her feel good. They allowed her to appreciate change and, most important, they made her feel safe because they would never go away once she brought them inside.

Like Katherine, Sarah was very mature for her years. She had a way of making everyone love her. Her smiled melted one's heart and reminded Katherine of Al.

Katherine tried several times to go back to school, but found it very difficult, especially when trying to raise Sarah. She finally decided, after her separation from Tim, to do a home study course. Katherine was proud to be only ten hours short of completing her training to become a legal secretary. It was her dream come true, her promise to herself and Al.

Meanwhile, she enjoyed working at the local library. This was convenient because she was able to study during the slow periods. What really made the job nice though, was that Sarah was allowed to join her, so she never had to worry about Sarah being at home alone. Katherine was happy as she centered her life around Sarah and her career goals.

CHAPTER TWENTY-EIGHT

It was a warm autumn day and Sarah had set out to collect leaves while Katherine went to meet with her counselor to discuss a paper she had written. Sarah sat down on a rock in the woods behind her house, then she placed her backpack and nature book on the ground next to her. She'd been walking the trail for almost two hours, looking for things to add to her leaf collection. She'd started this leaf collection three years ago when she'd decided she needed something to do to keep herself occupied. This gave her a reason to get out of the house that seemed empty since Tim left. Though her collection wasn't that big, she was satisfied just to be doing something.

This was the first chance in almost three months that Sarah had a free Saturday afternoon to do as she pleased. She'd been going to Tim's house most weekends. He lived ten minutes away. She rarely got the opportunity to look at leaves, let alone try to collect them, as Tim usually took her to plays and museums. This day, Sarah enjoyed her time to herself. As she closed her eyes and let the sun warm her face, she thought of how lucky she was. She had almost everything she could ever want, except the one thing she wanted most, to have her parents back together again.

Sarah desperately wanted to see them back together. They had said they were going to be separated for awhile, to see if their lives would get better. Sarah felt that her parents were miserable and lonely without each other, but they were too stubborn to forgive and forget. Sitting in the woods surrounded by the sounds and beauty of nature, Sarah began to think about that awful evening when Katherine and Tim told her they planned to separate.

She remembered sitting at the table facing her mother and father. She had known for weeks that this moment was coming, but she did not want to believe it. All the fights, the slamming doors, the arguments and dinners alone, were clues. Sarah thought about the look on Katherine's face—hurt, confusion, and pain written all over it. She thought about Tim. His facial expression had been stern and unyielding. She could tell that a great depth of emotion was hidden beneath the surface of his brown eyes, but he didn't let it show that evening.

Sarah remembered getting angry, as she shot out of her chair, ready to do battle with Katherine, and feeling it was mainly Katherine's decision. She could hear herself yelling. "What do you mean, he's leaving? He can't be! You can't make him leave! Okay…so you argue once in a while, that's understandable. Adults don't always get along. But this is ridiculous! You are selfish! All you think about is what you want and what you think is best! What about me? Aren't I a part of this family? This isn't best for me, and I don't care how much you think it is. I know it isn't! You sit here and tell me how much it hurts you to stay together, but you have no idea how much it hurts me for you guys to be apart!"

When she had seen no changes in their expressions; no compassion in their eyes; she started to beg and plead. She turned toward her father. "You don't want to leave. Tell her that! She will listen, she'll understand! She'll let you stay! You don't have to leave, Daddy. Things will work out, and you can be happy here! You were before, weren't you? Please, Daddy, please! Tell her you want to stay!"

Sarah remembered feeling defeated as she watched her parents cry, each begging the other to say something to her. It was Tim who spoke first. She could still hear and feel his last word before he left, as he walked over and hugged her. "Not much is going to change, honey. I'll see you every weekend, and we'll still have lots of fun together. I just won't be home every day. Okay? I have to go."

Sarah thought about how she'd felt when Tim walked out the door, and the way the door sounded as it gave a final click. Determined not to ruin the rest of her day, she stood, then wiped the tears away and headed home. While she walked, she thought about the past months. She realized everything wasn't her fault, and though Katherine's and Tim's relationship wasn't perfect, it was close enough. She saw Tim almost every weekend like he had promised. He would pick her up on Friday after school and bring her home on Sunday evenings. This particular weekend, however, he was unable to see her. He had to go out of town on business.

Sarah decided to stop by and see Martin before she went home. He was the one who got her interested in collecting leaves. Martin had been the school janitor ever since she could remember. He and his wife didn't live far from her house. Since all of their children were grown, they always welcomed her company. Martin was a nature expert. He knew everything about anything having to do with the environment. He'd loved it when Sarah showed him the additions she'd made to her collection.

But now, Martin's youngest daughter, her husband and their three-year-old son had moved in with them, after his son-in-law lost his job. Thinking about how noisy and chaotic it would be with the little kid around, Sarah decided to go home. She felt it would be best to talk to Martin at school. Furthermore, getting home early would give her some time with Katherine.

Sarah really didn't mind spending this particular weekend at home. Tonight she had made plans to spend the night at her best friend Diane's house. Because of her weekend arrangements with Tim, Sarah found very little time to spend with Diane, outside of school. Diane lived about a mile away, and she had been Sarah's best friend for eight years. They met when they were in preschool. They attended the same kindergarten, and had been the best of friends ever since.

Sarah told Diane everything, and Diane told her everything as well. There had been times when they fought, but they never stayed mad at each other for more than a day. This year, when they moved up to the middle school, their friendship seemed to grow. They had both been scared, since they didn't have all their classes together, and the eighth and ninth graders would occasionally pick on the seventh graders. But in the end, everything worked out, and they were beginning to like middle school.

When Sarah reached her house she was relieved that Katherine wasn't outside waiting for her as she often was. Sarah smelled hamburgers frying, as she walked through the door. This was her favorite, and Katherine loved to cook when she had the time. Sarah threw her backpack on the floor and ran toward the kitchen.

"Hi, Mom! I'm home. Something smells good and I know what it is. I can't wait to show you the beautiful leaves I found today. I had so much fun in the woods. I started to stop by and see Mr. Martin, but I decided the house would be too noisy with his grandson there."

"I'm glad you enjoyed yourself. I thought we would eat and then go out and do some fun 'mother and daughter' stuff."

"Okay, mom, but don't forget, I'm spending the night at Diane's house."

"I haven't forgotten, Sarah."

"Mom, you're the greatest," Sarah said, rushing out of the kitchen.

"Sarah, where are you going? Lunch is almost ready."

"I'm going to call Diane to make sure her plans haven't changed. I'll be right back."

"I've heard that one before." Katherine said, as she continued to prepare lunch.

CHAPTER TWENTY-NINE

The weekend had flown by. When Sarah arrived at school, Tracy, one of her classmates, walked up to her. "Hi, Sarah, how are you doing? Have you seen Diane? She's looking for you. It seems important."

"Where did she go?" Sarah asked.

"She was standing in front of the school when I saw her last."

"Thanks, Tracy, I'll try and find her. I'll see you in class."

Sarah looked around for Diane, but was unable to find her. It was time for class, so she hurried to Mr. Wright's math room. He did not like his students to be late. He would always say something to them when they walked into the room late, and Sarah did not want to be embarrassed.

Math was over, and Sarah was leaving the room when she heard Diane calling her. She could tell something was wrong. Diane was not only whispering, she was looking around as if waiting for someone to catch her in a heinous crime.

"What's the matter, Diane? I heard you were looking for me. I tried to find you before I went to math."

"Quiet!" Diane cautioned, as she pulled Sarah around the corner and out of sight.

"Diane, what's going on?" Sarah asked.

"Sarah, when I got to school, I heard Jenny was looking for you."

"Jenny, the bully?" Sarah responded with surprise."

"Yes, Sarah. She has taken the pleasure of informing several people that she plans to kick your butt after school."

"What?" Sarah was aghast as the color drained from her face.

"Sarah, she said you had it coming. She told several girls that she never liked you and Friday, during lunch period, you gave her a dirty look. She couldn't confront you after school on Friday, because her mother picked her up. Mary told me she would be ready for you today."

"She said what? I didn't! I never....oh my gosh, Diane! What am I going to do?" Sarah was frightened. Katherine had taught her to stand up for what she believed and not to let people push her around. She was the type of person who always thought things out before she acted, not wanting to hurt anyone's feelings. She knew she hadn't done anything wrong to Jenny. Jenny was just looking for someone to pick on. Sarah had never been in a fight before. Jenny was a big girl, and Sarah was not about to test her immature fighting skills against her.

"What should I do, Diane?" Sarah's voice cracked as worry shadowed her face.

"Well," Diane advised, "I'd avoid her. She can't get you if she can't find you."

"You mean I should run?" Sarah asked incredulously.

"It's either that or stay and fight"

"I think you're right, Diane, I'll avoid her. Hopefully, she will come to her senses and leave me alone. I'll see you later." Sarah walked away, trying to act as if she was not worried. She knew Jenny was the type of bully who would do anything just to prove a point. She had already beaten up several seventh graders, and now it was Sarah's turn.

Sarah spent the duration of the day taking the long way to class. She peered cautiously around every corner before turning it, and kept her ears peeled for the sound of Jenny's voice, behind or in front of her. She decided to skip lunch, and spent that period in library looking at various books. Never in her life, had she been so eager to leave school.

Before her last class, Sarah decided she would leave school early. She went to her locker, got her bag, and started out the front door. But as she approached the door, her apprehensions returned, as she heard Jenny's boisterous voice ahead of her. She abruptly turned on her heels and headed out the back door. She knew she would have to take the long way home by cutting through the woods.

Sarah pulled her bag up on her shoulder and started running. When she got tired, she walked, but she kept looking back to make sure Jenny was not following her. When she reached the path that had been made throughout the years by many other kids, she thought maybe she was doing the wrong thing. Maybe she should have stayed and dealt with Jenny. She was about to summon all of her courage and turn around, when she realized that this was not the day to play superwoman.

While walking down the path, Sarah spotted a beautiful multi-colored leaf on the ground in front of her. The yellow and red colors were brilliant. Sarah decided it would be a nice addition to her collection. Since she felt she was safe from the clutches of Jenny, she bent over to pick the leaf up and examine it. But as she did, a gust of wind arose and blew the leaf further along the path. When she was finally able to catch up to it, she stomped her foot to keep it from escaping. As she bent over once again to pick it up, a mouse scampered across the path. Sarah, who was terrified of all rodents, screamed and stumbled backwards.

As she stepped back, she fell down an embankment. Everything was a blur to her as the trees and ground melted into one. Although it was only a few seconds before Sarah came to a stop, it seemed like an eternity. She lay on her back for a few minutes, dazed and unable to move. She had scraped her hands and arms, torn her shirt, there was a large rip in her jeans and she was lying on a pile of branches.

"Just great! Just fricken great! I'm going to have a great time explaining this." Sarah voiced, as she gradually raised herself to a sitting position and looked up the embankment. After doing a quick analysis, she decided that, if she moved to her left a little further where it wasn't as steep, she would be able to climb up more easily. She would have been content to sit there for a moment more, until she looked at her watch. It was quarter of four, and Katherine would be home in less than ten minutes. Sarah was still a fifteen-minute walk from her house.

       *   *   *

Since the divorce, Katherine became upset whenever Sarah was late. Not wanting to face her upset mother after the type of day she was having, Sarah sprang to her feet. Unfortunately, she sprang up a little to fast. Her weight snapped a twig under her foot and she fell down again. Scared and irritated, Sarah didn't waste anytime trying again. This time, she decided to try positioning her hands in front of her to steady herself. When she leaned forward, her hand brushed against some type of cloth material. Instantly intrigued, Sarah cleared away the underbrush to see what it was. To her astonishment, she saw a green knapsack. It looked very much like the kind of bag the eighth graders carried to school.

This is strange, Sarah thought. It appeared to have a little weight to it. It felt like a bag full of dirty clothes. Being the good Samaritan that she was, Sarah decided to open the bag, hoping to find a name or something, so she could return the bag to its rightful owner. When she opened the bag, she found something much more surprising. It was filled with money. Sarah sat there shocked. The little green bag was filled to the brim with hundred-dollar bills. Sarah had never seen so much money in her life!

"Who? What?" Several questions were running through Sarah's head. The bag gave Sarah all of the energy she needed to get up and out of there. In a flash, she was sprinting up the hill and on her way home with the bag. Though Sarah was excited, she was by no means an athlete and she couldn't keep the speed up for very long. As soon as she was out of the woods, she had to stop. She clutched the bag protectively to her chest, and started walking toward her house. When she got home, she hoped she wouldn't see Katherine's car in the driveway, but it was there. Sarah took a deep breath and picked up a little speed. She hoped that Katherine had gone for a walk, but she knew that wish was too good to be true.

"Where have you been, Sarah? It's after four! You should have been home half an hour ago. What happened to you? Why are you so dirty?…"

"But mom…look what I found!" Sarah exclaimed, holding the bag in front of her.

"I don't care about what you found. Whatever it is doesn't give you a reason to come home this late, especially without a telephone call or anything. Were you and Diane in the woods? There are so many bad things happening to young girls these days. Even here in this safe haven of Alberville, I still worry. Just a phone call: 'I'm at my friend's house, I'll be late! I'm…', Katherine was on a roll. It was just what Sarah was hoping to avoid. She was not up to one of Katherine's lectures today, and she knew this situation could be brutal if Katherine continued.

"But—" Sarah said. "Mom—" she tried again, but Katherine kept talking.

"I know you might think I'm overreacting, but, Sarah, you're all I've got. I can't help but worry."

It was now or never. Sarah knew she had to interrupt this run-on lecture that Katherine was just getting tuned up for.

"MOM, I FOUND SOME MONEY…LOTS OF MONEY," Sarah yelled out, as she opened the bag.

Katherine stopped talking as she gazed down at the money in the bag. "What? Sarah!" said Katherine, speechless.

Sensing her mother's change of spirit, Sarah saw the opportunity to share the story of her discovery. Cautiously, she pulled a few of the hundred dollar bills out of the bag. Very cautiously, since Sarah was not sure how Katherine was going to react.

"Sarah, where did you find this? This is a lot of money…I don't understand." Katherine said, more anxious and concerned with each word she spoke.

"Mom, it's a long story."

Katherine rushed to close the front door as she prepared to listen to Sarah. She and Sarah went into the kitchen and sat down. Sarah slowly retold the story.

At first, Katherine was upset, not wanting to believe what Sarah had been put through, but she was also relieved that Sarah was okay.

"Sarah, I'm sorry. I was worried about you. I didn't know or even think…do you have any idea who's money this is?"

"No, Mom. When I opened the bag and saw all the money, the only thing I could think of was to run home and tell you. I have no idea."

Katherine turned the bag upside down and dumped the contents onto the kitchen table. The bills covered the table, and, in addition, several hundred dollar bills and a small envelope fell to the floor. The two of them were so engrossed in watching the money tumble out of the bag, they didn't notice the small brown envelope. When Katherine stepped forward to shake the bag to make sure all the contents were out, the envelope slid underneath the table, obscured by the tablecloth.

Sarah picked the money up off the floor, while Katherine stood looking at the money on the table. Her thoughts flashed back to the black briefcase and her encounter with Bobbie. She remembered how afraid she had been.

"Don't touch any of the money, Sarah. I don't want to be held responsible if any of it comes up missing. I'm going to put it back in the bag. I'll call the police."

"You mean we can't keep some of it? I found it."

"No, Sarah, that would be stealing! This is not ours to keep. We must call the police."

"But, Mom, I don't understand why we can't keep some of the money."

"Sarah, you're young, and I know it's hard for you to fully understand all of this right now, but believe me, someday you will. Remember, I have always taught you to be honest and never tell a lie?"

"Yes, but I found it! "Finders keepers, losers weepers'. You never told me that was wrong."

"You're right, but that's just a game of words kids and adults play. It's not right. We have to give this money to the police."

Katherine could tell by the look in Sarah's eyes that she didn't understand. She knew it would be important to help her understand the significance of this, but this lesson would take some time...time that Katherine felt she did not have at this moment. Having all of this money in her house made her nervous.

"Sarah, go and wash up. I'll finish dinner and we will call the police together. I'm proud of you. I love you, and I'm so glad you didn't get hurt," Katherine said, hugging her. Sarah walked off without saying a word.

While they prepared for dinner and their phone call to the police, a man walked through the woods looking for the money. He wore a long black overcoat and a large brim hat that shadowed his face. Unable to find it right away was beginning to frustrate him. He had been given specific details about where the bag was tossed. He searched the bottom of the embankment for a few more moments. While making his way up the embankment, he caught sight of something purple lying on the ground. It was a child's school bag. He opened it. The name 'Sarah Oberman' was written on all the papers.

"What the hell!" he sounded out to himself. Realizing that some kid may have his money, or more importantly, the envelope, he headed for the school he had passed on his way into the woods, hoping to find an answer.

Meanwhile, Katherine had completed her search of the bag's contents. She decided she would have dinner with Sarah before they called the police. Hopefully this would allow Sarah time to calm down.

"That's an awful lot of money, isn't it Mom?"

Katherine wasn't quick to answer. All she could think about was the money. She was smart enough to know that, in this day and age, people just didn't carry around thousands of dollars in a school bag, unless they were trying to hide it.

Across the table, Sarah was thinking the same thoughts. She was old enough to know a lot about drugs and crime, even if most of it came from the shows she saw on television. She knew the money she brought into the house wasn't put there to brighten her day. It must have been left for somebody, and that somebody would probably be looking for it, if they weren't already.

Sarah squirmed in the chair. She thought, *if only I hadn't been such a coward. If only I had kept walking, and didn't stop to chase after the leaf. If only I'd just left the bag there and hadn't opened it.* Thoughts of regret propelled through her head as tears appeared on her face.

"Sarah, don't cry. Everything will be alright. Don't worry. This is not your fault, this could have happened to anyone. We'll be alright, don't worry, Sarah," Katherine said, holding Sarah's hand. "Besides, nothing has happened. All we need to do is call the police and tell them what you found. They will pick the money up and you'll have an exciting story to tell your friends tomorrow. You'll be a hero!" Katherine knew she couldn't wait any longer.

As Katherine walked toward the phone, she had a feeling of *deja vu.* She had been in this situation before, but this time she was not afraid to call the police. She did not have to run.

"Hello, Alberville police station, please hold," a woman's voice answered. After being put on hold briefly, the woman returned. "Thanks for waiting. How can I help you?"

"Hello, my name is Katherine Oberman. I found...I mean my daughter found a large sum of money and I need to speak with someone."

"Mrs. Oberman, was the money found in Alberville?"

"Yes, it was."

"Please hold and I will transfer you to someone who can help you."

The call was being transferred to Detective Carl Ganeli, who seemed to be having one of his usual disorganized days. "What am I going to do? Those idiots said they had everything under control." Ganeli reached over and flicked off the small television sitting at the corner of the desk. He had just finished listening to the late afternoon news.

Carl Ganeli was a different type of detective. He had somehow earned his stripes by default, meaning no one wanted the job. Ganeli was known more for his appetite than for his accolades. On this particular day, he was sitting at his desk musing, while he tried to tidy up his outfit. Ganeli wore brown pants and a white shirt that was stained with sweat. He had a large stain on his tie where part of his jelly doughnut had fallen at breakfast. He'd usually spend the majority of the day sitting behind the desk in his stuffy office, filing papers. He had allowed himself to get too out of shape to be on the street. Because of the time he had been on the police force and the scarcity of police officers in Alberville, they kept him around.

While reading through a boring police report, he kept scratching at the fiery red hairs that covered his partially bald head. The walls in his office were bare. No trophies, no medals, or awards. On his desk was a picture of a woman and child, but they weren't his family. It was just the picture that came with the frame. He lived alone, just he and his two cats. Whenever someone asked him what he was going to do with his life, he always retorted with, "When is life going to give me a break so I have a chance to do something with it?"

He was just about ready to put the files away and go home when the telephone rang. The clerk had decided to call Ganeli, and have him take the report since everyone else was busy.

Ganeli at first just looked at the telephone. "Dammit! This better be good. I have enough to do already." He picked up the phone. "Yeah, who is it?"

"There is a call on line two. A woman calling about finding some money. I was going to transfer it to Officer Staton, but he's still on the telephone. Would you mind taking the report for him?" Momentarily stunned, he shook his head as he waited for the call to be transferred. "Detective Carl Ganeli, how may I help you?"

"Hello, my name is Katherine Oberman and I have a…well it's not really a problem, it's more like a situation."

"Well, ma'am, why don't you give me your name so I know who you are, then you can explain to me your situation."

"I did, sir. My name is Katherine Oberman."

"Can you spell that please."

"K-a-t-h-e-r-i-n-e O-b-e-r-m-a-n. Should I spell it again?" Katherine asked.

"No, thanks ma'am, please continue."

"I don't know exactly how to start."

"Why don't you start at the beginning, Miss Oberman?"

"Okay," Katherine said, taking a few deep breaths. "My daughter, Sarah, she's twelve…, Katherine paused, starting to feel very anxious. "Well she found something."

"What do you mean by something ma'am?" Ganeli questioned.

"Well, more like she stumbled upon something."

Ganeli was starting to get frustrated. He was hungry and Katherine was taking away his eating time. "Miss Oberson, can you be a little clearer? I'm having a difficult time understanding you."

"It's Oberman, and yes, I will get to the point. My daughter, Sarah, was walking along a wooded trail, in back of Alberville Middle School and she fell. When she fell, she found this bag. You know how kids are, right?"

"Unfortunately ma'am I don't, but go ahead."

"Well, kids like to explore, open things. So she opened the bag and found it was full of money, a lot of money."

Ganeli leaned forward and took a sip of the lukewarm cup of coffee. He was now getting interested, very, very interested. Little did Katherine know, but Carl Ganeli had just been offered a large reward if he found a bag of money that had been dropped in the woods. The call came from the local bank president, Mr. Dunn. Ganeli was told that the gentleman had lost the bag while hunting. He knew Ganeli would help. Ganeli had become known as an officer who would do anything for money.

"What did your daughter find?" He coaxed her gently.

"She found…, she found…, a lot of money. A whole, whole lot of money."

Ganeli spit his coffee out of his mouth and shot out of his chair. "How much is a lot," he asked, his voice changing octaves.

"I'm not sure. There appears to be thousands of hundred dollar bills."

"It couldn't be," Ganeli shouted.

"I'm telling you," Katherine replied. "It's a lot of money."

"No, no. No, I believe you, I believe you. Do you still have the money with you?"

"Yes, I do. I don't know where it came from. It might be drug money or something, and I figured there was no better place to turn then to the police, right?" Katherine said, hoping to be reassured.

"You're absolutely right. I'll come by and pick up the money. Let the police take care of handling the money, so you're not held responsible. I'll bring it back to the station and work on locating the owner. You never know ma'am, there might even be a reward! Not everybody is as honest as you are."

Flattered, Katherine replied, "Thank you, it will be such a relief if you come and get it. I don't want it sitting around my house any longer than need be."

"Give me your address and I'll be there in a matter of minutes."

No sooner had she hung up the phone than, Ganeli was dancing around his office.

"Hot damn! I'm going to be rich! I found it!" Ganeli was sure this was the money Mr. Dunn was looking for. He called him immediately.

"Mr. Dunn. I found the money. I just got a call from a woman. Her daughter found it."

"Ganeli, that's great! Remember what I said, no one can know about this. You pick the money up and meet me at..." Dunn gave Ganeli instructions.

Ganeli flew out of his office. He chose to handle this alone. The clerk watched him go by, and she was astonished. She hadn't seen him move that fast since it was announced the bakery next door was going out of business.

"It's alright now, Sarah. The police are coming. Everything is going to be okay."

"Really, Mom? You mean that?"

"Of course. Have I ever lied to you? If I say things are going to be okay, don't things always turn out for the best?"

"Yes, they do, Mom. Yes, they do."

CHAPTER THIRTY

While Katherine nervously awaited Ganeli's arrival, she decided to reheat their dinner. Sarah walked around with her headphones on, listening to her crazy music. Katherine removed Sarah's headphones, then sat her down and began to prepare her for questions she might encounter from the police. Sarah was instructed to be honest. Katherine assured her the police were coming to help them.

Katherine glanced at the clock on the stove. She'd called the police almost twenty minutes ago, so where were they? she wondered, looking at the clock, then the bag, and again at the clock. Katherine decided it would be best to go to the living room and watch the evening news while she waited. She sent Sarah upstairs to fix herself up before the police arrived.

"AGGGGHH!" Katherine voiced as she shook her head. *You're over-reacting!* She kept telling herself that this was not one of those Monday night movies as she turned on the television.

The news started with a cute story about a mother and daughter being reunited, then a feel-good story about a lost puppy finding its owner. She started to relax in her favorite chair when the top story was reintroduced.

"As reported earlier, another grim tragedy has rocked New York City's banking system. Today, the body of Richard Manelli was found washed up on the shores of Hudson Bay by two joggers. Mr. Manelli was reported missing several weeks ago by his wife, after she returned home and found the house in shambles and blood all over the living room. It is suspected that millions of dollars in investment bonds have been used illegally by his bank. The Police have been hopeful, but when no one in his family heard from him and no ransom note appeared, their hopes grew dim."

"For months, this city's banking system has been rocked with scandal, the first being the death of Richard Albright, a bank President, whose car went off the road just three months ago. Ultimately, his death was ruled accidental, but there is still much speculation. Days after his death, accusations of fraud were brought against his bank. Some believe he misused investor's dollars. An investigation is being conducted at present."

"The President of Third Manhattan Bank is accused of misusing investment funds to subsidize personal trading. An investigation was launched but no hard evidence has been found, despite the charges. The Vice President of the bank, William Marcus was found in his office last Friday, hanging from the ceiling fan. Typed on his computer screen, was a single sentence that read "I'm sorry, forgive me." What he was sorry for has yet to be established. To date, millions of dollars are unaccounted for in these scandals.

"Stolen, perhaps? Destroyed, maybe? Hidden, possibly. However, after the deaths of three most prominent leaders of the investment banking industry, a dropped investigation and missing millions, it certainly leaves reasonable doubt in one's mind. The feeling is that there are a lot of names to be uncovered in this entire scandal and, until they are, this carnage will continue. This is Sandra Jones, Channel Seven News. Please tune in to our eleven o'clock news for further updates."

Katherine sat still. The thought of money and murder frightened her to death, especially knowing she had thousands of dollars sitting on her kitchen floor. Before she was able to lapse into a panic attack, the doorbell interrupted her thoughts. Hoping it was the police, she flew towards it. When she looked through the peephole she saw a partially bald man, dressed in a white shirt, holding out a badge. Katherine cautiously opened the door.

"Hi, ma'am. I'm Detective Ganeli. You called?"

"Yes, please come in." Katherine breathed a sigh of relief.

When he stepped into the foyer and into the light, Katherine was a little startled by his appearance. Ganeli had not done much to improve himself. The stain from the jelly donut was still on his tie. His pants were so tight around his waist it appeared his stomach was about to explode. The calm protective detective that she expected was not the type who walked through her door. Ganeli looked nervous and disorientated, as if it was the first time he'd ever been inside someone's house. He pulled papers out of his pockets, all appeared to be used. He fidgeted from one foot to another as he looked around the room.

Katherine noticed how uncomfortable he was and invited him into the living room. Once they were seated, he seemed to settle down.

"Well, ma'am how are you today? I mean this evening."

"I'm fine, or at least I was..." Katherine said as Ganeli interrupted.

"Oh, I ate a stale doughnut this morning and I can still feel it settling on the bottom of my stomach, but I hope it will be digested by morning." Ganeli hoped to get a laugh, but instead he received a look of disgust.

After several awkward minutes, Katherine suggested she call Sarah. Ganeli agreed, as he continued to tap his feet while he searched for something clean to write on.

Katherine could hear Sarah at the top of the stairs. Initially Sarah just stood there trying to get a glimpse of the detective. Ganeli pulled out a black leather notepad from his back pocket, as he stood to greet Sarah. He seemed rather surprised that he had one. The notepad was so flat, Katherine thought it was his wallet. Ganeli used it more for writing grocery lists than for taking statements, but he figured he ought to write something down. After fishing around in his shirt and pants pockets, he pulled out a short pencil without an eraser.

Sarah finally made her way down the stairs. She stood quietly next to Katherine, staring at Ganeli. She nervously awaited his questions.

Wanting to get the interview out of the way, Ganeli instinctively took a step toward Sarah, then reached out to shake her hand as he introduced himself. Just as instinctively, Sarah took a step back and bumped into Katherine.

"It's okay, go ahead. He's here to help us, Sarah." Katherine urged Sarah to shake Ganeli's hands as she placed her hands on Sarah's shoulders.

"Well, Sarah," Ganeli started off. "Your mother tells me you had an exciting day today, huh?"

Sarah nodded.

"She tells me that you found a bag with a large amount of money in it."

Again Sarah nodded, not knowing what else to say.

"Umm geee, let's seee…," Ganeli was stumped. Sarah wasn't offering any information. Did this make her a hostile witness? he wondered. Or wait, did that only happen in court? He stood scratching his head. *Christ, what am I going to do?* he thought.

Katherine watched Ganeli. She wondered if he didn't know how to talk to children, or if he was just a little slow. She hoped it wasn't the latter. Wanting to get this man and the bag out of her house, she offered a little advice.

"Sarah, why don't you tell Detective Ganeli how you found the money?" Ganeli shot Katherine a grateful smile, as he opened up his little handbook, trying to redeem himself.

"Well, okay," Sarah said, grateful to have something to do besides stand there watching that grotesque looking man run his chubby hands through his greasy hair.

"I took the back way home from school to avoid getting into a fight. I went through the woods. I was—"

Ganeli interrupted her. "Wait a minute, you took an abnormal route home by way of transporting yourself through the woods, located at the rear of your school?"

Sarah puzzled, replied, "Yes."

Ganeli was quite pleased with himself. He made a big show of writing something down in his notepad. He carefully drew a perfectly round circle, with two eyes and a triangle nose, before he looked up at Sarah, as if to tell her it was alright to continue.

Picking up on the officer's cue, Sarah continued. "Anyway, I was walking home and I saw this really cool leaf. Since I often collect leaves for my nature scrapbook—"

"Wait a second," Ganeli interrupted again. "You collect nature things?"

"Yes, I do." Sarah responded.

"How long have you collected leaves and other things?"

Sarah didn't respond. Katherine could tell Sarah was getting irritated.

"Hummm, I see." Ganeli said, as he added a long neck, legs, and hands with stubby fingers to the interesting character he was drawing. When he thought enough time had passed for it to seem that he had recorded his observations accurately, he instructed Sarah to continue.

"Well, I saw this interesting leaf and chased after it."

"Do you make a habit of chasing after leaves?" Ganeli asked.

"Well, I guess I do, since I have to catch the leaf in order to add it to my collection. Anyway, when I finally caught up with the leaf and bent to pick it up a mouse scurried across the path and I—"

"Wait a minute," Ganeli interrupted. "Are you sure it was a mouse? Could it not have been a squirrel, chipmunk or another member of the rodent family? Are you just saying it was a mouse because you are scared of mice and you're looking for a reason to explain—"

"I DON'T KNOW WHAT IT WAS EXACTLY!" shouted Sarah. "It was small! It was brown! It had a tail and it squealed as it ran past me! I'm sorry that I didn't ask it to stop so I could inspect it!"

"Sarah, you apologize to Detective Ganeli! That is no way to talk to an adult! You apologize right now!"

Realizing that perhaps he was taking things too far, Ganeli took a minute to add some clouds and grass to his developing picture before asking Sarah to continue. Sarah finished in a flourish and ran up the stairs.

"I apologize for her behavior. It's really been a rough day for her. Please try to understand," Katherine voiced, disappointed.

Ganeli scratched his head and continued to write. He finished drawing a smiley face on the sun. "I think I have about all the information I need for now. I'll call you if anything else comes up. Please thank Sarah for her help." Ganeli headed towards the door. He had his hand on the doorknob when Katherine stopped him.

"Detective Ganeli, you forgot the money."

"Oh, thanks, Ganeli responded, embarrassed.

Katherine went to get the bag while Ganeli waited at the door. Katherine returned with the bag. Ganeli, cheeks red, thanked Katherine and left with the money.

Sarah heard the door close as she stood at the top of the steps. She ran down the stairs and joined Katherine. They watched Ganeli drive away. Katherine glared at Sarah. "Sarah, I'm very ashamed of your behavior, we will discuss this over dinner." Sarah didn't say a word.

The two of them, relieved the money was gone, headed towards the kitchen.

CHAPTER THIRTY-ONE

Meanwhile, the man in the dark overcoat had made his way to the Alberville school house. In his hand, he carried the purple school bag. As he approached the building, he noticed the school appeared vacant. There wasn't a car or school bus in the parking lot. As he got closer to the school, he noticed several lights were on inside the building. He tried to open the door, but it was locked. He walked around to the side of the building and looked through several windows. No one seemed to be inside. When he returned to the front of the building, he caught a glimpse of someone moving inside.

From afar, he could see a man, dressed in gray pants and a shirt, carrying a broom. It was Martin, the janitor, in his friendly state of mind and whistling as he swept the hallway. The man began to shake the doors, hoping to get Martin's attention. Martin seemed to be in his own world and at first did not hear the noise.

As Martin moved closer towards the front of the building, he heard a noise coming from the front door. He looked toward the door, but was unable to see anyone. Martin cautiously walked toward the door, clutching the broom handle tighter as he walked. He could now see the shadowy figure of someone standing at the door. He placed his hand on the door and was just about to open it, but decided he'd better ask who it was first. This was the time to practice what he had preached to the kids: never open the door until you know who it is. Just as he was about to open his mouth, the man yelled out.

"I found a school bag that belongs to one of the kids." Martin recognized the school's logo on the bag as the man held it up, and opened the door. To his surprise, the man seemed taller than he expected. Martin knew he was not from around Alberville, he was too well dressed. The man's dark coat and hat gave him a somewhat clergy-like appearance.

"Thanks for returning the bag, mister. I'm sure you've have made one of our kids a happy camper," Martin said and reached out for the bag.

The man pulled the bag back toward himself as he looked down at Martin. "Do you know where I can find Sarah Oberman? I would like to return this to her personally. You see," he said, "I was walking through the woods, looking at some property and found this bag. I know this child needs it. There appear to be some homework papers for tonight."

Confused, Martin looked at the man. He was not aware of any property for sale in the area. "Where did you say you found the bag?"

"That's not important. Just give me her address and I will return the bag," the man said.

Martin knew it was against school policy to give out a student's address or phone number. He also knew Sarah, Katherine and Tim very well.

"I'll return it to the 'Lost and Found' in the morning. I'm sure someone will pick it up," Martin said, again reaching out for the bag. The man again refused to part with it.

"I would like to give this to Sarah Oberman personally. I'm sure she needs the bag to do her school work."

"Don't worry Sir, I'll make sure this Sarah gets the bag," Martin said.

Growing obviously intolerant, the man sternly asked, "Do you know where the girl lives or not?"

"No, I don't know where she lives." If you'd like to leave the bag here, I'll see that she gets it tomorrow."

"That's quite alright. I'll stop by tomorrow," the man said, as he walked away with the bag. When Martin could no longer see the man, he decided to call Katherine and tell her what happened.

Meanwhile, Ganeli had decided to take a detour away from the police station. Instead, he headed west out of town. According to Mr. Dunn's instructions, the plans were to meet him with the money at a specific location on the outskirts of Alberville. Ganeli decided to call the boys at the precinct so they wouldn't worry.

"Hey, Doris! It's me. You know, Ganeli."

Doris just listened. She knew Ganeli had a knack for rambling on.

"Hey, Doris! Are you there?"

"Sure, Carl. How can I help you?"

"Hey, don't sound so uppity. I know it's only me. Ha ha ha."

Ganeli enjoyed his humor alone. "Hey, Doris. I'll be a little late. I got a little tip I'm working on. Tell the boys not to worry."

"Sure, Carl," Doris responded, in a slow, tired voice.

Ganeli hung up the phone as he drove along, resuming his jovial state of mind.

Doris looked at her phone wondering what Ganeli was eating, and thinking that the last time he had a tip was the night Beefer's had a special on Barbecue rib tips.

CHAPTER THIRTY-TWO

Katherine and Sarah had just finished dinner. Sarah was still in tears from her scolding as she reached for her napkin to wipe her face and accidentally knocked over her glass of Kool-Aid. As she grabbed several napkins to wipe up her spill off the floor, she noticed a small brown envelope under the table. She picked it up thinking Katherine must have dropped it while going through the mail.

"Mom, you dropped one of your letters!"

"You must have dropped it when you opened the mail today."

"Sarah, I was so worried about you I forgot to get the mail," Katherine responded as she reached for the envelope. The envelope was sealed with no address or name on the back or front. Katherine opened the envelope and pulled four sheets of paper out of the envelope. The papers had a list of names written on them. *This seems quite strange*, she thought, as she read the names on the first sheet. None seemed familiar. To her surprise, the second sheet contained the name Detective Carl Ganeli, Alberville. This was written next to Mr. Tom Dunn, Bank President. *I don't understand*, she thought, as she continued to read the names. It was a list of men, banks and various locations.

In the background, the early evening news was about to begin its second round of stories. Katherine kept a small television in the kitchen. She enjoyed watching the evening news as she washed dishes.

"Our top story this evening is the discovery of the body of Richard Manelli. He was found washed ashore at the Hudson Bay by two joggers today. This happens to be one of several mysterious deaths of bank executives over the last several months. As you know…just two months ago, William Marcus, the Vice President of Third Manhattan Bank, was found in his office hanging from the ceiling."

At that moment, a cold shiver ran through Katherine's body. She glanced toward the news and then re-read the list of names. On page two of the list, were the names Richard Manelli and William Marcus. She looked at the list again, somewhat confused, yet alarmed. She began to think about the earlier broadcast.

Why were the names of all those men on this list? Why do I have this list in my house? How did it get here? What did these men have in common? Katherine ran over to the television and turned to another news station. They were just starting their story. "Today the body of Richard Manelli was washed ashore on the Hudson Bay. The body was sighted by two joggers. This is the sixth of several mysterious deaths or murders that have rocked the banking industry. Just months ago,...Richard Albright...Raymond Trimmer...all found dead. There are still no answers."

The news went on as Katherine looked through the list. All of the names mentioned were found throughout the sheets she held in her hand. What baffled her even more was that she saw the name John Walters, New York Investor, on the list. The sight of that name rekindled her fears.

Frantically, she turned to other news stations as she tried to decipher what she had discovered. The name John Walters was not mentioned on any of the news shows. What could that mean? Was he the next to be murdered, or did he have something to do with this? It was as if the past had resurfaced. What about Nick Walters, she wondered, frantically looking over the list. His name was not there.

Marcus, dead; Albright, dead; Trimmer, dead. Ganeli, alive, she thought. "Oh my God! Ganeli! He must know about the murders," she cried out, as she stumbled back toward the kitchen sink.

"Mom, what's wrong? Are you alright?" Sarah asked, as the terror in Katherine's eyes grew.

"Mom, what's wrong?" Sarah asked, getting up from the table.

Katherine was speechless. A flurry of questions dashed through her head. She looked around the kitchen and out the window. It was dark. Katherine looked at Sarah, and Sarah's eyes were filled with fright.

"Mom, what's wrong? Please, tell me what's wrong? I'm scared!"

Katherine didn't know what to say. Suddenly the telephone rang. Katherine jumped as her heart raced.

Sarah rushed towards the phone. "Don't answer that!" she yelled. Sarah stopped in her tracks.

"I can't take this. Tell me something!" Sarah cried cry out. "I know something is wrong. Please, Mom, please talk to me."

The phone continued to ring, and each ring seemed to get louder. Katherine didn't know what to do. She knew it wasn't Tim. He was out of town, or could it be...? Unable to stand the thought of not knowing, Katherine picked the phone up, but didn't say anything.

"Mrs. Oberman? Mrs. Oberman," a pleasant voice called out. "Mrs. Oberman, it's Martin, the janitor at the school." Katherine let out several deep breaths as her pounding heart echoed through her body.

"Mrs. Oberman, are you there?"

"Yes. Yes, Martin, I'm here."

"Are you and Sarah alright?"

"Yes, but..." Katherine paused...

"Mrs. Oberman, something really strange just happened. I thought you should know—"

"What happened?" Katherine blurted out the question before Martin could finish.

Martin went on to tell her about the man at the school who had found Sarah's bag. He told her the man's story about looking at some property when he stumbled across Sarah's bag. He explained how the man seemed to get irritated when he wouldn't reveal their address.

"What did he look like?" Katherine asked, afraid.

Martin went on to describe the dark overcoat and large brim hat that the man wore. He remembered he had a mustache, but that was all he could remember. Martin explained how uneasy the man made him feel.

"Did he say where he was going when he left?" Katherine asked.

"No he didn't, Mrs. Oberman, but he kept Sarah's school-bag."

"Sarah, did you have your book bag when you left school?"

Sarah thought for a quick moment. "Yes, mom. Why?"

"Where is it?" Katherine asked.

Sarah remembered that she last saw it when she fell.

"I...I...I left it...in...the...woods," Sarah said shamefully, realizing, from the look on Katherine's face, that she knew.

"Oh God, what am I going to do?" Katherine shouted.

"Mrs. Oberman, are you okay?"

"Yes," Katherine responded reluctantly and hung up the telephone.

"Mom, you're scaring me! Did someone find my bag?"

"We can't stay here. A man found your bag. He was at your school asking Martin for our address. He kept your bag. I don't know if that man found our address or not, but I don't think it will be safe to stay here and wait for him. Sarah, we must leave and get some help. Right now!"

"Why can't we wait for the man to bring my bag? Why must we leave? What did I do?"

"You didn't do anything. The papers in the envelope had information that may be important to the man..., information I shouldn't have seen. I'll explain everything to you later. We have to get out of here, right now! I need your help. Go to your room and pack a few things. You have five minutes. Hurry!"

Katherine peeped out of the window to see if there were any cars coming. She couldn't see anything. It was dark. All she could think about was getting out of the house. Sarah bounded up the stairs. Katherine ran into the kitchen and grabbed her purse, locked the back door, then ran upstairs to her room to gather a few of her belongings.

Katherine had a bag packed in less than two minutes. She was just about to leave the room and check on Sarah when she remembered she needed her good luck charm. This was her five-leaf clover pin. She kept it packed away in her trunk, a place where

she locked away her special memories. She grabbed the pin and headed to Sarah's room.

Katherine found Sarah sitting on her bag trying to get it zipped. Not wanting to waste another second, she grabbed Sarah's bag, and the two of them hurried down the steps. Sarah grabbed her favorite doll that was sitting on the chair next to the door, as they dashed out of the house. Katherine took one final look at the house, then they got in the car and she backed out of the driveway and sped away.

CHAPTER THIRTY-THREE

Ganeli sat hunched over the wheel of his beat-up brown Malibu Classic, driving down a secluded alley on the outskirts of Alberville. The evening was rather foggy. He was getting close to where he was supposed to meet Mr. Dunn. He'd just passed the abandoned schoolhouse that Dunn had described. Looking ahead, he could see lights flashing. Moving closer, he realized it was Dunn's car. He pulled up next to it, but he did not see anyone inside. Ganeli thought maybe Dunn was playing 'hide and seek' so he decided to turn his engine off and duck out of sight, thinking Dunn would appear, but he didn't. *That's strange*, Ganeli thought, as he got out of the car.

"I know you're in there, Dunn. It's me, Ganeli," he said, stepping lightly as he walked up on Dunn's car. As he got closer and looked inside, he noticed it was empty. Ganeli looked around and wondered, *where could he be?* The fog had thickened, and it was quiet. Ganeli was upset. He wanted his share of the money. He had plans.

"Where is that idiot? He said he would be here! His car is here! Here I am, driving around like a jack fool, trying to find this damn alley and I'm left to meet an abandoned car. I should just take all the money. I guess I would, if I were not a good cop." Ganeli was talking to himself.

He let out a string of curses as an alley cat jumped in front of the car. "Where in the hell is he!" Ganeli shouted out. "I can't take too much more of this shit. I'm getting mad!"

After a few more minutes of standing and waiting, he reached into the back seat of his car and pulled out a doughnut. He stood there, chomping on the doughnut and thinking. He knew he had the money and this made him feel he had the power. He liked the way he was starting to feel. He had not felt this way since he gave Mrs. Brown—the little old lady at the church—a parking ticket for parking in the handicapped space; not realizing she had a handicap sticker on her car.

Ganeli knew that his involvement was wrong, but he was beyond the point of caring. He needed something to look forward to in his life. When he'd received the phone call from Dunn offering him a lot of money for a little of his time, he couldn't resist. All he had to do was misplace a little police evidence, lose a couple of files and forget to ask a few questions. He would get a fair amount of money, retire early and spend the rest of his life enjoying the fat of the land.

This was the plan, but getting Katherine's phone call made it easy. He did not have to cover up anything. He had the money, the report and the pictures he drew, all to himself. It could not have gone any smoother, except for the absence of Mr. Dunn.

Several minutes had passed. Ganeli polished off three more dough-nuts and was about to get into his car, when from afar, he could see the headlights of a car approaching. The dollar signs began to flash in his head as he waited. A black car pulled up in front of him. As the car stopped, its tire sprayed a puddle of dirty water all over his pants. Ganeli let out a scream. "Dammit!" He was about to continue when he saw two tall white men get out of the car. Ganeli decided it would be best to shake off the excess water and forget the incident.

The two men were about the same height, well built and dressed alike. Ganeli could see their white shirts, ties and dark overcoats. He noticed that they were wearing black gloves. As they approached him, Ganeli reached for his gun. He felt the two of them could do some serious dam-age. He was unable to get his gun out. It seemed he was having trouble with the snap. It had been quite some time since he had to use it.

Ganeli panicked as one of the men stepped directly in front of him and grabbed his hand while the other one leaned against the car.

"Ganeli?" The man in front of him called out as he clutched Ganeli's hand.

"Yeah, that's me. Who in the hell are you, and how do you know my name? You better let my hand go before I—"

He was silenced by a kick in the gut as he fell toward the man, who pushed Ganeli up and pasted him against the car. Ganeli just moaned.

"Listen here, you fat fuck! I don't have time for your heroic bullshit. I want the money."

"Yeah, I...know," Ganeli responded." "Who...in...the hell....are...you...? Where is Dunn?"

"Dead! Just where you will be," the man said, belting Ganeli in the gut, this time with his fist. Ganeli slumped forward.

"Dead? What in the hell is going on here? Who in the—" Ganeli silenced himself, as he saw that the man leaning against the car was displaying his gun.

"I want the money, Ganeli," the man voiced.

"It's in the bag..., in the car," Ganeli responded.

"Check the bag out," the man signaled to his partner who was leaning against the car.

"Where did you get the money, Ganeli? the man standing in front of him asked.

"You don't need to know," Ganeli said, feeling a little reckless.

"I said...fatso, where did you get the money?" he released Ganeli's hand and grabbed him by the collar.

"Like I said, it's none of your—. " Ganeli found it difficult to talk as the man clutched his collar. He could see the other man frantically searching through the bag. All the money had been dumped on the car seat.

The man who had been searching the bag, walked over to the other and whispered into his ear. Ganeli tried hard to listen, but found it difficult as his attacker clutched his throat. The next thing Ganeli knew, a knife was pressed against his throat. He tried to remember what the police book would tell him to do in this situation, but nothing came to mind. Realizing he no longer had control and never did, Ganeli quickly divulged the story of the phone call and his visit to the Oberman's house. He closed his eyes waiting for his throat to be slit.

Just as Ganeli was about to open his mouth and plea for his life, the lights of an oncoming car shined on them. The car approached recklessly down the alley. The man clutching his throat let go, then jumped to the front of Dunn's car.

Ganeli stood there, trying to catch his breath. He was between shock and reality, relieved he was not dead and scared to death about what would happen next, as he looked into the headlights of the vehicle. Everyone had moved except Ganeli and a lonely alley cat, who had come out of its hiding place. Unfortunately, the cat was crushed underneath the wheels of the car.

Ganeli got sick. Despite everyone else's opinion of him, Ganeli did have a soft spot for animals. The car came to an abrupt stop, just short of the other cars and, once again, Ganeli was sprayed with muddy water. He pretended not to notice, hoping that whoever was in the car would help him.

Ganeli watched, as a tall man in a dark overcoat and large brim hat stepped out of the car.

"What's going on?" the man asked as he walked towards Ganeli.

"Slick, you damn near killed me!" Ganeli's attacker shouted as he moved from behind the car.

"I'm sorry, Bob, I get turned on when I drive in fog, especially down a dark secluded alley. Believe me, I had everything under control. What's going on?" Slick asked.

"Slick, we've taken care of Dunn. I can't believe he was going to double-cross your father just to save his hide."

"My father thought he would help bring Riggins down. Riggins must have put heavy pressure on him. What about Ron?" Slick asked.

"We found him, but it was to late. Someone put a bullet right through his heart." Bob responded.

"Damn! My father said he was scared to death when he called. Ron thought he had shaken Dunn's men when he ran through the woods."

"I'm just glad he realized what Dunn was up to do when they met." Bob said as he looked at Ganeli.

"Have you found the list?" Slick asked Bob.

"No, but we followed Dunn to this alley. Slick, you should have seen his face when I stepped out of the car. Man, it gave me such a rush! We searched his car, but found nothing. After a good beating, he told us he was meeting a cop name Ganeli. He pleaded for us to help him leave the country, confirming Ron's story about his fears of Riggins. Somehow Riggins found out about the list. I can't believe he was going to snitch just to save his hide. We're lucky Ron could not be bought. Sam and I took care of him and waited for that pathetic cop over there."

"Did he have the list?"

"No, but I think he knows where the list is. That's the only reason that buffoon is still alive! The money was all there," Bob said, as he pointed towards the back seat of the car.

"Right, you son-of-a-bitch!" Bob yelled, as he looked toward Ganeli.

"Ganeli knows," shouted Bob. Ganeli wondered what they thought he knew, as he watched Slick walk toward him.

"Know what? I don't know anything," Ganeli said, as Slick moved closer, and he tried to back away. "Well you see, here's what happened…" Ganeli was silenced by a murderous look.

"Was I talking to you?" Slick asked, towering over Ganeli. "You're the crooked cop Dunn told Ron about."

Ganeli stood there trying to decide if his body was shaking or if he was shitting. "Oh…oh…no…I…just—"

"Then shut up," Slick demanded. "Get the bag. Bring it here," Slick instructed Ganeli.

Hastily, Ganeli went to his car. His legs were shaking so bad you could hear his wet pants flapping. He placed the money back in the bag and took it to Slick. Ganeli expected Slick to recount the money, but to his surprise, Slick paid no attention to the money. After a thorough search of the bag, Slick turned to Sam and Bob. "You're right. It's not here."

Not knowing what Slick was talking about, Ganeli stood there with a broken smile on his face. His smile vanished quickly when all three men surrounded him.

"Hey, guyssss…, what's going on? The money is all there," Ganeli said.

"Listen, you idiot," Slick said. "We don't give a monkey's ass about the money. We want the list."

"List, what list?" Ganeli asked, obviously puzzled.

Slick snapped open a knife and held it at Ganeli's nose. He did it so fast Ganeli did not have time to swallow.

"The list! I want it now!" Slick said.

Ganeli knew he only had seconds to respond."Oh, that list! I didn't see a list. I could make one for you. Mister. Dunn promised me—"

"Wrong answer, you asshole! I don't think you know who you are fucking with. Slick pushed the tip of the knife into Ganeli's nose, just enough to get a trickle of blood.

"I…I thinnnnk, I…I sa.. sa…sa…saw some…something…wa…when I…pick…picked up the ba…ba…bag."

"Where is the girl? She must have the list."

"Girl?" Ganeli responded.

"Just answer my damn questions!" Slick demanded.

"Let me finish him Slick." Bob said, as he moved towards Ganeli. Slick waved him off.

"Let's go," said Slick. "Ganeli will take us to the girl."

Slick got into his car. Bob, Sam and Ganeli got into the other car. Bob called someone on his car phone, and instructed them to come to the alley and do away with Dunn and Ganeli's cars.

"Hey, that's my Malibu classic," said Ganeli. " I need my car. What do you mean, do away with it?"

"Don't worry, you won't need that car where you are going," Bob assured Ganeli as he looked at him through the rear-view mirror.

While the two cars were heading towards the Oberman house, Katherine and Sarah fled in the opposite direction. Katherine drove well over the speed limit. Her heart and mind raced, as the premonition of the worst possible scenario surfaced. Over and over in her mind she could hear Martin's voice telling her, "a man in a dark coat and hat was at the school looking for Sarah."

Looking ahead she could see the lights of oncoming cars, but she registered nothing. Katherine thought only of the safety of Sarah and herself. She tried to think about what she should do with the list. Throwing it out the car window came to mind. *What if the man found them?. Maybe he would let them go if she gave it to him, but maybe not*, she thought. Before she realized it, she was at the Alberville precinct. She clasped the papers and Sarah's hand, then went inside.

She walked through the doors of the precinct, convinced that what she was about to do was right and that her nightmare would soon be over. However, like a spell, as soon as she stepped into the building, the feeling of safety was replaced by instant dread. The first police officer who passed before her eyes made her freeze in her tracts. Could she trust any of them? Time stood still as Katherine stood holding the envelope in her hand.

The ringing phone, the clicking of shoes on the tile floor; all faded into a dim roar as she focused on a poster in the background. The poster displayed a large man pointing a finger, at the bottom were the bold words OUR JOB IS TO PROTECT YOU. The irony of the situation and the sign made her stumble out of the building with Sarah in tow.

"Miss...Miss, can I help you?" It was Doris. She could see that Katherine seemed troubled. Katherine was moving so fast, she did not hear anything or anybody as she hurried towards her car. She dropped her keys while trying to start the car, and she took shallow breaths trying to calm down. Katherine then looked over at Sarah and what she saw nearly broke her heart.

Sarah had been quiet since they left the house, but Katherine had simply attributed this to the manner in which she railroaded her out of the house. Not knowing quite what to say, she vowed to pull herself and her daughter out of this mess. She started the engine and, with no destination in mind, she set out for the open road.

CHAPTER THIRTY-FOUR

The two drivers shut off their lights as they pulled into the driveway of the Oberman residence. Ganeli got out, aided by the nudge of Sam's gun. He watched, fascinated, as Sam and Bob simultaneously removed black caps from their pockets. It was just like on TV, Ganeli thought. Wanting to disguise himself, he frantically searched his pockets, but all he was able to find was a pair of green earmuffs and a mismatched pair of cotton gloves with a half-eaten sucker stuck to one of them.

"I can't wait to take care of you. I'm going to make you wish you never were born, you fat piece of shit," Bob said, moving toward Ganeli.

Slick stepped between them. "Cut the bullshit. We have a job to finish, then you can have your fun. I told you we need him for now." Slick said, and pushed Bob away.

"You need him, but I want him, and I can't wait," Sam said, as he kicked dirt toward Ganeli.

"Hey! alright! cried Ganeli. You don't like me, but at least respect me. After all, there's enough money for all of us. I don't want the list. You guys can have it. I don't even want to see it, so let's work together."

"Come on, Bob, let's go. Don't let this stupid cop get to you," Sam said, moving toward the house.

They moved quietly up the stairs onto the screened porch. Bob lead, followed by Sam, while Ganeli and Slick held up the rear. Ganeli dared not turn around. The mere sound of Slick's breathing scared him to death. He tried to act like 'one of the guys', keeping in step as they moved toward the front door. Within seconds, Bob had the door to the house open and walked inside. Ganeli noticed with disdain that they hadn't checked to see if anyone was home, and he feared for Katherine and Sarah. Noticing the house was quiet and dark, Ganeli prayed that it was also empty.

Once inside, as if by instinct, Sam and Bob separated, leaving Ganeli in the foyer with Slick. Not knowing what to do, he decided to go into the living room where he and Katherine had talked.

"Where in hell are you going? Sit down!" Slick ordered, then shoved Ganeli onto the couch.

"Wait a minute…I'm on your side," Ganeli yelled. "Hey, man!"

"Man?" Slick responded.

"I mean Ship," Ganeli said.

"Ship?" Slick voiced with a pestilent glance.

"I'm sorry, I'm nervous…I mean Slick. I'm in this with you. My ass is on the line here. I promise, if you let me go, I won't tell anyone. You can keep the money."

"Shut up! If you had done your job right in the first place, we would-n't be in this situation. What kind of a cop are you? Who would hire you? You're a disgrace to the police force."

"I'm a good detective. In 1972, I got an award for giving out the most parking tickets in one week."

"I can't believe this shit," Slick said, as he decided to disengage himself from Ganeli. *What an idiot,* he thought. Slick looked around the cozily decorated room. It felt like he had been there before. His thoughts and feelings were interrupted by a loud crash!

Ganeli damn near jumped to the ceiling. It was Bob and Sam dumping things onto the floor. They were turning over trashcans and dressers and breaking glass as they ransacked the house.

Ganeli took the liberty of turning on the television, as he watched Slick walk around the room. Ganeli felt he should do something to convince Slick that he was a bad guy also, so he leaned over and picked up a couple of pillows that had fallen to the floor when he sat down. He began to rip them apart like some type of wild man, scattering feathers all over the place.

Slick could not believe his eyes. He moved to a corner and watched Ganeli make an ass of himself. He wanted to laugh, but he dared not. *This man is truly deranged. A sicko, a real sicko*, Slick thought, as Ganeli finally fell to the couch exhausted.

Within minutes, all three men were gathered behind him. Ganeli shot out of the couch and stood up in a vain attempt to face them eye-to-eye. Whatever threatening phrase he was trying to conjure up was lost when he saw the cold stares in their menacing eyes.

It was Bob who decided to address Ganeli. "It's not here."

Ganeli, not clever enough to think of anything else, decided to play dumb. "What are you talking about?"

"You know what I'm talking about, you dumb…The list, the thing we drove all the way out here to look for! The thing you said you saw, you fat liar!"

"Oh, that list. It's not here?" Ganeli asked, as he made a big show of scratching his head as if he were thinking diligently. "Why don't we look some place else?" Ganeli suggested, continuing to scratch his head. The expression on Bob's face turned from one of impassiveness to one of exasperation. Ganeli, rather pleased with himself, displayed a huge smile that showed his yellowed but fully intact teeth. Bob rewarded him with a fist in the mouth.

Sam burst out laughing as Ganeli went sprawling across the couch. Ganeli just lay there and felt the room spinning around him. When he was finally able to look up, he was face to face with Slick.

"I don't know what kind of game you're playing, Ganeli, but it ends now! I don't care what you have to do, I want that list! The mother and daughter obviously know what they've found, because it's apparent that they left this place in a hurry. I don't care what you have to do, Bob, just do it! I want that list!" Slick walked away.

Bob pointed his gun toward Ganeli's head. "It's bye-bye time, you Colombo reject." Ganeli's heart did a mad dash through his body as he closed his eyes, awaiting the fatal bullet. His body was drenched in sweat.

"Oh, dear God!" Ganeli cried out.

"God won't help you now." The trigger clicked, as Bob cocked it. Seconds seems like hours for Ganeli, as the suspense built. CLICK!!!

"LOOOOOAAAAARRRRRDDDDD," Ganeli shouted. Sam laughed as he watched Bob scare the shit out of Ganeli. Both he and Slick knew Bob had a toy gun. They had played this game before.

"You fuuuuuuu…" Ganeli began to shout, once he realized what they were doing.

"Say it, and I will kill you! What a wasted piece of flesh you are," Bob said, throwing the toy gun onto Ganeli.

"Get up, Ganeli," Slick instructed. "If that list gets into the wrong hands, my family goes down. If that happens, I will cut your fat ass up so small, they will have to gather your parts with tweezers. Now get the hell up!"

On that note, the men left Ganeli sprawled on the floor looking for his lost tooth. Ganeli was so frightened, he felt he would have been better off dead.

Mad and scared as hell, he shouted out at Slick. "Who in the hell are you?" Ganeli held his mouth as the blood ran between his fingers. "I want to know! Who in the hell are you? You can't treat me like this! I'm not some type of animal! Kill me! Why don't you kill me?" Ganeli sobbed, as he prepared to accept the end of his mortality. "Kill me, dammit! Kill me!" he yelled out.

"To you, I'm Slick. If you don't help me find what I'm looking for, I will be your worst fucking nightmare! Not only will I do away with your fat ass, I'll annihilate anyone and everyone who harbors a piece of your pathetic genetic code. As I said, get the hell up!"

Ganeli lay there wondering how he was going to pull himself out of this mess. He felt as if he wanted to die. He was ashamed of all the corrupt things he had done in his life and knew this was God's way of getting back at him. He thought if only he had another chance, if there was some way he could prove himself all over again. He knew his soul could not touch the caliber of the three men that had him trapped.

CHAPTER THIRTY-FIVE

Katherine traveled down the road at an alarming speed. Her only thought was that she needed to put as much distance between herself and Alberville as possible. Indeed, she would have gone on driving at breakneck speed had she not seen the flashing lights ahead of her. As she got closer to the lights, she could see that it was an emergency vehicle.

She drove for miles, conscious only of trying to find someone who could help her. She started having flashbacks of her childhood. She thought of Al and wished he were there to help them.

"Officer Glen, that's it! Officer Glen," Katherine yelled out, as her picture of hope surfaced. Sarah looked at Katherine as if she lost her mind.

"Mom, what are you talking about? Who's Officer Glen?" Sarah asked.

"Sarah, we're heading towards New York. I know a man...I mean a police officer there. I'm sure he will help us. I met him when I was younger, just a few years older than you. I know he will help us."

Katherine wanted to ease Sarah's worries. She decided to lighten the mood by offering to play music or a game, trying to treat this like an ordinary road trip. Katherine played the alphabet game with Sarah. Driving down the road looking for 'l's and 'm's was a lot less stressful than envisioning them caught with the papers, not knowing what that outcome would be. Sarah decided to play along. She knew Katherine was trying to divert her attention, and she wanted her to do so as they headed for New York.

As they continued to drive, Katherine looked and felt much more relaxed. Sarah listened to music on the radio as they continued to play the alphabet game. Finally Sarah got tired of the alphabet game and decided to play the license plate game. She and Tim would do this often when they traveled. They would see how many different states they could find. Soon, Sarah had Katherine involved in the game.

"Look, Sarah. There's an Ohio license plate passing on the right."

"Yeah, mom, there's a car from Pennsylvania ahead."

"You're right. This is fun, Sarah." Katherine felt she had put Sarah's mind at ease, but she realized that neither of them would be safe until they got help and rid themselves of the papers.

Sarah was now eagerly trying to read the license plates of all the cars she could see. She spotted an orange truck. She was fascinated when the license plate read New Mexico. She turned to Katherine. "Can you believe it, New Mexico. Those people must have been traveling for days."

"You're right if that's true. Remember it's possible they rented the truck with those plates attached."

"Yeah, that's a possibility. It'd be cool if they really were from New Mexico. It's weird how your license plate tells so much about where you come from, or even who you could be, huh?" Sarah was content with trying to make Katherine feel she was okay.

Katherine impressed by the complexity of Sarah's thinking continued to drive, when suddenly the impact of Sarah's words hit her. Katherine looked at Sarah. Sarah's eyes widened as she too realized the impact of her statement.

"Oh, Mom," Sarah said breathlessly. "What are we going to do?"

"We could cover up the license plates and no one could see it," Sarah suggested.

"We can't do that, Sarah. Everyone would notice our car and we would surely be pulled over by the police."

"You're right, Mom. What a stupid thought. I was just thinking out loud. Let's think of some other ideas.

Although it was dark, it would only take one police car to spot their license plate. This thought scared her so much that, every time she saw a car behind her, she thought it was the police checking out her license plate.

The two of them sat, quietly pondering…trying to figure out what they were going to do. It was Sarah who spoke first. "Driving isn't the only way to get to New York, Mom. We can take a train or something, right?"

Katherine, deep in thought, did not respond. She realized that life was beginning to repeat itself. Over twelve years ago she had left New York City with Al, running to save her life from the threats of John Walters. Now she was running back to New York, seeking rescue. The difference was that, this time, John Walters was not threatening her, although he was involved somehow.

"Mom are you listening?"

"Mom!" Sarah shouted, and Katherine was shaken from her deep thoughts.

"I'm sorry, Sarah. What did you say?" Sarah wanted to say just forget it, but she decided this was not the time to be rude. She repeated her idea. "Driving isn't the only way to get to New York."

Picking up on Sarah's lead, Katherine got an idea. "You're right, Sarah, we could abandon the car and take a train or bus. That's the way your grandfather and I left New York City. We rode a bus." Following that thought, Katherine became concerned about something else.

"But wait. Wouldn't they check the train and bus stations? They could find the car in the parking lot and easily determine where we went, unless…" Katherine thought out loud as Sarah listened. "Unless…unless…we leave the car somewhere and find a ride to the station."

Unable to think of anything better, Sarah agreed. Katherine turned off the highway and onto a dark road. The two of them sat quietly, scared to death, but feeling assured they were doing the right thing. After driving at a snail's pace, Katherine could see the lights of some homes spread out ahead. She felt this would be an ideal place to leave the car.

"It's dark and scary. I think we should turn around and go back to the highway. I don't think this was a good idea," Sarah said, looking out of the car windows.

"What will we tell the people, Mom, when we knock on their door? It better be good. Something pretty terrible had to happen to make us come to such an area seeking help. It better be good," Sarah said, this time waiting for a response.

"We will tell the people your father abused me and we are on the run. I'll tell them we need to get to New York to my parents for safety. " Katherine went on as Sarah listened, but the plan bothered Sarah.

"I don't like that idea. My dad was not abusive. I don't want people to think that."

"You're right, Sarah, but this is something we have to say. I don't want to tell the truth and get someone else in trouble." Katherine hoped for Sarah's understanding.

"Okay, mom, I'll play it your way, but I don't like it."

"Thanks, Sarah. I knew you would understand. Okay, Sarah this is what we'll do…," Katherine detailed every word to Sarah, as she laid out the plan. Finally, Katherine was finished.

They got out of the car and hurried down the path toward the homes.

CHAPTER THIRTY-SIX

As they walked, they tried to ignore the indefinable shadows and hidden noises. Finally, Katherine and Sarah stood in front of a rather small two story white house, with a cozy swing on the front porch and window boxes.

Katherine and Sarah approached the front door, hoping that the warmth they perceived on the outside also rested within. Katherine took a second to regain her composure before knocking timidly on the door. The drama classes Sarah had taken at school proved to be worthwhile for both of them. Having rehearsed her role thoroughly with Sarah, Katherine felt that she could act it. Sarah knew she could act, and the show was about to begin. Before Katherine knocked on the door, she signaled to Sarah. The two of them messed up their hair to add the special effects. Katherine knocked on the door.

Finally, a soft, yet reassuring voice spoke from within. "Who is it?"

"It's Katherine Oberman. I'm with my daughter, Sarah," Katherine said, waiting for a response. The door opened. In front of her stood a little old lady with white hair. She wore a dark green plaid robe and cute little teddy bear slippers. She looked rather puzzled as she stared at Katherine. Katherine didn't know if this was brought about by her unfamiliar face or her Don King hairstyle. Realizing it was show time, she began to tell her story.

"Ma'am, I'm sorry to disturb you, but we need your help. My ex-husband isn't quite right in the head, and he wanted to see our daughter," Katherine said, pulling a somber-looking Sarah in front of her. Sarah stood there, lips drooping, eyes sad with a few crocodile tears, as she looked up at the old lady. Katherine continued with her story as she watched the woman stare at Sarah. It was probably her junior Don King hairdo that captured the woman's attention. Sarah had gone a little overboard, a bit of a shock motif.

Katherine continued her story. "We're going through a divorce, and I didn't trust him alone with her because of his violent temper. He said he wanted to meet with me to settle the details of our divorce. He sounded sincere and it seemed like the right thing to do for everyone. But, when my daughter and I went to leave, my car wouldn't start. He offered to take us home. I know I shouldn't have trusted him," Katherine cried to seal the special effects, as the women listened. "I never thought…, I never thought..," Katherine paused to gather herself. The show was just beginning. "I never thought he would leave us stranded in the middle of the night on a cold dark road. He refused to take us any further unless I changed my mind about the divorce," Katherine wailed and Sarah followed her lead. The two of them made such a scene, the little old woman invited them into the house.

"Please come in. The two of you must be tired. I'll fix you something warm to drink and then I'll call the police."

"No!" Katherine and Sarah yelled in unison. The woman was startled.

"I don't understand," the woman said. She looked to Katherine for an answer, and Katherine searched her mind for acting lesson 101 to come up with one, but the words did not come. Sarah decided she'd better help out. After all, she was the true actress in the family.

"You see, Miss…Miss…"

"Please, young lady, call me Miss Phyllis."

"You see, Miss Phyllis, my mother is ashamed to tell you that my father is a police officer." Katherine stood there in shock, wondering where Sarah was about to take this story. Sarah went on.

"You see, Miss Phyllis, we have called the police in the past. No one will do anything because my father is a policeman. That is why my mom and I left and moved back to New York with my grandparents. If you call the police, they won't help us. They will let my father know where we are, and he will come after us. All we need is help getting to the bus or train station. We can go back to New York and be safe with my grand-parents. Please don't call the police," Sarah begged.

"I'm sorry, honey. I didn't know your dad is a police officer. I under-stand and I won't call the police, but please, don't cry. Let me get the two of you something warm to drink, then you can sit and relax for awhile. Would you like to come with me?" Phyllis asked.

"Sarah, my name is Sarah."

"Sarah, would you like to come with me? That's a pretty name."

"Thank you. I would love to."

Sarah and Phyllis walked toward the kitchen. Sarah looked back and gave Katherine a wink. Katherine began to think about what she should do next. She knew she had to get to New York and get in touch with Officer Glen. She hoped that he would remember her.

Katherine and Sarah had been so busy putting their plans together they didn't even bother to glance back at their abandoned car. It's a shame they didn't, because although the car appeared to be well hidden, it was not.

CHAPTER THIRTY-SEVEN

Back in Alberville, Ganeli was being driven to the police station by Bob and Sam. Slick wanted the license plate number and description of the vehicle. The search of the house left them without any major information except for the address of Tim Oberman. Slick decided he would go to Tim's house to see if Katherine and Sarah were there.

Ganeli sat in the back seat of the car with Sam. He was worried. He feared taking them to the precinct, knowing there was only a skeleton crew on duty. The car pulled into the parking lot of the precinct, and Ganeli instructed Bob to park in his usual parking space next to the dumpster.

"Wait here, fellows. I'll go in and get the information. It will only take a few minutes," Ganeli said.

"Sit your ass down, you fat son-of-a-bitch. You're not going anywhere until I say so!" Bob said, as he pointed his gun at Ganeli. What Ganeli didn't know was that Bob and Sam were well-read regarding the Alberville police force.

"That's not necessary," Ganeli said, glaring at the gun.

"Do you think I'm stupid, you fat fuck? You're not going in there alone. I'm going with you and, if you try anything, I'll blow your ass away along with that rookie cop inside. Ganeli did not say a word. He knew Bob was not bullshitting.

"Listen, tubs, Bob continued, I'm going in there with you. We will use the side door. If anyone should say anything, just tell them I'm a friend of yours and you wanted me to see the office. If I detect any funny stuff, you and your cronies will feel the heat of metal as I blow your asses away! Do you understand?"

"Yes, Ganeli answered, I understand. I don't want anyone to get hurt. Let's not overreact. Please, don't harm anyone inside, just to prove a point."

"Let's go. Remember, you're in the driver's seat, Officer Fuckup. If I detect one wrong signal…"

"I know. Don't worry, I understand you," Ganeli said, as he moved toward the side door of the precinct. Reluctantly, he stuck his key in the doorlock. The precinct seemed rather quiet. Ganeli could see the rookie cop at the front desk. He decided to wave, letting the rookie know everything was okay.

Sticking to his usual routine, Ganeli walked by the jail cells. He noticed Harry, the town drunk, was locked up again. He told Bob about Harry, trying to make small talk. Stone-faced, Bob did not say a word.

Finally Ganeli reached his office. Bob stood so close to him that their shadows interlocked. "Okay, fatso, get the information. I don't want to stay in this pigsty of an office any longer than I have to," Bob said, as he leaned against the wall by the door.

Ganeli typed the name Katherine Oberman into his computer, hoping some of the surrounding county police would pick up on it. He willed himself not to look up at Bob as he entered the data. While he waited for the computer to complete its search, he began to clear some of the papers off of his desk. He could see out of the corner of his eye that Bob was getting antsy. Bob wiped off his gun while he watched Ganeli.

"What in the hell are you looking at, fatso? My patience is running out. You better—" Before Bob could finish, the computer beeped, signaling it had found a match. Bob walked over to Ganeli's desk and stood behind his chair.

"She drives a black Blazer, license plate K…" Ganeli said, as he wrote the information down. It frightened him thinking at any moment he might get a bullet in his back.

The intensity of the moment was heightened by a knock on the door. Bob leaned over Ganeli's chair, whispering in his ear, "It's your fucking call. Dead or alive? I like dead. You choose, fatso." Bob cocked his gun.

The knock came again. "Ganeli, are you in there?" It was the rookie cop. Ganeli developed a sinking feeling in his stomach. Bob walked over to the door and stood behind it, signaling Ganeli to answer. Finally, with his gut tied in knots, he mustered up enough strength to move towards the door, then opened it.

"Ganeli, I just got a phone call from the Clark County police." Ganeli listened, hoping nothing would set Bob off. The rookie went on. "They said they found the car you were looking for in a field about a hundred miles outside Alberville. Here's the information. Do you need me to do anything for you?"

"No. Thanks, Jerry." Ganeli closed the door as he looked at the slip of paper. Seconds seemed like years as he stood there, then Bob snatched the paper from him, and he jumped in alarm.

"Where in the hell is this place?" Bob asked.

"Not too...too...far from...here," Ganeli responded haltingly.

"Let's get the fuck out of here. I want you to take us there. Let's go, now!"

Ganeli led Bob out the back door, avoiding Jerry. He could not understand why Bob didn't react to knowing the Clark County police had been notified.

They got into the car, this time with Sam driving. Bob sat in the back seat with Ganeli. Bob called Slick to let him know what had happened and arranged for a meeting place as they set out to find the car, hoping to locate Katherine and Sarah nearby.

*　　　　　　*　　　　　　*

In the warm serenity of Phyllis's home, Sarah and Katherine sat at the kitchen table enjoying cookies, cocoa and a cup of tea. Phyllis didn't pester them with any further questions, concerned that they had already been through enough. The plan was for Phyllis to take them to the bus station in the morning. Although Katherine wanted to keep moving, Phyllis told her the next bus would not leave until then.

While enjoying the snack, they talked about the weather, politics and other frivolous topics. After polishing off a second cup of cocoa, Sarah excused herself and went into the bathroom. Katherine took that moment to talk privately with Phyllis. "I hate to impose on you any more, but I need to use your phone. I need to call my parents to tell them everything is okay, and to make arrangements for them to pick us up when we get to New York. I'm sure they are worried to death about Sarah and me."

"Certainly, dear," Phyllis said, then directed Katherine to the guest room where she could use the phone in private and rest. When Sarah came out, Phyllis led her to a comfortable couch in the living room where she could relax. In the bedroom, Katherine called Information to locate the telephone number of the Seventeenth Precinct. Glen had been working there when she left New York. It took a while, but Katherine finally got in touch with the precinct. She was relieved to know that it still existed.

The phone rang several times. Finally a man answered. "Hello, Seventeenth Precinct, may I help you?"

"Yes, please. My name is Katherine Oberman and I need to talk to Officer Glen. It's an emergency."

"I'm sorry, Miss, we don't have an Officer Glen here." Katherine's heart sank.

"I need to know where he is. Please, this is an emergency."

The clerk sensed the panic in Katherine's voice. "Miss Ober."

"It's Oberman."

"I'm sorry. I need to try and get more information. You mentioned this is an emergency?"

"Yes. I need to find Officer Glen. He's the only one that can help me. Please, this is urgent.

"Are you sure he worked here?"

"I'm not sure where he works now, but, when I left New York, he worked in the Seventeenth Precinct," Katherine said, as she went on to describe Glen.

"Please hold, Miss."

"Hey, Mike, I have a woman on the phone trying to get in touch with an Officer Glen. She says it's important, and I sense it is. I checked the roster, but there was no listing of a Glen. Her description sounds familiar. Tall, six plus feet, blue eyes and a single dimple."

"Yeah, Rick. That's Tony Glen. He's a detective now, but he used to work here. He transferred to the Fifteenth Precinct about a month after you came. He earned the award for Officer of the Year before his promotion."

"Thanks, Mike," Rick said, as he returned to the telephone.

"Miss, I think I found him. He's a detective now. I need to take your number and have him call you. I'm not allowed to give you his phone number.

"Dammit! You don't understand! My daughter and I are being chased by some men who might kill us if they catch us. Have you heard about the Manelli, Marcus and Trimmer murders? I have information that might be linked to them, and I need to talk to Detective Glen now!

Rick was stunned. "Miss, I believe you," Rick said, trying to calm Katherine down. "I'll call the Fifteenth Precinct while you hold. I'll try and put you in direct contact with Detective Glen. Please, I must get your phone number in case we get disconnected."

Katherine noticed that Phyllis had taped the number to the phone. She gave the number to Rick as she waited, hoping the next voice she heard would be Glen's.

Within seconds, Rick was back on the phone. " Miss Oberman, I found him. Please hold, Miss Oberman. Good luck."

"Thanks for your help, "Katherine said, nervously waiting to hear Detective Glen's voice. The silence of the phone line created an uneasiness. She wondered....

Then the voice of Detective Glen came on the line. "Hello, this is Detective Glen," he spoke in a groggy voice. It was Glen, Katherine could tell by that deep husky voice. It had not changed.

"Hello, Officer Glen? I mean Detective Glen?"

"Speaking…" Glen had been informed by the clerk that a woman by the name Oberman was trying to get in touch with him. He had no idea who this was. After the clerk mentioned her comments about the Manelli, Elder and Marcus murders, Glen felt compelled to investigate further, but decided to be cautious. He wanted to make sure this was not just another prank call, as he had received several hundred of those since the investigation into the murders began.

"Detective Glen, this is Katherine, Katherine Oberman."

"Katherine Oberman…do I know you?" Glen asked, unable to recognize the name or voice.

"Detective Glen, it's me, Katherine Mills, from New York. The one that aced her algebra exam years ago." Katherine knew that, if this did not jog his memory, nothing would.

"Katherine, it's been so long…what the heck?" Glen glanced over at the clock on his desk. It was almost three in the morning. "I mean how are you? What's going on."

"I'm in trouble, Detective Glen, and I need your help. You're the only person I can trust."

"This sounds serious, Katherine."

"It is. Are you familiar with the New York City Banking deaths?"

"Who isn't?" Glen responded. "My department has the lead on the investigation."

"I think, I might have something."

"What? I don't understand, Katherine. What is going on?"

"I have information that may help."

"Please explain, Katherine, I don't understand."

"Today, no…yesterday, as Sarah was walking home from school—"

"Who's Sarah?"

"Sarah is my daughter, she's twelve."

"Oh, okay, "Glen responded.

"She was walking home from school and found a large amount of money."

"How much?'

"I don't know…a lot. It filled a large bag, and it was all one hundred dollar bills."

"Okay, continue. I'm listening."

"Well, she found the money in the woods and brought it home. That's another long story I would like to tell you about later. Anyway, she didn't realize that, when she picked up the bag with the money, she'd left her school bag behind. She brought the money home and naturally I panicked and called the police. They sent a detective out. While I was waiting for him I decided to watch the news. The story about Richard Manelli's body being found in New York appeared. It really didn't mean anything to me, at first."

"Richard Manelli. Yes, he was just found in the Hudson Bay. "Katherine, go on. I'm listening."

"Then the detective came. Carl Ganeli…," she paused waiting to see if the name would register. Glen picked up on the cue as he responded. "Haven't heard of him."

Katherine went on. "Well he came, asked a few questions and took the money. I thought that was the end of things, so Sarah and I went to finish our dinner. Then Sarah knocked over her drink, and she found an envelope on the floor while cleaning up her mess. At first she thought it was a letter of mine, but, after opening it, it was apparent it had fallen out of the bag with the money. It contained a list of names. On the list were the names of Richard Manelli, William Marcus, Raymond Trimmer, along with Carl Ganeli and others. Ganeli was the detective who came to my house. Even John Walters' name was on the list. He owned the investment firm I was working at just before I left New York City.

"A list! That's hard to believe," Glen responded, curious.

"That's what I was thinking. So I frantically searched the television stations until I found the story on a different channel, then realized that several of the men on the list were...were..."

"Dead," Glen finished for her.

"I immediately wanted to pick up the phone and call the police..."

"You didn't?"

"No, I knew if Ganeli was involved in this, then others might be. I don't think it actually hit me until I walked into the Precinct."

"Precinct! What precinct?" Glen asked.

"That's another long story." Katherine said as she went on. "Then, I got a phone call..." Her voice began to quiver.

"You got a phone call..." Glen said, prompting Katherine to continue.

"I got a phone call from a neighbor, the school's janitor, who said that a man had come to the school and was looking for Sarah. He said he wanted to return her bag, but he wouldn't leave it at the school. He said he had to give it to her in person. I got scared. I didn't know what else to do so I ran. We drove for almost two hours, then I left my car in a field. I was afraid someone would find us in the car. A very nice woman took us in."

"Does she know what's going on?"

"No, she doesn't."

"That's good, the less people who know, the better. Katherine, I need to get to you. I need to know where you are."

"Detective Glen. I need you to be honest with me. What are my options? Somehow I feel no matter what happens, Sarah and I will not be safe. I need to know. Please tell me."

"Katherine, you should get the document to the proper authorities. I can protect you. You're not the running type, you're a fighter." Glen waited for Katherine to respond.

Katherine looked at herself in the mirror that sat in front of her. What she saw was a terrified and tired woman, a woman who didn't have the courage, skills, or the strength to spend the rest of her life running. She saw a woman who did not want to risk death now or later by any murderer's hands. The thought of living the rest of her life in fear meant, she would live no longer. She looked into the mirror again. This time she caught a glimpse of the locket she wore around her neck. In the locket was a picture of Sarah now, and a picture of Sarah on the day she was born.

"Katherine, are you alright?" Glen asked.

"Yes," Katherine responded. "I'm okay."

"Katherine, tell me where you are. Are you safe there?"

"Yes, I think so. I hid my car. I don't think anyone will find it."

"Tell me, Katherine, where are you?"

Katherine searched the nightstand for something with Phyllis's address on it, but there wasn't anything in the drawer that bore the address. She could hear Phyllis washing dishes and humming some unfamiliar tune. Just as she was about to enter the kitchen, she noticed a mail rack hanging on the wall. She reached in and grabbed a couple of envelopes. Phyllis Tyler was the name on the envelope and the address followed. Katherine scurried back to the bedroom and reads the address to Glen.

"Katherine, it seems you're a couple of hours away," Glen said as he located Lumberville, New York on the map. "I'll gather a few things and leave right away. I still look the same, maybe a few gray hairs."

"I can't trust anyone but you. If I don't see your face at the door, my daughter and I will not go. We will run! I mean it! We'll run if you can't guarantee that you will meet us here. I mean it."

"Katherine, calm down. I will meet you. Take down this phone number. Be careful. Are you sure you're safe?" Glen asked, awaiting reassurance.

"Yes, Sarah and I are safe for now."

"Katherine!" Glen's voice was gravely serious. "Be careful! If you notice anyone suspicious, get out of there. Remember what I used to tell you?" Katherine listened, waiting for Glen to continue. "You're a survivor, Katherine."

"I needed to hear that," Katherine responded in a somber voice.

She was on the verge of hanging up the phone, when she heard Glen call out.

"Katherine! Katherine!"

"Yes?" Katherine responded.

"It will be okay. I'll be there soon."

"Hurry," Katherine said as she hung up the phone and walked out of the bedroom. By now the house was quiet. She walked into the living room and found Sarah asleep on the couch, covered in a beautiful multi-colored quilt.

Katherine took a seat opposite Sarah in the large recliner and stared at the door.

CHAPTER THIRTY-EIGHT

Katherine awakened to the smell of freshly-brewed coffee. The first few rays of dawn shone through the window. She looked over at the plaid couch and noticed Sarah was not there. It was almost six in the morning, and Glen had not arrived. Katherine hopped out of the chair, ran down the hall, and almost collided with Phyllis.

"I'm sorry, Phyllis. I was looking for Sarah. Have you seen her? Did anyone come to the door?" Katherine's asked, as Phyllis stepped back. "I woke up and she was—"

"She's in the bathroom washing up. We decided not to disturb you. You were resting so peacefully. Sarah wanted to surprise you and make your favorite breakfast, pancakes. She tells me you love pancakes. Why both of you are early risers. No one has come to the door. I'm a very light sleeper. Are you expecting someone?"

Katherine didn't know how to answer Phyllis's question and she felt foolish, knowing she must have scared Phyllis to death. "It's the pressure and strain of the last twenty-four hours. I must have dreamt that my husband had come after us. I'm sorry if I alarmed you."

At that moment Sarah walked into the kitchen. "Good morning, Mom. Did you get some rest? I hoped to surprise you, but I guess Miss Phyllis and I didn't get up early enough. That's okay, I'll go ahead and fix your breakfast anyway. Right, Miss Phyllis? We won't let Mom's early awakening change our plan."

"You're right, Sarah, let's go. Let's show your mom how these chicks can flap those cakes." Sarah enjoyed Phyllis's humor. Katherine wondered what she should do. She knew Sarah was okay, but she had to focus on the next matter at hand. Where in the world was Glen? *Something must have happened*, she thought, as she walked into the living room, thinking she'd better call and see what was taking him so long.

Meanwhile, Slick and his crew with Ganeli in tow, were in the process of searching the houses nearby, having found her car less than an hour before and hoping to locate the pair. The early morning fog had made it quite difficult to locate the car, and now that they had found it, the fog hindered their view of the surrounding homes.

Ganeli was rather upset, because Bob had decided to get rid of his radio communication. By the time they got to the car, the officer had left. The only trace of his presence was the sticker he left on the car window.

Although Ganeli was mad as hell at Bob, he was relieved that the officer was gone. He knew Bob would have killed him or anyone else he found, just to keep them quiet. As they walked, Ganeli said a prayer hoping that Katherine and Sarah were nowhere to be found. He regretted the day he allowed himself to get involved in this mess. Ganeli never thought this job would involve killing someone, especially an innocent mother and daughter. He knew there was no way these thugs would spare Katherine's and Sarah's lives. They knew too much, especially if they had the list the thugs were looking for.

Ganeli watched Slick moving toward a house. It was like watching a fox stalk his prey. Every step was calculated, each an equal distant from the other. Hands so tightly fixed in his coat pocket, you would think they were locked in place. Slick was more determined than ever to find the list. He had become almost psychotic as his compulsive mind searched for clues. Ganeli knew something must have ignited this. It seemed, after Slick's search of Tim Oberman's house came up empty, his behavior changed. This change in Slick's demeanor even scared Bob and Sam. He had them jumping like little puppets on a string.

Finally they reached a small green house. Slick signaled for Bob to go to the door. The plan was to portray themselves as policemen searching for a missing kid. A tall old man with blue-gray hair opened the door.

He seemed rather happy to have company. The man smiled at Bob, showing his gums.

"Come on in. I just finished milking my goat. You know there is nothing like a little goat's milk to get the heart ticking in the morning."

Bob stepped back as the man lifted a pail up to his face. It was obvious he didn't appreciate the man's offer.

"Thanks, but no thanks. My name is Detective Walden," Bob said. "We are looking for a young girl who has been missing for several days. There is strong suspicion she may be in this area. It is believed she may be with a woman...a woman who kidnapped her. Have you seen anyone?"

"I sure did," the man responded very quickly. "I believe you have found her. Come in. I knew something was suspicious about that woman dragging that little girl around," the man went on.

Bob looked back at Slick, giving him and Sam a signal to move forward. Ganeli could not believe what he was hearing. He nervously walked into the man's home.

Once inside, neither of them could believe what they were seeing and smelling. The place was filthy. Papers and clothing were scattered over furniture and the floor. Numerous cats were visible in addition to those moving beneath the piles of clothing. The three of them stayed close to the front door. Even Bob, the stalkers' advocate, stood steadfast as he held his hand over his nose and mouth.

"Where's the girl?" Bob asked in a muffled voice. It was obvious he didn't care to search any further than he had to.

"Right here." The old man said, pointing to the television that stood in a corner. "Right here."

The looks on Bob, Sam and Slick's faces were indescribable, as they saw the old man pointing toward the television. Ganeli did everything he could not to laugh. The man was pointing at a television that did not have a picture tube.

"Right here," Bob echoed the man's word. "I don't understand, old man. I asked you about a young girl and a woman."

"I know you did, and there they were. Just last night I was sitting here watching television. A little girl was running from a woman who was trying to kidnapped her."

"That television?" Bob shook his head trying to reconfirm what he heard.

"Yes. Is there something wrong with my television?" Again he pointed to the television.

"No. There isn't a thing wrong with your television." Bob said as he walked out the door cursing to himself. "I should...," Bob said, reaching into his belt. Slick grabbed his hand.

"I want the list! You have nothing to gain by killing a stupid old man. Let's get the hell out of here. My patience is wearing thin."

Ganeli rejoiced as they headed up the road. He knew he had to control himself. He was not up for another encounter with Bob, at least not at the moment. Ganeli felt sorry for the old man. He decided that, if he got out of this alive, he would send someone to the man's house to help him.

The fog was beginning to clear. In front of them was a little white house with window boxes. That would be their next stop.

CHAPTER THIRTY-NINE

Inside the house, Katherine savored her morning coffee, realizing this was a difficult place to find, and trying to give Glen a few more minutes. Sarah amused herself by reading the comics from yesterday's papers, as she enjoyed her breakfast. Phyllis, just happy to have company, stood at the kitchen stove humming away as she prepared tea.

Katherine finished the last sip of her coffee, then instructed Sarah to help clean off the table. Katherine wiped the crumbs off the table while Sarah carried the cups to the sink. Suddenly, there was a loud crash, as Sarah dropped all of the dishes. Startled, both women jumped.

"Sarah, what's wrong?" Katherine asked.

At first Sarah didn't answer or move. "It's…it's…the detective that was at our house," Sarah said, pointing out the window. "He's coming up the path with some men!"

Katherine rushed to the window. She instantly recognized Ganeli. His stumpy physique and confused hair style was unmistakable. Shadowing him were three men. Katherine remembered Martin telling her there was a man in a dark coat and hat looking for Sarah.

"We have to get out of here!" Katherine said, looking at Sarah. Sarah's eyes focused on Katherine's as their thoughts connected. Not wanting to waste anytime, she grabbed Sarah's hand and pulled her away from the window.

"Is there a back way out?" She asked Phyllis.

"What's this all about?" Phyllis demanded, feeling she deserved an explanation. "I don't understand!"

"Phyllis, you've been very kind to us and I'm eternally grateful. There are four men coming this way and they are extremely dangerous. The less I tell you, the better off you will be. I'm begging you. Sarah and I need your help."

Phyllis looked at Sarah. She had never seen a child so frightened.

"Please," Katherine begged, grabbing Phyllis's hand. "Please, when they come, stall them. Please help us."

"You lied to me!" Phyllis yelled out.

Not bothering with a rebuttal, Katherine pleaded. "Please, if not for my sake, for Sarah's."

"Alright! Go out the back door! There's a path to the left that leads through the woods and onto a busy road. You should be able to catch a ride," Phyllis said, as she looked into Sarah's tearful eyes. "Be careful—"

Before Phyllis could finish, Katherine and Sarah were fleeing past her. The words "thank you" lagged behind as Phyllis heard the back door close.

Phyllis watched the pair slip into the woods, as she heard a knock at her front door. She closed the door to bedroom facing the back of the house, patted down her hair and moved toward the door. She pretended that she had been awakened.

"Who is it?"

"Detective Bob."

"Yes, may I help you?" Phyllis asked, opening the door.

"Morning ma'am. Sorry to bother you this early, but I have some important business to conduct. Last night a women kidnapped a young girl." Bob gave a description of Katherine and Sarah based on Ganeli's recollection. "We have reason to believe that she may have been in the vicinity."

Phyllis placed her hand over her heart in what might have been interpreted as shock, but was really an effort to calm her beating heart. She could not believe what she was hearing. The description fit Katherine and Sarah to a 'T'.

"Oh my!"

"Yes ma'am, I'm afraid it's true," Bob said, realizing that he was getting to the little old lady. He then pulled out a picture of Sarah. It was a picture that Slick had found at Tim's house. Phyllis looked at the picture. It was Sarah. Bob could sense that Phyllis knew something.

"Have you seen her?" Bob asked.

Phyllis thought about Katherine's desperate plea and the look in Sarah's eyes. She couldn't do it! Even if the story she was hearing was true, she could not tell what she knew. Phyllis thought about how happy Sarah and Katherine were as they enjoyed their time together in her home. *If this was a kidnapping, it was happy reunion*, she thought.

"Um," said Phyllis. "Yes, they stopped by here." Bob signaled for the others to come closer as he listened. "They didn't stay long. They wanted shelter. Being an old woman, and knowing nothing about them, I directed them further down the road. I told them there was a farm about two miles away, owned by the McNeals. They like to help stray people, so I directed them there." Phyllis knew that the McNeal's were on vacation and would be away for several weeks.

"What time did they come through here?" Bob asked, as he glanced back at Slick.

"About, about eeeee....eleven o'clock last evening." Phyllis answered.

"Do you mind if we take a look around?"

Phyllis, despite her best intentions, waited a little too long to reply. Slick pushed Bob forward, almost knocking Phyllis down as they entered her home.

Katherine and Sarah sat huddled on a hill that overlooked Phyllis's house. Katherine wanted to see which direction Phyllis would lead the men and to make sure Phyllis was safe.

Phyllis tried to make light conversation as the men moved about her home. "Are you men thirsty? Would you like some tea or coffee?" Phyllis asked, hoping they would just say 'no' and leave. Slick's presence frightened her. He was standing so close she could smell the fabric of his coat.

Ganeli decided to talk with her and try to help her out. "So you live here by yourself?" Ganeli asked, as he tried to break the tension.

"Yes," Phyllis responded. "My husband Charles died about five years ago, and I've been taking care of this place all by myself."

"Must be pretty hard, huh?"

"It was at first, but I think I've gotten use to it. Would you gentlemen like some coffee?" Phyllis said, as she moved away from Slick.

"Yes, please," Ganeli quickly responded.

Phyllis hurried into the kitchen, then took a minute to calm her nerves while she listened to Bob and Sam search the house.

Ganeli decided to sit on the couch, but stopped when his rump rested on a doll. He pulled it from under him and instantly recognized it as the one sitting on a wicker chair in the foyer of the Oberman's home. Ganeli tried to stash the doll under the sofa. He was spotted by Slick.

"What do you have there, Ganeli?" Slick asked, walking over to him.

"Huh?" Ganeli said, as he pretended he had been picking the doll up off the floor.

"What do you have in your hand?"

"Just this doll. Pretty, huh?"

"What were you doing with it?" Slick asked.

"Nothing," Ganeli responded. "I was just admiring it; my mother collected dolls, ya know? She had them sitting on every window seat and every shelf in the house she…," Ganeli stopped himself. He realized in trying to help he'd done more damage than good. A quick glance around the place showed no signs of any other dolls. In fact, the doll was out of place. Something wasn't right and Slick knew it. If he didn't, the stupid look on Ganeli's face told him. Slick grabbed the doll from Ganeli. He could hear Phyllis returning.

"Ganeli, if you open your mouth, I'll close it for good," Slick instructed. Ganeli wasn't sure what Slick's comment was all about, but he knew he'd better listen. Phyllis walked into the room with a tray of coffee and donuts. Slick placed the doll behind his back and began to question Phyllis.

"You collect dolls, ma'am?"

"Heavens no! They are frivolous things; I never could stand them when I was young. I preferred cooking."

"Do you have any grandchildren or neighbors who have dolls? Slick asked."

"Can't say I do. I don't have any children. I wish I did. I wouldn't be so lonely. Most of my neighbors are either too old, or just don't care about dolls." Ganeli watched helplessly as Phyllis answered Slick's questions.

"Well, I find that surprising, ma'am…" Slick pulled the doll from behind his back.

The color left Phyllis's face. She had totally forgotten about Sarah's doll. She tried to laugh it off. "Oh that's…, that's…, that's…my…." Phyllis was unable to put the words together.

Ganeli watched in horror as Bob and Sam pulled out their guns. They had heard the entire inquisition, and realized the old woman knew a lot more than she said.

Bob moved toward Phyllis. "You old bitch, you're lying! Where are they?"

Phyllis screamed and knocked the tray to the floor. "Please, don't hurt me! I'm an old woman. Please!"

"Yeah, you're old. You're also a lying bitch!" Bob shouted. Ganeli knew there was no way he could sit there and let this happen.

*　　　　　　　*　　　　　　　*

Katherine felt that something was wrong. The men were in there too long. She knew she couldn't let Phyllis die as a result of her kindness. Needing to make a quick decision, she searched for a place for Sarah to hide.

*　　　　　　　*　　　　　　　*

Inside the house, things did not look good for Phyllis.

"Okay, I want to know the truth. Where are they?" Bob yelled, then he threw her onto the couch next to Ganeli. A look beyond terror appeared in Phyllis's eyes.

Ganeli was furious. He stood up and was just about to open his mouth when he saw someone at the window behind him. He wasn't the only one, as the other men saw her as well.

"Hey, Slick, look!" Bob gestured toward the window. They saw a woman running up the hill.

"There she is," Sam yelled. "It must be the mother. Let's get her." Ganeli looked out of the window. He recognized Katherine but he didn't say anything. Sam moved towards the door.

"Silence her!" Sam shouted to Bob.

"No!" Ganeli yelled, but before he could stop Bob, Phyllis was hit in the head with the butt of the gun and she fell to the floor, her body lifeless.

"You! You!" Ganeli screamed, glaring at Bob.

"You what? You fat pig, I'll finish your ass right here and now!" Bob cocked his gun in Ganeli's face. "Say something, pig! Your ass is worthless now! Say! Say something!"

"Cut the bullshit, Bob!" Slick demanded. We need him. He knows this area better than any of us. Until I'm sure I've found them, he has to stay alive. Let's go," Slick ordered. Ganeli glared into Bob's eyes as they stood looking at each other.

"Move it! Now!" Slick yelled, as he shoved Ganeli out the door.

"Move it, fatso! Your ass is mine! I can't wait!" Bob snarled as he walked past Ganeli.

CHAPTER FORTY

Realizing she had been spotted by the men, Katherine ran like the wind. She knew she had to reach the ravine where Sarah was hidden. Ganeli stopped running and hobbled up the hill, but Sam gained on Katherine and Bob was right behind him. When they reached the top of the hill, Katherine had disappeared, and Bob suggested they separate.

By now Katherine had reached the ravine and she jumped into the ditch with Sarah. Desperately needing to catch her breath, Katherine forced herself to be quiet as she held Sarah in her arms.

Katherine and Sarah huddled together until they heard the men run past them. Katherine looked out. The coast was clear. "Sarah, there's the trail that leads to the road. I want you to stay right behind me. If I say run, you run. If I say get down, get down. Okay?" Sarah was too afraid to speak, so she simply nodded her head. They would have to take side trails through the woods to avoid being seen.

Bob and Sam had reunited and had reached a point where they could see nothing but trees and an empty trail. They heard something or someone moving in the brush behind them, and perked up their ears. Simultaneously, they ducked behind trees, hoping it would be Katherine and Sarah. They were disappointed to see a heavily sweating Ganeli. He was panting and heaving. They signaled him to be quiet, but, either he didn't see the signal, or he decided to ignore it, because he began waving frantically and shouting.

"Hey, guys! I'm over here! Hey, guys!"

"What in the hell were you thinking? You idiot! If you can't keep up, then at least shut up!" Sam whispered.

"Oh! Sorry, guess I wasn't thinking. Where are they? Don't tell me you didn't catch her!" Ganeli went on, realizing he was adding fuel to an already smoldering fire.

"You fat Fuck!" Bob leaped out toward Ganeli, but Sam stepped between the two of them, and tried to calm Bob down.

"Come on, Bob, remember what Slick said. His time will come. We can't afford to lose it. Let's stay focused on business."

"I'm sick of this shit, Sam! If we were working with Bobbie, this fat fuck would have been dead a long time ago," Bob said, as Sam held him back.

"You're right, Bob, but cool it for now. I don't—"

At that moment, Slick appeared. "What in the hell is going on here? Where are they?" Slick asked.

"They're around here somewhere," Sam responded. Ganeli and Bob did not say a word.

"Time is running out. We can't afford to let them get away. We have to get that list. Get moving, they can't be far away," Slick instructed.

The men scattered like mice, as Ganeli stood in the middle of the path, not quite sure what to do. He knew he had just survived another episode of Bob's wrath. He also knew that he had no sense of direction, but figured the others would come looking for him in the end. He thought back to when he was a Boy Scout and they'd gone on hikes and he hadn't been able to keep up. He was often left behind at the campsite.

Looking back, Ganeli felt his entire life had been a screw-up. He was always the one left behind; always the one trying to be like everyone else, but not quite succeeding. He guessed that's why he became a policeman. He'd thought that, maybe if he could help people, he would be liked. If he had more money, he would be able to buy friendship. What Ganeli was quickly learning, was that money wasn't the answer. Being a cop and a good one was much more important.

Ganeli knew he could easily leave at this point, allowing Slick and his crew to find Katherine and Sarah and do as they pleased. But, for some reason he couldn't leave. As Ganeli set out to involve himself in the chase, he had come to his own personal realization. Never would he relive the scenario in Phyllis's home.

CHAPTER FORTY-ONE

Sarah and Katherine stood pressed against a tree, not far away from the site where the men had gathered. Thanks to Ganeli, they were able to see the men. Katherine discussed her plan with Sarah, as they broke twigs and stuffed them in their clothes and hair. Katherine looked ahead and Sarah glanced back making sure they weren't being followed.

"Mom? Mom, what's wrong? Why have we stopped?" Sarah asked.

"I can't find the trail, Sarah. I'm trying to determine which way we—" Katherine stopped in mid-sentence, as she saw a figure moving in the distance. She pulled Sarah to the ground and they quickly scrambled under a pile of brush, then lay face down in the dirt. It was filthy and slimy. They could feel ants crawling on them, but they didn't move.

At the same time, Ganeli moved in their direction. He could see two pair of legs, and he noticed that Sam was about to walk right into them. Ganeli frantically searched for something to divert Sam's attention.

Katherine could hear the rustling noises get closer. She was terrified as she and Sarah clung tightly to each other. She was sure they had been spotted. There was nothing she could do.

"Hey, Sam! They're over here!" Ganeli shouted, waving his hands. Katherine heard what was going. She continued to lay still as the sounds of the crunching brush become more distant.

"I see them." Ganeli pointed in the opposite direction. Katherine was too afraid to look up.

Sam ran over to Ganeli. "Hey man, shut up! Do you want them to hear you? Where are they?"

"Over there. Follow me," Ganeli said as he continued to lure Sam away from Katherine and Sarah. Katherine realized, at that moment, Ganeli was trying to help them. She knew they had to leave and fast.

"Sarah, are you okay? Listen, when I say go, quietly get up and stick close to me. Try to make as little noise as possible."

Katherine looked around. She could see Ganeli, talking to a tall man at a distance. Not wanting to waste any time, Katherine grabbed Sarah's and began to run.

Ganeli could see that Katherine and Sarah were escaping as he continued to distract Sam. "You're right, I'm sorry. I didn't mean to yell, but come on, how was I supposed to get your attention? Jump up and down until you looked in my direction? I'm sorry, but my heart just can't take that type of action! Follow me, I'm sure I saw them." Ganeli said to Sam as he walked away.

Ganeli glanced behind him to make sure Sam was following. When he did, he also looked to see if Katherine and Sarah were out of sight. However, he looked one time too many.

Sam caught Ganeli looking behind him. As he turned to see what Ganeli was looking at, he saw the blurred shadows of two people fleeing, and he knew Ganeli had betrayed him. "What the hell…! Bob was right, we should have killed your ass a long time ago. You…you…" Sam said, as he reached for his gun. Reflexively, Ganeli grabbed Sam. Within seconds Ganeli found himself fighting for his life. He thought he was going to faint but he knew he had to hang on, as they struggled.

"I'm going to kill you." Sam said, kicking Ganeli in the gut as they both held onto the gun. Ganeli grunted as the kick knocked the wind out of him. He fell to the ground, holding onto the gun, and his weight pulled Sam down with him. Ganeli struggled to free the gun from Sam's hand. He knew this was his 'do or die' moment and decided to bite into Sam's arm. Sam screamed as the gun fell between the two of them. Ganeli grabbed for the gun and so did Sam. The gun went off. Ganeli lay slumped over Sam. As he rolled away from Sam, he noticed that his shirt was covered with blood. He looked over at Sam who was also covered with blood. The bullet had gone into Sam's chest.

Exhausted from the struggle, Ganeli stood up, his eyes fixed on Sam. He knew he was not a killer, yet, before him, a man lay dead. Ganeli watched as Sam's blood mixed with the dirt.

Ganeli knew this was a death without options. It was an accident he told himself as he struggled with what he had done. Ganeli felt for some reason God had chosen him to go on, and he felt humble.

Having wrestled with his conscience, Ganeli turned his attention to the problem at hand. The last thing he needed was for Slick or Bob to find Sam. He decided to hide the body in a sunken area near a cliff that was a few yards away. He remembered stepping into it when he'd wandered around.

Bob heard the shot and was quickly within yards of Ganeli. He could see Ganeli dragging Sam's body. Bob fired two shots. Ganeli looked up, then stumbled backward and fell over the cliff.

"That fat fuck. I should have put a bullet in his ass a long time ago," Bob said to himself as rushed over to the cliff to take one last look at Ganeli. He could see that Sam had been shot in the chest and there was no sign of life.

Bob stepped to the edge of the cliff to look. Before he knew it, a hand clutched his ankle. It was Ganeli, who had landed on a ledge just beneath the cliff's edge. His shoulder was wounded and his head was grazed by the bullets. Bob tried to reach for his gun, but the force of Ganeli jerking his ankle and the fear of falling kept him unsteady.

As Ganeli watched, Bob gave a long yell and his body united with the earth below. "Who's the fat fuck now, you ball of shit," Ganeli yelled, vindicated.

CHAPTER FORTY-TWO

Back at Phyllis's house, Detective Glen and his right hand man, Detective John Johnson, had arrived. Glen was worried, knowing it had taken longer than he had anticipated to find Phyllis's home. He hoped Katherine and Sarah were okay, but, as he drove up to the house, his thoughts told him otherwise. He saw a car parked nearby. Normally this would not be important, but the New York City license plates alarmed him.

They circled the outside of the house, and everything seemed calm. Glen felt it was safe to go in. When he knocked on the front door, it opened. With guns held high, Glen entered, with John following. Inside, he could see that a struggle had taken place. Several living room chairs were turned over. Phyllis's coffee cups, donuts and an overturned teapot were scattered on the floor. As Glen moved toward the couch, he noticed something red on the floor. Glen brushed his finger over it and smelled it. It was blood.

He signaled for John to search the upstairs, as he looked around the main floor. As Glen made his way toward the kitchen, he heard a faint moan. He cautiously opened the door. On the floor was Phyllis, holding her head, blood seeping through her fingers. Her hair and the carpet beneath her were soaked with blood. Beside her was the overturned telephone.

Glen surveyed the room, and it appeared safe. He rushed over to Phyllis. "Ma'am, don't worry. I'll get help for you. Can you understand me?" Phyllis moaned. She had lost a lot of blood and was too weak to speak.

"Please squeeze my hand, if you can," Glen asked. "I need to know if a young woman name Katherine and her daughter were here." Phyllis gave his hand a soft squeeze.

"Glen, I didn't find anyone upstairs." John stood in the doorway surprised that Glen had found someone.

"John, hurry! Call for help!"

"Please, I need your help ma'am. Try to hang in there. Help is on the way. I'm going to ask you a couple of questions. If the answer is yes, squeeze my hand. Just like you did before. Please try. I need to find Katherine," Glen pleaded.

"Did Katherine and her daughter leave here with some men?" There was no response from Phyllis.

"Did they leave here alone?" Phyllis squeezed his hand.

"Did several men or a man come here looking for them?" A faint squeeze.

"Did the men find them here?" no response.

"Did they leave before the men got here?" a faint squeeze.

"Did the men see them?" a faint squeeze.

"Did the men go after them?" a faint squeeze.

Glen decided not to press Phyllis any further. He had gathered enough information to help him. He could hear the emergency vehicles and police squad approaching. John ran outside to direct them. The paramedics were the first on the scene.

"Hurry!" John yelled out. "This woman has been beaten. She has lost a lot of blood, and I think she has gone into shock."

The paramedics worked on Phyllis as Glen and John moved out of the way. They were just about to walk out of the front door, when a well-built man of medium height, with brown hair and wearing a navy-blue suit walked in. He was followed by several police officers.

"Who are you?" The man asked.

"I'm Detective Glen and this is my partner, Detective Johnson. We're from the New York City police department," Glen said as he showed his ID and gave the man his card.

"I'm Detective Rice from the Lumberville police department!" The detective responded as he glared at the two of them. "Now, tell me why are the two of you here?"

"Detective Rice, a young woman and her daughter are in deep trouble. Several men followed them to this house. They beat the old lady, but the mother and daughter had escaped earlier. The men are after them. They may have information related to the New York investment scandal murders, and I must find them. These men will stop at nothing."

"Ralph, call for backup! I want this entire area searched! Get me men, plenty of men! Get moving! I want backup, now!" Rice shouted out orders.

"Listen, Detective…, what's your name again?" Rice asked.

"Glen. It's Glen."

"I want you and your man to get out of here. We appreciate your help, but we can handle things from here out. By the way, what are the names of the woman and child?"

Glen, feeling shafted, decided to get in his final dig. "I thought you could handle things!"

"Dammit! You city detectives! Don't bullshit me! I'll have your ass brought up to your superiors for withholding evidence!"

Glen's initial reaction was to feed Rice another line, but John flashed him a look suggesting he cool it.

"The woman's name is Katherine Mills. I…I…mean, Katherine Oberman, and her daughter's name is Sarah. They lived in Alberville."

"Thanks." Rice said, then walked away. Glen could hear him talking to a couple of the police officers as he and John stood on the porch. Glen and John decided it was time to leave. Glen wanted to find Katherine.

"Hey, Glen," yelled Rice. "We will call you when we find her. Remember, it's in our hands now."

Glen did not bother to respond, as he and John got into their car and drove off. "John, these upstate bureau boys really piss me off."

"You're right Glen, they're all the same. I don't want to go home. This is as much our case as theirs," John remarked.

"Wait a minute, John, who said anything about going home? We're going to find Katherine and Sarah. I have a stake in this case."

"But, I thought…Glen, you said you were leaving!" John was confused.

"No, I didn't say that. Rice suggested we leave, but I have no intention on turning back. Let's see what we can find out. Katherine and Sarah have to be nearby."

CHAPTER FORTY-THREE

Katherine pulled an exhausted Sarah behind her as they continued to run to safety, having no idea where they were going. They were lost, yet determined. They might have kept their rapid pace if they hadn't reached a clearing and found themselves besieged with fatigue. The clearing was about the size of a baseball field, and surrounded by trees.

Katherine heard the shots. She hoped nothing had happened to Phyllis. She thought about Glen and wondered where he was. She thought about Al, knowing that, if he were with them, he would know exactly what to do.

What Katherine and Sarah could not see was Ganeli approaching. He had somehow gathered enough strength to climb off the ledge. He tied off his shoulder with his torn shirt, and was able to stop the bleeding. Ganeli was surprised that, for the first time in his life, he didn't feel like he was trapped within his uniform. But before he could revel in his thoughts, he caught a glimpse of someone. It was Slick.

Katherine and Sarah lay in the grass catching their breath, until they heard the snap of a twig. Both of them jumped up and looked around, trying to detect which direction the noise had come from. Katherine's instincts told her that this noise was not made by an animal. She felt they were being watched and they were trapped. Katherine needed to hear more sounds to determine which direction to run, as she knew the wrong move might run them right into the arms of their assailants. Suddenly the calm, peaceful, and serene scene they had basked in momentarily, became a deep trap.

"Mom, what are we going to do?" Sarah whispered in fear.

"Listen," Katherine said as she tried to instill calm as she too, looked around.

Ganeli carefully moved toward the clearing. He was able to get a better view of the person hiding behind the tree. It was definitely Slick. They were within fifty yards of each other, but Slick had not seen Ganeli; he was focused on something else.

As Ganeli followed Slick's direction of concern, he saw two figures in the distance. Although several trees distorted his view, he knew this had to be Katherine and Sarah.

Slick could tell by their stillness that they had heard the twig snap. He also knew if he moved and they saw him, he might risk losing them again. Slick noticed several rocks next to his feet.

Ganeli could tell that Slick was up to something as he watched him pick something up off the ground. Ganeli pulled out the gun he'd confiscated from Sam. His hand shook. From the waist down, his body had become one large cramp. Ganeli watched Slick bend over again. This time he saw the rock. He knew he had to stop him. Before he could think about it, he fired the gun. The bullet just missed Slick. Katherine heard something fall behind her. Another shot fired.

"Run! Run! Ganeli yelled out.

Katherine and Sarah dashed forward as they heard a third shot. Sarah screamed as Katherine pulled her along. Slick lay on the ground, trying to focus on who was shooting at him, and which direction the bullets were coming from.

Ganeli cautiously moved closer, thinking he had hit Slick, since he could not detect any movement. Just as he was about to move in, he saw Slick reach for his gun. Ganeli fired another shot. Again it missed Slick. To Ganeli's amazement, Slick had his gun in hand and had spotted him. Ganeli jumped behind a tree as Slick fired his first shot. He fired back, causing Slick to retreat. Ganeli was running out of ammunition. He decided to run in the direction opposite from Katherine and Sarah, hoping that Slick would follow, but Slick decided to maintain his ground. He wanted to make sure there wasn't someone else waiting for him. He felt sure he could get Ganeli.

Katherine and Sarah finally reached the road after running in a breathless fury. They looked back to make sure no one was on their trail. The road was bordered by trees, and further down they could see a sharp curve. Katherine decided to move in that direction and hide while they waited for someone to come along.

When Katherine heard a car coming her way, she started waving her hands. The old lady did not stop her car as the sight of Katherine scared her. Katherine continued to wave, hoping the woman would turn around, but the woman kept going. Katherine knew time was running out. She saw a semi approaching, then speeding past her. She knew it would not be long before the men caught up with them. She looked over at Sarah. Sarah was sitting next to a bush, her clothes torn and dirty. She looked like one of those bag ladies that Katherine remembered seeing in the train station when she was growing up in New York. It seemed Sarah had aged beyond her years over the last twenty-four hours.

Looking at Sarah caused Katherine to realize how she must look, and she knew her appearance was probably frightening. She figures that if drivers saw the two of them they might stop. She could see a car approaching. The two of them waved, hoping for a miracle.

A young woman drove past them. When she looked into her rearview mirror and saw Sarah crying and Katherine consoling her, she turned the car around and stopped near Katherine and Sarah.

"Can I help you?" The woman asked. Katherine and Sarah were so relieved they opened the car doors and jumped inside before the woman could say another word. Before the woman knew it, Katherine was sitting in the front seat and Sarah in the back. They were breathing so hard the windows fogged.

"Are the two of you alright? Where are you going?" The woman asked, somewhat startled.

"Anywhere. Just get us out of here, please," Katherine said, winded. "Please, just drive!" Katherine pleaded.

The woman looked in her rear view mirror. Sarah's big beautiful brown eyes and her tired looking face, captured her heart.

Just as the car pulled away, Slick emerged from the woods.

CHAPTER FORTY-FOUR

Katherine settled down as the car moved along. The only things she thought about were finding a safe place for her and Sarah and getting help. Where was Glen, she wondered.

"Hi, my name is Angie." Katherine was deep in thought as she looked into the woods. "Hi, I'm Angie," the woman repeated. This time Katherine heard her.

"I'm sorry. My name is…" Katherine thought for a quick second and realized she should not tell this woman her true name. "My name is Gretchen," Katherine said, thinking of her days at Walters and Vein, "and that's my daughter."

"What happened to the two of you? Did you get lost in the woods or did your car break down or something?" Angie asked.

"Umm…yeah, I think the battery died. My daughter and I walked, looking for a gas station. I didn't think a gas station would be so far away." Katherine looked at Angie, trying to detect if she was taking in all of this. Katherine went on. "However, after walking for a while without a gas station or house in sight, I didn't know what to do. So, I decided to try and see if we could get a ride. I really don't do this often. I'm glad that you stopped," Katherine cast a fleeting glance towards Sarah. "I had my daughter to think about, you know? I can't tell you how much I appreciate your kindness."

"I know a place in Locksmith, where you can get help. I'll drop you off there, if that's okay?" Angie asked.

"Sure, that will be fine." Katherine responded.

"Where's home for you two?"

"Well, home for me is New York City."

"So that's where you're headed?"

"Yes, but you don't have to take us all the way. I just need a place where I can make a phone call and make arrangements regarding my car."

"Well, I'm going shopping. You'll find plenty of telephones and help in Locksmith. I'm just glad I was able to help. I hope someone would do the same for me someday, but in this day and age, you really have to be very careful about who you pick up. I don't think I would have stopped if I had not seen your daughter looking so heartbroken."

"Well, I'm glad you did. I can't tell you how much we appreciate your help," Katherine said, cautiously relaxing as she listened to Angie's endless chatter about the weather, her boyfriend and her family. Although Katherine's thoughts were miles away, she really did not mind the entertainment. At least she knew she and Sarah were safe for now.

Meanwhile, back in the woods, there were police and barking dogs everywhere. Detective Rice had everyone searching for Katherine and Sarah and their assailants. The gunshots had heightened their alarm. Rice had given the men instruction to be cautious. They were to shoot to kill if they had no choice, but he wanted Katherine and Sarah alive.

Rice walked down one of the wooded trails when he heard one of his men call out. "Hey, over here! I found someone!" The dogs barked out of control. "Hey, over here." Rice and several of his men rushed over to see what the commotion was all about. When they arrived on the scene, they could see a body on the ground. Rice's men had discovered Sam's body. All of them stood there and looked at the blood-soaked corpse. They could tell that the shooting had been recent, and Rice was sure it had to be one of the shots they heard.

"Brent, call for more backup," Rice instructed. "Call the chief, he needs to know what is going on. I think we have stumbled onto something big, something real big! Let's get homicide in here. Be careful, I don't want to distort any evidence."

Rice continued his instructions. "You men continue to search, but be extremely careful. I need to speak to the chief before I move on. Signal me if you find anything. Remember be careful. I want the woman and girl alive."

At the same time, Glen and John were driving down one of the roads behind the woods. Ahead of them they could see a man waving. It was Ganeli. He had reached the roadside.

As they approached, they could see that Ganeli was hurt. The blood had soaked through his shirt. Glen and John prepared for the worse as they held their guns in hand, hoping they would not have to use them. They pulled up next to Ganeli and stopped on the far side of the road. John got out and stood behind the car.

"Don't move! Who are you?" John said, pointing his gun at Ganeli.

"Don't shoot! I'm a detective! I can show you!" Ganeli went to reach into his coat.

"Freeze! I said don't move! Get on the ground face down! Now!" John demanded, as he cocked his gun. Ganeli slowly laid face down on the ground as directed. Cautiously John approached him, his gun fully cocked. Glen protected John as he looked around.

"Don't say a word!" John demanded, pointing his gun at Ganeli as he searched him.

"Glen, it's okay."

"I can help you," Ganeli said as he tried to get John to listen.

"Shut up and stay down until I tell you to get up," John said as he passed Glen Ganeli's wallet.

"Glen, this guy seems to be legit." He's a detective named Ganeli. He's been shot.

"Ganeli. Ganeli." Glen repeated the name as he looked through the wallet.

"Get up," Glen instructed. John helped Ganeli to his feet. Initially he grabbed him by his injured arm and Ganeli let out a painful groan.

"Let's get him into the car. I need to get him out of here before Rice and his boys come. We need to get him someplace where we can talk." Glen said.

CHAPTER FORTY-FIVE

Angie dropped Katherine and Sarah off in Locksmith, which was about an hour away from New York City. The town was similar to Alberville, except there were taller buildings, more stores and fewer trees. Katherine thanked her as she and Sarah got out of the car. They watched as Angie drove away, then stood in front of a Sunoco gas station, trying to decide what to do next.

Katherine felt the men had to be close on their trail. They needed a place to hide—a place where she and Sarah could rest and call Detective Glen. Sarah was exhausted. Katherine decided the best thing to do was to get some clean clothes and camp out in a hotel. As she reached into her pocket to make sure she had some money, she pulled out the list. *Just get rid of it,* she thought, but she couldn't. She quickly tucked it in her jacket pocket then counted her money. She had enough cash for a few items and a hotel.

Katherine decided to go to one of the local stores. She bought a couple of hats and clothing. Now she had the task of finding somewhere to stay. She had about two hundred dollars left, and would have to pay for the hotel and possibly transportation into New York City.

As they walked around Locksmith, Katherine noticed several cheap hotels. There was one in particular that caught her attention. It was the Sleep Light Inn, sitting off on one of the side streets. It was the words Sleep Light that attracted her.

Katherine had Sarah wait outside, as she walked into the hotel foyer. There was a young woman on duty.

"Hi. Can I help you?" the clerk asked.

"Yes. I need a room," Katherine said as she took a quick glimpse toward the door, making sure Sarah was okay. The clerk could not see Sarah.

"How many are in your party?"

"Two…I mean, one. Sorry, it has been a busy day," Katherine said.

"And how will you be paying for the room?" The clerk asked, busily typing the information into the computer.

"Cash," Katherine answered.

"I'm sorry, we don't accept cash. You must use a credit card to guarantee payment of your room."

Katherine was taken aback. Using her credit card was not an option. What was she to do? Katherine decided it was Oscar time again. "Please, may I speak to your manager?" Katherine's voice stern and confidant.

"Surely. Please wait a second while I get him." The clerk stepped into the back room. A very tall and plain looking gentleman came out, along with the clerk. He seemed nice as he stood there in his white shirt, navy blue tie with a friendly smile.

Katherine determined. "Sir, I need help! Just a room for one night! My husband is after me," Katherine looked around the lobby. "He…he…has been beating me. He's after me. I only have a few dollars. I…I…had to run out of the house while he was asleep. I…I…don't have my credit card. I didn't have time to get my purse…Pleeeeeese…I…I have more than enough cash to pay you for the room. I won't damage a thing. My mother will be here to pick me up in the morning. Pleeeese…help me!" Katherine cried out. She could see another couple coming in the front door.

"Ma'am, please! Don't worry about the credit card," the manager said as he tried to calm Katherine and avoid chasing the other customers away. He did not fully believe the story. "I'll call the police for you."

"Oh! Please don't. That won't help. I just need to get away. My mother is the only person that can help me, thanks for your kindness."

"Your name, please," the manager asked. "I'll go ahead and get you registered."

"It's Kat…I'm sorry. All of this has me so shaken. My name is Gretchen Moore."

"Here's your key, Mrs. Moore. Your room is around the back. Just go outside and turn to your right. Take the elevator to the third floor."

"Thank you, sir. I can't tell you how much I appreciate everything you have done for me." Katherine walked outside and Sarah followed. She and Sarah dashed around the corner to find their room.

*   *   *

Slick was picked up by a nice old man driving a pick-up truck. Slick's first instinct was to do away with the man, but he realized he needed the man's help. The man had jimmy-rigged the truck with a weird handle on the gearshift. Watching him operate the vehicle gave Slick a headache.

Several police cars passed the truck. Slick assumed that Ganeli had ratted on him. He knew his worst enemy at this point was time.

*   *   *

By this time Glen and John had driven some distance from where they had picked up Ganeli. They passed through Locksmith and were within an hour of the Bronx River Bridge leading into New York City. Ganeli's wound was superficial and the bleeding had stopped, so Glen continued to pump him for information. He needed to know more about the assailants, especially this Slick character that Ganeli kept alluding to. Glen felt Ganeli was holding something back.

"I'm telling you the truth. I don't know anymore. Believe me, I had no idea the money was tied to the investment scandal and murders. I was in this for the money only. I don't know or want to know names. I haven't seen a list or want to see a list. Please arrest me, do something. I can't take this anymore. I have my own guilt to live with. I'll never forgive myself if something should happen to Katherine and Sarah. I know I was the one who got them involved. I should have never told those bastards where the money came from. I was trying to save my hide. I didn't...!" Ganeli said, ashamed.

Glen looked over at John as they listened to Ganeli. Glen's demeanor alarmed John.

"Are you alright?" John asked.

"I'm fine John, trust me," Glen thoughtlessly responded as he watched Ganeli through his rear view mirror.

"All of us do things we regret, Ganeli. I think we all need a Fairy Godmother to protect us," Glen said as he started the car and headed back towards Locksmith.

Fairy Godmother? Where did that come from? John thought to himself as he flashed Glen a peculiar look.

CHAPTER FORTY-SIX

Katherine and Sarah made their way to the hotel room. Katherine anxiously unlocked the door. Katherine rested against the closed door. She didn't have the strength to take another step as she watched Sarah fall across the bed.

After a few moments she mustered up enough strength to close the drapes. Then she decided it was time to call Detective Glen. As Katherine sat down countless thoughts raced through her head. The doubts and disappointment were diminishing Katherine's hope so much so that she pulled out the list and read it again. She did not remember seeing Detective Glen's name on the list, but she had to make sure.

Sarah had fallen fast asleep. Her face was dirty and her hair reeked of musk from the woods. Katherine stroked her hand across Sarah's brow, as the warmth of Sarah's smooth placid skin radiated up Katherine's arm. Katherine wondered if she could have done anything different...

She pulled the piece of paper with Glen's number out of her pocket. She listened intently as she anticipated someone answering.

"Hello, Fifteenth Precinct, may I help you?" a woman asked.

"Yes, I need to speak to Detective Glen."

"I'm sorry, he's not here. May I take a message?"

Katherine did not know what to say. She couldn't believe he was not there, especially since he had not shown up at Phyllis's house. Her thoughts were interrupted by the voice on the other end of the telephone.

"Miss, may I take a message?"

"No," Katherine responded. "But could you please tell me where he is or when he left?"

"I'm sorry, miss. I am not allowed to divulge that information."

"But, you don't understand. He would want me to know. He was supposed to meet my daughter and me several hours ago. I need to know where he is. It's a matter of life and death."

"Miss, I will do everything I can to help you. If you like, I can have you speak with one of the other officers, or I can take your number and have Detective Glen call you."

"So, you do know where he is?" Katherine asked.

"Miss, I will do my best to help you. Please, let me have you speak to another officer."

"No! I don't want to speak to anyone else," Katherine said, emphatically.

"Miss, I just want…"

Katherine hung up the phone. As she looked at Sarah, she thought of Nick. And as the thoughts grew stronger, so did the feelings of the chilling night Bobbie came to her apartment. It was such a vivid recollection her hands began to shake.

Katherine rushed into the bathroom. She did not want Sarah to see her like this. "Oh, God! I'm sorry for my sins! I should have told Nick! Please forgive me! I need help! Please help me!" Overwhelmed, Katherine fell to her knees. She looked into the mirror in front of her, and saw the reflection of a woman she had never seen before.

There were bags under her eyes. Her hair was frazzled. Her skin was dry with multiple abrasions. What alarmed her most were the eyes that looked back at her. These eyes were unfamiliar. They appeared stern, yet strong and firm, eyes searching for a soul. The eyes were that of a strong woman, a survivor.

As she stood up with eyes fixed on her image in the mirror, her legs no longer felt weak and her mind unclogged. She knew she had to fight to the end. As Katherine walked out of the bathroom, she noticed that her surroundings seemed different. Sarah was still sprawled across the bed. Above the bed was a beautiful scenic view of trees and running streams. *I'll visit that place someday*, Katherine thought to herself as she walked over to the bed and lay down next to Sarah. She decided they would wait until dark, then catch a bus and head into New York City.

CHAPTER FORTY-SEVEN

Slick made his way to Locksmith. As they drove through town, Slick searched for clues that Katherine and Sarah were there. He had to find them. As the man drove on, Slick thought about how or why he got involved in all of this. It just seemed to happen. At one point in his life he was in love, and the next thing he knew he didn't care about anything. Slick's thoughts were interrupted as he noticed a car up ahead. It looked like the car that had picked Katherine and Sarah up on the road. As they drew closer Slick became sure this was the car. He ordered the driver to stop, then thanked the man and tossed him a fifty-dollar bill.

The car was empty and the doors were locked. He decided to wait for the driver. Slick noticed a small diner behind him, so he went inside to wait.

In the diner were several people drinking coffee and watching the news. As Slick walked over to a table and sat down, he heard an alarming news broadcast. "We interrupt this story to bring you a special broadcast. Two bodies were found this morning in Lumberville, New York. One of the men appears to have been shot. As you can see, the police are everywhere behind me, trying to piece together what happened in this small quiet town. The names of the victims are still unknown, as are the reasons behind their deaths. There is some speculation this may be tied to the strange investment Bankers' deaths that have plagued New York City. Per recent information it appears all these men may have been murdered. The details are very sketchy at this point. We will keep you up to date as this story unfolds. This is Barbara Tyson from Channel Two News."

Slick was sure the two men were Bob and Sam. This would explain the shots and the reason they had not caught up with him. He knew that it would only be a matter of time before cops would be all over the place looking for him, especially if that snitch, Ganeli, had his way. Slick waited impatiently for the driver of the car to appear, as he drank his cup of coffee.

Glen, John and Ganeli arrived in Locksmith. Ganeli seemed to be familiar with the area, and he had a hunch that Katherine and Sarah were there. Glen and John decided to rely on Ganeli for direction. They were convinced that Ganeli wanted to find Katherine and Sarah safe and alive as much as they did. Ganeli became more animated as he began to direct the two of them. Glen watched Ganeli and listened to him carefully. It was like working with a one armed Colombo.

They planned to search all the local restaurants, hotels and stores. John was to contact the local police station to see if they turned up there. Ganeli searched the hotels, while Glen searched the restaurants. They agreed to call the Fifteenth Precinct and leave a message if they found anything. Each man was to check in every two hours. Before they set out, Glen checked out Ganeli's wound, wanting to make sure Ganeli would be up for the chase. "Ganeli, if you find yourself getting weak or tired, go to the car. I'll assume you're there if you haven't checked in. Okay?" Glen asked.

"You got it." Ganeli gave Glen the thumbs-up sign and wandered down the street.

"Ganeli," Glen called out. "Let's avoid getting caught alone at night."

"What's the matter, are you New York boys afraid of the dark?"

*   *   *

Back in Lumberville, the police were searching the woods for clues. Just as Slick suspected, they had blocked off all the roads leading in and out of Lumbersville. Detective Rice worked with Homicide as they tried to piece together the events. Rice thought that Phyllis was the main link, so he called the hospital. The latest update was that she was still in serious condition. Rice decided to leak the fact that Phyllis was alive to the news media.

CHAPTER FORTY-EIGHT

Glen, John, and Ganeli continued their search, but they hadn't come up with any clues. Ganeli walked into the Sleep Light Inn and was about to approach the clerk, when the newscast in the background caught his attention. "We bring you further coverage of our top story today. Earlier, we reported that the bodies of two men were found in the woods of Lumberville, New York. These men are still unidentified. As we reported earlier, these deaths may be connected to the New York City investment murders, but that information is still sketchy. We have heard, since our last broadcast, that there may be a witness. An elderly woman, who remains hospitalized, might be able to help the police. We understand that this woman was brutally beaten, possibly by the dead men or others who might still be in the area. We will bring you further updates as this chilling story unfolds. This is Barbara Tyson of Channel Two News."

Ganeli knew the woman had to be Phyllis. He was relieved she was still alive. This was the best news that he had received today. He went to the desk. "Hello, my name is Detective Ganeli. I need your help."

"How can I help you, sir?" the clerk greeted him.

"I'm looking for a young woman and her daughter. Their names are Katherine and Sarah Oberman. I believe they might have checked into your inn. I understand the information is confidential, but believe me, they are in trouble and I need to help them." Ganeli showed her his badge.

The clerk looked at Ganeli's badge. Her young innocence made her feel this was someone she could trust. "Sir, no woman with a child has checked in today." Before she could start her next sentence Ganeli was on the attack.

"Would you at least check your registry for the names?"

She looked to see if the manager was behind her. Then she looked down at the screen. She wanted to help Ganeli, but she was unsure if she should go any further without the manager's consent. Ganeli picked up on this.

"Please, call your manager. I'll talk with him or her if you are unable to help me."

These seemed to be the words the young clerk needed to hear. She punched a few keys on the computer.

"Sir, how do you spell that last name?" The clerk asked.

"Oberman. O. b. e. r. m. a. n., first name Katherine."

The clerk punched a few more keys. "I'm sorry sir, we do not have anyone by that name registered. I wish that I could have helped you."

"Thanks, I appreciate your help. If someone should show up by that name, here's my phone number. Please call. It is truly a matter of life and death."

"I will, and again, I'm sorry, sir. I wish I could help."

Ganeli walked out. He had checked every possible lead and had come up empty. It was getting late, and he needed to check in with Glen and John.

*   *   *

Several blocks away, Slick had heard the same broadcast that Ganeli had. He was back at the diner. The owner of the car had not returned. Slick knew the woman on the newscast had to be the little old lady they had roughed up. He did not plan to verify whether she was dead or alive. He was just about to order his early evening meal, when he noticed a woman walking towards the car. It was Angie. At first he thought she was going to walk by it, but she stopped and placed her bags on the trunk, then pulled out her keys.

Slick approached Angie. "Hi, that's really a nice car you have there. What year is it?"

Angie looked up and, to her surprise, there was a tall, dark and handsome man talking to her. At first she thought it was too good to be true. *Maybe this is my lucky day, or then again, maybe he has mistaken me for someone else,* she thought.

"Wait," Slick said as he placed his hands on the trunk. Angie smiled.

"I'm sorry. I did not realize you were talking to me. Please, I don't want you to think I am a rude or snobbish person. I had so many things on my mind, I didn't hear you." Angie said with a smile.

"I really admire beautiful cars, and when they come with beautiful women, that's even more intriguing. What do you say we go for a bite to eat? I'm sure you're hungry after all your shopping."

"Why not?" Angie said, and closed the trunk. Slick realized she thought they were going into the diner. He needed to get her someplace secluded in case things got ugly.

"Let's not eat here. Let's go some place nice and quiet. I saw a nice restaurant down the road on my way in. Let's go there." Slick suggested.

"Sure," said Angie. "Why not? Let me lock up my car. I'll ride with you."

"No way, not on our first date. My mother always told me to allow the lady to drive. That way she would not feel the man was trying to take advantage of her," Slick said, hoping Angie would fall for the line.

"I like the way your mother thinks. She sounds a lot like my father. Get in. I know a couple of nice places."

As Slick got into the car, Officer Glen entered the diner. He was so pre-occupied with finding Katherine and Sarah, the couple getting into the car did not attract his attention. Slick and Angie drove off...

       *   *   *

Dusk was fast approaching as Slick and Angie headed towards the other side of town. Slick immediately pumped Angie for information. "Tell me, how was your day? I can see you like to do a lot of shopping."

"Sometimes I do," Angie responded. "It really depends on the mood. I'm sure you don't have that problem."

"Hey, believe me, sometimes I do. It really depends on how my day starts off. I had plans today to do a little shopping. On my way into town, I picked up a hitchhiker. I felt so sorry for the man that I gave him a few bucks. By the time I got in town, I lost my desire to shop. I could not get that poor man off my mind." Slick looked skeptically at his watch.

"That's strange. My day started off similar to yours. I picked up a mother and daughter earlier. I only stopped because I felt sorry for the young girl. They were good people, a little dirty and smelly, but really nice people."

"That was kind of you. I'm sure they really appreciated the lift," Slick said.

"I think they did. They said their car had broken down and they needed to get to a service station. I dropped them off at the Sunoco station in town. I hope everything went well for them. There was something about the daughter that really captured my heart. She really didn't say much, she seemed very tired."

"You say the young girl appeared tired?" Slick asked.

"Yes, it seemed she was."

"What about the mother? Did she seem okay? You really can't tell what these parents will do today, especially after that Susan Smith story."

"You're right, but she seemed rather nice. She reminded me a little of myself, except her hair was shorter."

"You mean she had dark brown hair as pretty as yours?"

"Well…well, not quite as pretty," Angie said with a smile. " I hope everything works out for the two of them."

"That was nice of you to help them. Did they say where they were going?" Slick asked.

"I'm not really sure. I think they might have said something about New York City. I know they would not be going too far until they get their car fixed."

Nightfall was upon them and Angie was fast approaching the restaurant. Up ahead, Slick could see a roadside telephone. Slick felt this would be the opportune place to stop. He remembered he was still wearing his pager. He flicked the button and sounded the beep.

"Someone paged you?" Angie asked.

"Yes, probably the job." Slick pulled the pager out pretending he had a message. "I need to stop and make a phone call, its important. Would you stop at that pay phone coming up?"

"Sure! The last thing I want to do is keep a man from his business. That is, unless I'm the business," Angie said as she gave Slick a seductive smile, then pulled the car off to the side of the road. Slick didn't get out. He looked at Angie, and flashed her a wink.

"Why don't you go ahead and answer that page? Let's plan dinner at my house instead."

Slick's eyes gleamed and he leaned towards Angie. She closed her eyes as she anticipated his kiss. In place of the kiss, Slick hit her in the back of her head with a rock. He searched for a place to dump her, but the surroundings were too barren, so he bound and gagged Angie and placed her limp body in the trunk.

CHAPTER FORTY-NINE

Sarah awoke confused and disoriented. She was so tired that she slept through the entire day. She glanced over toward the window at the partially drawn drapes. Between the crack in the drapes was nothing but darkness. It took a few minutes for Sarah to remember where she was. Her neck felt stiff as she rose to stretch. She looked down at Katherine who was stretched out across the bed. It was obvious she was still in a deep sleep. Not wanting to wake her, Sarah tiptoed around the room, looking for the television remote. Finally locating it, she turned on the television, pushed the mute button and began flipping through the channels.

She channel-surfed for several minutes before coming to the conclusion that nothing was on. Growing increasingly restless, she flipped through the hotel brochure and looked at the pictures, before going on to the room service menu. Finally, she flipped through the bible that was in the nightstand drawer. Nothing seemed to hold her attention.

Sarah spent several minutes gazing out of the window, staring down at the busy streets. It seemed that this little town had developed a little night-life. She watched as several people crossed the street and entered the corner pub. She noticed the diner. It was the neon light shaped like a bagel that caught her attention. Her hunger pains were starting to get to her so she decided to take a quick walk over to the shop.

To Sarah, it appeared to be the right thing to do. She knew Katherine loves a good strong cup of coffee when she wakes up and Sarah felt a bagel and cream cheese would be great. Sarah could not think of a better way to ease her restlessness. Sarah put on the hat that Katherine bought for her and helped herself to a few dollars. She knew Katherine would be upset, but she thought the smell of fresh coffee and bagels would put her in a good mood and she would forgive her. Sarah took the key and headed out of the door. Before she locked the door, she took one last look at Katherine to make sure she was still asleep.

Feeling very grown up, she stepped into the elevator. When the elevator stopped on the second floor, alarm filled Sarah's eyes. A middle-aged man entered. Her first instinct was to run, but the gentlemen seem preoccupied on his cellular phone. She remained on the elevator. The doors opened onto the main floor. She started to go into the lobby, but she remembered no one was supposed to know she was there. She turned and exited through the side door.

When she got outside, she contemplated going back to the room, but the prospect of a warm bagel and melted cream cheese ran through her mind. It was the smell from the diner that changed her mind. Sarah was totally unprepared for the crowd of people who greeted her. Some appeared agitated as they shouted out their orders. Sarah knew it would take a little while to get what she needed. She glanced back towards the hotel and worried that Katherine might wake up and find her gone. Sarah got in line.

CHAPTER FIFTY

Ganeli and the men reunited back at the car. They could not believe that they came up empty-handed. Glen was sure Katherine and Sarah had to be nearby. Ganeli worried that Slick might have caught up to them and killed them. Glen felt this had not happened. His gut instinct still told him they were not only alive, but also close by. The three men sat in the car, trying to decide what they should do next. It was John who came up with the most sensible idea.

"Hey, guys, I think we may be going about this all wrong. From what the two of you have told me, this Katherine is a pretty smart chick. We need to put ourselves in her shoes. The more I think about this, the more sense it makes. If you were a parent and you knew someone was after you, what would you do?" John asked.

"I would hide somewhere," Ganeli answered.

"Right, Ganeli," said John. "But how would you throw off your assailants?"

"I would change my appearance," Ganeli responded.

"That makes sense, but what else would you do if you had to stay in a small town like this?" John asked.

"I would still change my appearance." Ganeli said.

"Ganeli," said John. I see something different happening here."

"So do I," Glen said.

"They would probably change their appearance, not only physically, but in numbers," said John.

"You're right, John," said Glen.

John went on. "Ganeli, when you checked the hotels, what did you look for?"

Ganeli thought before he responded. "I told them I was looking for a mother and a daughter. That made sense to me."

"You're right, Ganeli. That does make sense, but I bet Katherine thought the same thing. I bet she not only checked in under an assumed name, she did not register Sarah," John said, awaiting a response.

"Bingo!" Glen yelled out. "I bet…You're damn right! Katherine knew that anyone coming after her would be looking for two people. Why in the hell didn't we think of this earlier?"

"What do you mean *we*, Chief Detective?" John laughed.

"Alright, John, good job. We need to backtrack to all the hotels in the area. Let's think like Katherine. If I were her, I would not stay on the main drag. Do the two of you agree?"

"Right," John responded as he and Ganeli agreed. Glen went on.

"So, from that conclusion, we are down to three hotels. Is that right Ganeli?"

"You're right." Ganeli answered.

"Each of us must take one. Let's follow John's lead and search for a single woman. Forget the name. Any single woman is fair game. We'll meet at that coffee shop or diner, whatever it is, in a hour." Glen said. The three of them got out of the car, for a last attempt to find Katherine and Sarah in Locksmith.

*   *   *

Slick made his way back to the inner part of the town. He decided that he would first look around the bus station. He was sure he would eventually find them there. When he arrived at the bus station, all seemed quiet. There were only a few people waiting. Slick saw a little old lady wrapped up in her shawl. He walked toward her to make sure this was not a disguise. The woman instantly looked up as he neared, and she was as old as sin. Several other women were scattered around the small bus station. He scoped them out, then decided to check the restrooms to make sure they were not hiding there. The restrooms were empty.

Slick walked over to the ticket clerk to check the bus schedule again. The last bus for New York City was still leaving at eight p.m. He purchased a ticket, just in case he had to board in a hurry. He knew if he didn't find them tonight, it would be all over, including the family fortune and numerous bankers' careers. The thought of having to tell his father he was not able to get the list was not an event he savored. He decided to go back to the diner and have dinner before the bus departed.

CHAPTER FIFTY-ONE

Katherine awakened looking up at a yellowed and cracked ceiling. She lay there for a moment, enjoying the peace and quiet. It was as tranquil as if she were at home in Alberville. After a few seconds, the comfortable silence turned into an eerie one. She didn't hear any noises except the ticking clock. The bed was empty.

She scanned the room so fast it made her dizzy. She noticed the closed bathroom door. She was sure Sarah was inside. "Sarah?" Katherine shouted. There was no response. Katherine knocked on the bathroom door. The door opened. Katherine's heart dropped. There was no Sarah. She gasped and stepped back, not wanting to believe what was happening. She opened the room door and looked down the hall. She didn't see Sarah.

Katherine ran down the hall and looked around the corridors as she called out Sarah's name. Each shout grew louder. The terror eclipsed anything and everything she'd felt the past few days. Katherine feared that the men had come to their room while she was asleep and took Sarah away. What she could not understand was why they did not kidnap or kill her, unless they had found what they needed. *The list!* she thought, as she rushed backed into the room. She noticed that the hat she bought Sarah was missing. *She couldn't, she wouldn't!* Katherine thought as she wrestled with the idea that Sarah had left on her own. Katherine rushed over to the chair where she'd left her jacket. She checked her pocket; the list was still there. She rushed over to the window. She quickly threw on her jacket and hat, then rushed out the door.

Sarah stood in line listening to the music as she studied the menu. She debated whether she should order Hazelnut or Irish Cream coffee for Katherine.

Katherine made her way to the lobby. She noticed the staff had changed shift. She felt it would be safe to ask about an adolescent girl.

"Have you seen a young girl? She's about five feet tall, brown hair with a blue hat." Katherine said, as she noticed the clerk was pre-occupied. She was having problems with the computer.

"Pardon me, ma'am." Katherine's voice was stern, as she leaned over the desk. "Have you seen a young girl, about five feet tall and wearing a blue hat?"

"What does she look like?" The woman finally responded.

Katherine described Sarah again to the woman. "I haven't, but kids usually go over to the diner across the street. I suggest you look there," said the clerk.

Katherine hurried across the street. She was in the doorway of the diner in a matter of seconds. She did a fast furious scan and when she saw Sarah in line, relief washed through her, then her anger raged. She stomped over to Sarah. Despite the curious looks of many onlookers, she grabbed Sarah right out of line and pulled her none too gently over to the side.

"Sarah, what were you thinking?"

Sarah's displayed the 'deer in the head-lights' look. She knew Katherine was upset and things were not looking pretty. The stress, pressure and fears had taken its toll on the two of them. It was breaking Sarah's heart to think she had caused additional pain for Katherine.

"What were you thinking?" Katherine said as she shook Sarah again. Sarah's eyes widened. "Do you know what I went through when I got up and you weren't there? Do you have any idea? Haven't you learned anything these past few days?" Katherine shouted.

"I'm sorry! I wanted to surprise you! I didn't mean to scare you! Sarah pleaded for forgiveness.

"Didn't you think...? What if something happened to you? You know how difficult it has been! Tell me, what was on your mind? Tell me! This is all your fault!" Katherine shouted as she clutched Sarah's shoulders.

Sarah cried out. "I'm sorry! I'm sorry! I was just trying to help! I know it's all my fault! I'm sorry," Sarah wept. The customers glared at Katherine. One man even yelled out, "Leave her alone!"

It was then Katherine realized what she had said as she looked at Sarah. The pain, regret and sadness caused Katherine to turn away. What had she done? What was she doing? What did she say? The echoes of Sarah's cries were breaking her heart. How? How? Katherine kept asking herself. Why? Why?

"Stop crying, Sarah. I'm sorry, I didn't mean what I said. I'm sorry. I know you were just trying to help. Please, forgive me," Katherine embraced Sarah. "Please forgive me." Katherine led Sarah to an empty booth in the back of the diner.

"Sarah, you know, I think a good cup of that flavored coffee and a bagel would be a great idea." Sarah smiled through her tears.

Katherine noticed a pay phone in the corner. She decided to try to get in touch with Detective Glen before she and Sarah set out for the city. The time in Locksmith had given her some security. She knew this was not the end, but she felt the chase had come to a halt for now. Katherine asked Sarah to order as she made her way over to the telephone.

"Fifteenth Precinct, may I help you?"

"Yes, I would like to speak to Detective Glen, this is Katherine Oberman calling again." The clerk immediately recognized the name. The phone calls from Glen and John had prepared her.

"Miss Katherine, I mean Miss Oberman. Where are you? Detective Glen is not here. He's looking for you. He has given me instructions, if you should call, I need to find out where you are. Are you and your daughter alright?" She asked.

"My daughter and I are okay." Katherine said, relieved that Glen was searching for her.

"Miss Oberman, please tell me where you are. I'll make every effort to locate him and have him meet you. Is there a phone number where I can reach you? The moment I get in touch with him, I will call you, I promise. If I can't get in touch with him, I will call you back with directions."

"Okay, but please hurry. We are sitting in the back of a diner in Locksmith, New York," Katherine replied. "The diner is called Friendly's and the number is…six-six-three-two-nine-four-seven. If I don't hear from you within half an hour, we will get on the bus and head into city."

"Miss Oberman, please stay there. I would rather have Detective Glen escort you into the city. I'll do everything in my power to get in touch with him. I'm sure he is not far away from you." The woman hung up the phone and immediately called Glen on his car phone.

"Mom, what happened?" "You were on the phone for a long time. Did you talk to the detective?" Sarah asked.

"No, Sarah, I did not talk to Detective Glen, but I found out that he is looking for us. He did not abandon us. We can expect a call shortly and everything will be okay. I feel we are safe for now."

"But, mom, what if she can't find him? What will we do then?"

"Sarah, let's try to stay positive. Remember, if she can't find him, we can always go back to our original plan. The woman on the phone said she would call us with directions if she could not contact him."

"Okay," Sarah said, as she took a bite out of her bagel.

CHAPTER FIFTY-TWO

Detective Glen walked into the Sleep Light Inn. "Hello, my name is Detective Glen. I'm with the New York City police department, and I need your help. You see, a young woman and her daughter are in deep trouble. I need to find them before something bad happens." Glen showed the clerk his identification as he continued to speak. "I believe the mother might have registered at your hotel. I know one of my men checked here earlier. I think the woman may have registered under a different name. Would you please take a moment and see if you have a single woman who checked in today?"

The clerk looked at Glen's identification. Although he seemed legitimate, she felt uncomfortable giving a strange man information on a single woman.

"One moment, sir. I'll check, but I'm not sure how much I'll be able to help you."

"Anything you can do that might help would be greatly appreciated," Glen responded, as he waited impatiently.

Punching up the guest list, the clerk noticed there were two single women who had registered that day, a Rebecca Cole and a Gretchen Moore. She hesitated for a moment, and then she looked up at Glen. He could tell from the look in her eyes that she had found something.

"Sir, I mean Mister Detective, I have to get my manager. I can't release this information to you. Glen knew he had landed something. He watched the woman go into the back room to seek out the manger. He noticed that in the clerk's haste, she did not clear the screen.

He took that moment to lean over the counter and look at the screen. He saw the names Rebecca Cole, room 224, and Gretchen Moore, room

336. Glen did not wait for the clerk to return. Glen rushed to room 224 and knocked on the door.

"Who is it?" A woman asked.

"It's Detective Glen. I'm looking for a Katherine Oberman."

"I'm sorry, you have the wrong room," the woman said, looking through the peephole. She feared the strange man at her door.

"I'm sorry ma'am. Please have a good evening." Glen rushed to the stairwell and onto the third floor. When he got to room 336, he stopped. The door of the room was open.

Glen pulled out his gun and slowly entered the room. He knew he had stumbled upon something. As he stepped into the room, there was no one in sight. He looked behind the door and searched the bathroom, closets and under the bed. He could tell the bed had been slept in, noticing the pillows were in the middle of the bed. He also noticed a few articles of clothing on the chair. Glen walked over and looked them over. The first garment was a flannel shirt that appeared to be a woman's. The shirt was very small and had a flower embroidered on the pocket. It had a peculiar smell, something he could not place, although it seemed familiar. He then noticed a pair of blue jeans. He picked up the jeans. Again they appeared to be those of a small woman, or possibly a young girl. When he's lifted the jeans, small pebbles of dried dirt that fell on the floor. There were smudges of dirt on the seat and legs of the jeans. He searched the pockets and found nothing. The smell of the clothing caught his attention. This was the smell of the earth around Phyllis's house. He remembered it, as he thought back to a comment he made to John regarding the odor of the outdoors.

Glen knew he had found Katherine and Sarah or at least their clothing. He searched every corner of the room for the list. By the time he finished, it looked as if a hurricane had hit the room. Glen wanted to make absolutely sure the list was not left behind. He rushed out of the room. He needed answers and he hoped the clerk would be able to help him.

When he arrived in the lobby, the clerk and her manager were standing at the desk. The clerk pointed in his direction as she spoke to the manager. Glen was winded, yet eager to have some of his questions answered. "I'm sorry, sir, but I need you to answer a few questions. I'm a detective," Glen pulled out his identification again. "The woman and daughter I'm looking for were here in room 336. Their lives are in grave danger." Glen tried to catch his breath as he described Katherine and Sarah to them.

The manager was very upset. This detective had violated the hotel policy, and he was reluctant to help him. "I'm sorry, Detective, but you have placed my establishment in jeopardy. I could be sued for your action," the manager said.

"I'm sorry, sir, but I have no time to waste. I'll make sure the blame falls back on my department. I'll take full responsibility for my actions."

"Try the diner across the street. Everyone seems to end up there," the manager suggested.

"Thanks, you have been very helpful. I'm sorry for the trouble I have cause you," Glen said as he rushed out the door. What Glen was not aware of, was that, while he was searching the inn, Slick had arrived at the diner and Katherine and Sarah were again running for their lives.

*   *   *

Katherine and Sarah had waited patiently in the back corner of the diner, hoping to hear from Glen or the clerk at the precinct. Katherine looked up and saw the lights of a car shining into the diner. At first she thought it was probably another customer, although she hoped it was Detective Glen. The lights of the car did not seem unusual, but a feeling came over Katherine. She saw a man getting out and, as the figure moved closer to the door, her attitude of patiently waiting turned to sheer fear. It was the man in the black coat and that hat she had seen walking with Ganeli earlier. She could tell that by the way he walked.

"Oh, my God! It's him!" Katherine whispered to Sarah. Sarah was about to turn around to look, but before she could, Katherine whispered, "don't turn around. We have to get out of here."

They inched down under the table and moved to the back, behind the booth. She had noticed earlier, while on the telephone, that there was a rear exit.

Slick was walking in the front door as Katherine and Sarah made their way out the back door and began running down the street, wondering where to go. Katherine thought of the bus station, but the sight of her assailant made her forget this idea. She saw several cars coming her way, and tried to thumb a ride. She dashed out into the street so fast; a motorcycle driver nearly hit her.

"You stupid bitch!" The man shouted. Katherine did not say a word.

A car stopped and the driver asked, "Do you need a ride?" Katherine, breathing faster than the car engine was turning, responded in an exhausted voice, "Yes! Please! My daughter and I need to get to New York City."

"Ma'am, I can't take you that far, but I can get you to the bridge if that's okay?"

"Anything! We'll take it!" Katherine said, as she and Sarah got in...

CHAPTER FIFTY-THREE

Inside the diner, the waitress approached Slick. He had about forty-five minutes before he had to be back at the bus station. He looked at the television. Several men sitting at the counter were engrossed in a basketball game. He knew he would not hear any updates about Lumberville unless there was some new-breaking news. He looked out the window at the car he was driving, and thought about the body of the young woman in the trunk. The waitress interrupted his thoughts.

"Sir, are you ready to order?"

"Yes, I am ready to order. I'll have a cup of coffee. Do you have any pasta?"

"As a matter of fact, we do. Our chef makes the best spaghetti and meatballs in this area. I think you will really enjoy the dish."

"That sounds good," Slick said as he looked around. "Is it always this quiet around here?"

"Sometimes," the waitress replied, "but, if you wanted excitement, you should have been here a little earlier. There was a woman in here that went ballistic with her daughter because she did not tell her where she was going. We thought she was going to hit the child!" The waitress rambled on and on.

"What happened to them?" Slick asked.

"Oh, they're still here. They're sitting in the booth in the back," the waitress replied, as she looked toward the booth. It was empty. "That's strange, they were there a minute ago," she said.

Upon hearing this, Slick decided to walk toward the booth. As he approached, he noticed the bagels had been barely eaten and the ice was still fresh in the glasses. It was quite obvious that whoever was there had left in a hurry. Slick noticed a piece of paper on the seat. The words

'Detective Glen, New York City' and a telephone number were written on it. He remembered Angie's comment about the mother and daughter going to New York City. He was sure the two had occupied the booth. He quickly searched the bathrooms, and then he noticed that the rear exit door was slightly ajar. He walked out the door. Although he didn't see anyone as he looked down the dark alley, he knew his instincts were right. He went back through the diner, got into his car and drove down the alley behind the diner. He noticed a couple of people on the street corner at the end of the alley.

"Hey, guys, have you seen a woman and a young girl within the last few minutes? I'm trying to find my wife and daughter. They were supposed to meet me on this corner." The men walked over to the car. They looked big and scary in the shadows of the moonlit evening. Slick stuck his hand in his pocket, ready to use his gun if necessary, not sure what the men had in mind.

"Did you say a woman and a girl?" the burley man asked.

"Yes, they left the diner a few minutes ago."

"I believe we did. There was some crazy woman with a young girl trying to flag down a car. A motorcycle almost hit her. A car stopped and picked the two of them up. They headed that way," the other man said, pointing in the direction of the bridge.

"What kind of car was it? Slick asked, searching for details.

"I'm not sure, but it looked like a black Lincoln."

Seconds later, Detective Glen walked into the diner. He quickly scanned the room looking for Katherine and Sarah, then started questioning the waitress; the same one who gave Slick the tip that sent him in hot pursuit of Katherine and Sarah.

"Did you see a woman with a young girl within the last half hour?" Glen asked.

"Yes, I believe they were here. They were sitting in the booth in the back. I sure wish I was as popular as them."

"What do you mean?" Glen asked, puzzled.

"Well, there was another man looking for them a few minutes ago. He seemed rather anxious also."

"Another man? Describe him to me!" Glen hoped it was Ganeli or John.

"The man wore a dark coat and hat—"

Before she could finish Glen interrupted. "Which way did they go? Which way did the man go?" Glen asked, anxious.

"I'm not sure about the woman and girl. I didn't see them leave. The gentleman left through the front door after he searched the place. He just drove away."

Glen recalled a car driving off as he approached the diner. That must have been Slick, he thought, as he dashed out the door. In the background, the telephone rang. "Hello, Friendly's Diner," the waitress answered.

"Hello," Martha responded. She knew it was not Katherine on the other end of the telephone. "There is a woman waiting for my call. She told me she would be sitting in the back booth."

"She ain't sitting there no more. I need to find out what she's got."

"What do you mean?" Martha asked.

"There have been two men in here looking for those two. She's gone. She's disappeared, and the men left. I'm sure they went to look for her."

Martha thanked the waitress, then hung up and put in another call to Glen's car phone. By this time, Glen along with Ganeli and John had returned to the car. Ganeli and John came up empty. Glen filled them in about his discovery as they headed down the road, hoping to catch up with Slick's car. Glen knew he would recognize Slick's car if he saw it.

Just as Glen was about to call into the precinct, the car phone rang. "Hello?"

"Hello, Detective Glen?"

"Yes, Martha, what is it?"

"Listen!" Martha was excited. "I heard from Katherine Oberman. She was in a diner with her daughter. When I could not reach you, I called back. A woman answered. She told me that Katherine was gone and two men were looking for her."

"I know, Martha, I was one of those men. I'm afraid the other is a tough guy called Slick. Did Katherine say where she was headed?"

"What I detected was, she wanted to come here. I asked her to await my call for instructions."

"Martha, I need you to prepare some back-up help for me. If I'm not mistaken, Katherine, Sarah and this Slick are heading toward the city. This road leads to the Bronx River Bridge. Prepare the men. I think it will all happen there. Just prepare them. I don't want them there until I give the signal. I'll call you when I get closer. I'll talk to you later." Glen was about to hang up the telephone, then he remembered something.

"Martha?"

"Yes, Detective Glen."

"Martha, if Katherine calls again, please call me right away," Glen instructed, as he headed toward the city.

"I understand," Martha replied.

CHAPTER FIFTY-FOUR

Katherine and Sarah made their way to the bridge. Their ride had dropped them about a block away. Katherine could see the lights of the New York City and some familiar buildings on the other side. This was the area where her childhood friend, Melody, had lived. Katherine knew that if she got to the other side of the bridge, she would not be far from the precinct. Sarah stood at her side. The bushes and trees cast shadows that frightened her. Everything appeared larger in the darkness. Sarah shivered, not because she was cold but because she was scared. She wanted to go back to the hotel.

As Katherine began to inform Sarah of her plan, she could see the headlights of an approaching car. The two of them hid behind some bushes. The car passed them as it crossed the bridge. They ran across the clearing and were about to cross the embankment and step onto the bridge when Katherine looked back and saw the headlights of another car approaching. She searched for a place to hide, but there was no place in sight. She remembered hiding and playing under the bridge as a child, so she grabbed Sarah's hand and they climbed down the embankment. She could hear the car above them getting nearer. There was nowhere to go, except for the murky water beneath them.

Within seconds, Sarah let out a horrific scream. Her feet were slipping down the embankment.

"Sarah! Sarah! Hold on!" Katherine cried out, as she clutched Sarah's arm. The darkness that surrounded them made it impossible to judge the depth of the water below.

Sarah screamed again as she struggled to implant her feet. "Mom! Help! Don't let go!" Sarah cried out.

"I won't Sarah! Oh, God!" Katherine cried out, as Sarah was pulled from her grip.

"Mom I'm falling! Mom!" Sarah screamed, holding onto some bushes, her feet uncertain in the muddy earth. "Mom, help me! I'm falling!"

Katherine knew she had to do something, even if it meant sacrificing her own life. She could see the mingling of moonlight and terror in Sarah's eyes. "Hold on Sarah! Grab my hand! You can do it!" she said as she lunged, supported only by her guts and the roots of a decayed tree.

Their hands met and, as they did, the list fell out of Katherine's jacket pocket toward the bottom of the embankment, the papers floating into the dusty darkness as Katherine grasped Sarah's hand tighter and pulled her to safety. They held each other in a deathly embrace, as the impact of the event captured them.

They made their way back onto the bridge. As they reached the other side and looked outward, they could see an abandoned parking lot with several demolished cars and several men standing around a burning trash can. Katherine notices her friend Melody's building, which appeared abandoned.

Katherine thought about what almost happened under the bridge as the sight of Sarah's weakened and fearful figure broke her heart. Katherine had to find a place for them to rest before they continued. She headed in the direction of the abandoned, yet familiar buildings as she placed Sarah's arms over her shoulder and her arm around Sarah's waist.

What Katherine did not see were the cars that crossed the bridge behind her. Slick was in one of those cars. While Slick waited for the stop light at the end of the bridge, he saw two figures crossing an empty lot. Something told him he had found his victims.

    *   *   *

Back in Locksmith, Detective Rice and his men combed the town. They discovered the Sleep Light Inn. After hearing the story from the manager and clerk about Detective Glen, they searched the room. From the looks of things, they knew Katherine and Sarah were in deep trouble.

The clerk told them where she directed the woman. Detective Rice followed the lead to Friendly's Diner. He spoke with the waitress and she told him what had happened. After speaking to several men outside the diner, Rice realized the chase was headed toward New York City. Earlier, he had informed the FBI about the possible connection to the New York investment murders. Rice decided he would try to get in touch with Glen. He needed to know if Katherine and Sarah were with him, as he pulled out the card Glen had given him and called the fifteenth precinct.

"Hello, Fifteenth Precinct," Martha answered.

"Hello, this is Detective Rice from the Lumberville police department. Is Detective Glen there?"

Martha knew right away who Rice was. She remembered Glen telling her about him. "No, I'm sorry, Detective Rice, he's not."

"Do you know how I can get in touch with him?" he asked.

Martha's first instinct was to say 'no', but she had not heard back from Glen.

"When I last spoke to him, he was heading toward the Bronx River Bridge. He thought the man chasing Miss Oberman and her daughter were headed in that direction."

"Thanks for the information," Rice said. He knew he had to get moving.

"You're welcome," Martha replied.

"Men, we're heading toward the Bronx River Bridge. I think we might find something there," Rice said.

CHAPTER FIFTY-FIVE

Katherine and Sarah moved toward the front door of the building. The door opened easily, and she helped Sarah inside. It was dark and the stench was awful. Katherine knew that if they could just rest in the entryway for a moment and gather their strength, they could move on. As she and Sarah rested their fatigued bodies against the wall and were about to sit down on the floor, a huge ungodly figure stepped in front of them. His face was detestable. The gray hairs of his eyebrows were so thick and long, they shadowed his eyes. His clothes were layered, torn and dirty. The offensive smell increased as he moved closer. Sarah let out a scream. The man towered over the two of them.

"Get the hell out of here! This is my home! Get out!" the man yelled. Katherine stood up, pushed Sarah behind her as they stepped backwards, out of the door. The two of them, mustered up enough strength to run to the next building. Katherine assisted Sarah, although in reality they were supporting each other.

Katherine grasped the doorknob and, at first, the door seemed locked. She shook the door, but it did not open. Finally, she pushed the door with her shoulder and it opened. She stepped inside, signaling for Sarah to follow. It was dark yet familiar. This was her old turf. It was quiet except for the sounds of the River. There were papers all over the floor and it smelled like a damp musty basement, although to Katherine this smell was like potpourri compared to what she and Sarah had just experienced.

The quiet was interrupted when Katherine heard a car approaching. She looked through the crack in the door. A car was moving slowly, coming toward the buildings. Katherine's instincts told her to open the door and seek help, but, for some reason, something beyond instinct controlled her actions as she held steadfast and continued to watch. The driver turned off the headlights as the car neared the buildings. Katherine could not tell who was inside the car, nor did she want to wait around and see. With all that had happened, she felt the best thing she could do was to find a place to hide. Unknown to Katherine, she was on the right track. The figure inside the car was Slick.

Katherine and Sarah moved further into the building. Katherine noticed several doors. She remembered the basement parties she and Melody had attended here. She was right; this was the door to the basement. She grabbed Sarah's hand and they cautiously made their way down the steps. With each step came a creaking noise. As they reached the bottom of the steps, they saw trash-cans and shadows, as the moon shone through the broken window. Katherine noticed a door that led to the outside of the building, but she knew they needed to rest, especially Sarah, before they attempted to move on. Katherine decided to hide under the steps.

Slick entered the first building. He opened the door and the stench almost knocked him out. To Slick, the smell was a combination of rotten eggs and horse shit. He moved cautiously into the building. He could hear the rustling of papers as the soft night wind blew through the broken windows. He was about to take another step when a man stepped out from behind a wall and stood in front of Slick smoking a cigarette. Slick jumped back. The pungent odor along with the man's grotesque appearance repulsed him.

"What in the hell do you want? Get the hell out of here!" the man yelled.

"I don't think you know who you're fucking with, you worthless piece of shit!" Slick said, as he stepped back.

The man did not flinch. He moved closer to Slick, as he spoke. "That gun doesn't scare me! People come in here all the time with guns! I have nothing! Get the hell out of here! You're wasting your time! I have nothing!"

"You're right! You don't have anything I want. I'm looking for a woman and her daughter. I believe I saw them come this way."

"I chased them away. I told them to get the hell out of here, just as I am telling you! Get out! Get the hell out!" The man shouted as he bounded toward Slick.

Slick reflexly fired his gun. The bullet hit the man in the chest and he fell to the floor. Slick left the building without taking the time to see if the man was dead or alive. He also didn't notice that the man's cigarette had fallen onto several papers.

Drenched with fear, Katherine and Sarah heard the shot, but did not move. It took all of Katherine's strength to hold Sarah steady. They were terrified as they experienced a sinking tranquillity while hiding underneath the steps. It was almost like being buried alive Katherine thought. Sarah's fearful shaking provided a quiet rumble. Their worries intensified when she heard the sound of a squeaking door above.

Someone had entered the building. Katherine was sure of this when she heard the footsteps above them. They were trapped. Even if she wanted to run, Sarah couldn't. She hoped that it was Glen or the dirty old man.

CHAPTER FIFTY-SIX

Glen, Ganeli and John had just crossed the bridge when John noticed smoke coming from a building in front of them. Glen saw something even more alarming, the car in the abandoned parking lot looked like the one he had seen pulling away from Friendly's Diner.

"John, I think that's the car!" Glen said, as he pointed toward the lot.

"Are you sure?" John asked.

"If not, we'd better make damn sure," Glen replied, as he drove toward the car. They came to an abrupt halt next to the car. Glen was the first to jump out.

Glen approached the car with caution, gun in hand. The car was empty, but, as he opened the glove compartment, he noticed traces of blood on the front seat. The car was registered to Angie Smith. Glen was just about to close the car door when he heard a thump coming from the trunk. He thought that John or Ganeli had made the noise, until he heard it again.

"John, open the trunk. I heard something!" Glen yelled out.

John grabbed a crowbar from his car and, within seconds, the three men stood aghast as they looked upon a woman, her hair soaked with blood. Ganeli and John carefully removed Angie from the trunk. She was still alive and she began to fight viciously, screaming like a cat striking a haunting dog. It was evident that she was in shock.

While John called for help. Glen headed toward the front of the building and directed Ganeli to check out the back of the building. As Glen entered, he saw a fire in the distance. He checked to see if John was following, then put a silencer on his gun as he waited.

"I've called Martha, she's sending back-up. Someone had already reported the fire, so help should be soon. I hope we're not to late," John said as he rushed up to join Glen.

"Let's go," Glen said, holding the gun to his side. John led the way into the building. There was smoke everywhere and neither man could see a thing.

As John yelled, "Let's get out—," his words ceased abruptly as he was struck by two bullets. He fell toward Glen, who pushed his body into the fire and ran out of the building. Glen looked for Ganeli, but saw no one, as Ganeli was moving in the opposite direction circling the buildings.

*   *   *

As Katherine heard the footsteps coming closer she held Sarah tightly. She knew they would be found. What could she do….?

"I know the two of you are down here. Come on out, I won't hurt you. All I want is the list," Slick said, as he reached the bottom of the stairs.

Katherine's fear surged. Their assailant was within a few feet of them. Peering between the garbage cans that separated them, she could see his feet. Just then, a mouse ran across Sarah's foot and she screamed. Slick moved toward them, knocking over one of the garbage cans. Impulsively, Katherine leapt toward him and the fight for survival was on. Sarah continued to scream.

Katherine grabbed Slick and held on, yelling, as he flung her around the dark indistinct basement room. "No! No!" she shouted. "We haven't done anything! Run, Sarah! Run! Get out of here!" Katherine screamed hysterically as she fought.

The gun went off toward the ceiling and, before Katherine could see it coming, a piercing blow struck her face and she plummeted to the floor. Slick fired another shot in her direction. Katherine did not move.

Ganeli heard the shots and screams as he entered the building, his gun in hand. He ran toward the sounds, his hands shaking as he moved toward the basement door. Glen also heard the shots and ran toward the back entrance.

Sarah's screaming was relentless as Slick grabbed her and pointed his gun at her head. His torn shirt draped across Sarah's face.

"Where's the list?" he demanded. Sarah continued to scream. "Shut up! I said, where's the list?" He clutched Sarah so tightly she could hardly breathe.

Katherine tried to move. The bullet had only grazed her head. As she looked in the direction of Sarah's muffled voice, her blurred vision saw two figures. She knew one of them was Sarah.

The back door to the basement flew open as Glen kicked it in. He immediately fired a shot at Slick. As Slick fell toward Katherine, pulled Sarah down with him. One arm was clutched around Sarah's neck; the other arm stretched out in front of Katherine.

"The only one getting a list today is me," Glen said, as he beamed his flashlight in Slick's direction.

"Oh, my God! No!" Katherine screamed. The arm lying in front of her bore a five-leaf clover tattoo. It was Nick. "Nick! Nick, why? What are you...?" she yelled, devastated.

Nick turned toward her, still holding onto Sarah. "Katherine...Katherine..."

"Don't hurt her! Don't hurt her! She's your daughter, Nick! Please don't hurt her!" Katherine cried as she tried to come to grips with what was happening. "Please...."

"Katherine," Nick muttered, then he passed out.

Ganeli stopped on the stairs when he heard Glen speak.

"Isn't this cute? Mom, dad and the secret daughter, all together again. Forget that fatherly bullshit! I want the papers!" Glen snatched Sarah away from Nick and pointed the gun to her head. "Give me the papers, Katherine, or I will kill her!"

"Officer Glen! Please! Why are you doing this? It's all my fault! Please...let Sarah go!" Katherine pleaded, terrified.

"Why? I'll tell you why. It's the least I can do before you take your last breath. Money—damn money! It's all about money. My mother washing floors and my father cleaning shit off toilet seats for a living. Both of them are dead without a damn thing to show for it. I'm not going to die penniless, remembered only for the dirt that covers my grave!

"When Riggins called on me to help secure his fortune, he paid me well. I lied for him, I protected him and I killed...Manelli...and Marcus...and Trimmer and Albright! All of them had threatened to expose Riggins. They were the ones who stole millions from their clients. The only thing Riggins did, was show them how to do it, and for that favor, they had to pay him money. When those corrupt bastards got tired of paying, they threatened to expose him. He paid me to protect him. Yes! I did it for the money! The money was good and will get even better when I give him the list."

"Now, you know why I want that list. And...I want it now! No one will ever see a name or connect him to anything. Where's the list?" Glen shouted.

In disbelief, Ganeli moved quietly up the stairs and out of the building. Outside, people were beginning to gather. He heard the distant sirens of the fire trucks. He concentrated on helping Katherine and Sarah as he moved to the back of the building.

As Glen's demands for the list became almost psychotic, Katherine continued to protest. "I don't have the list! It fell out of my pocked when we crossed the bridge. I had to let it go or I would have lost Sarah. Please, let us go. I don't know who's on the list, I swear to you! Please let us go, Officer Glen!" Katherine begged and began to cough as smoke seeped into the basement.

"You liar! Do you think I'm some kind of fool?" Glen shouted, as he clutched Sarah tighter. Sarah listened, gasping for air.

"No!" Katherine screamed, moving toward Glen.

"Move again, and I will kill her! By the time I count to ten, you'd better produce the list, KATHERINE!" Glen was desperate. "One!"

"Please!" Katherine cried out. "I don't have it. Kill me! Please let Sarah go."

"Two...three...four...five..." Glen continued to count.

"I swear to you on my father's grave, I don't have it. Please, let her go. It's my fault that I lost it, not Sarah's. Please let her go," Katherine pleaded.

"Six...seven...that's it!" Glen shouted.

"No!" Katherine cried out, coughing.

"EIGHT!" Ganeli yelled out, as he fired two shots into Glen's back. Glen fell to the floor.

Ganeli helped Sarah and Katherine to their feet and embraced them. As they approached the door, several police officers came running in. "Is everything alright? What happened?" one asked.

"Everything is okay. The man in the corner has been badly injured. The other is dead. I have these two," Ganeli responded.

He gently escorted Katherine and Sarah out of the building.

EPILOGUE

Rice and his men arrived on the scene as Ganeli led Katherine and Sarah out of the smoke-filled building. Rice's eyes widened as his car approached the building. It was like a scene out of the movies. The noise was deafening as shrill sirens, blaring voices and patrol cars filled the streets and police directed the traffic. There were ambulances and people everywhere, along with reporters and cameramen who were trying to catch a glimpse, or a picture, of Katherine and Sarah, or their assailants and finding out what led to the climatic ending to one of New York City's biggest stories.

The flashing lights from the cameras were blinding, and the overhead lights from the helicopters could be seen from miles away. There were young children standing with their eyes bubbled open as they clung to their mothers' waists, not understanding what had happened.

The stench of the burning building was everywhere as Rice ejected himself from the car. In the midst of all the noise and confusion, Rice saw Katherine, Sarah and Ganeli. His pace quickened as the reality of their survival ignited him. Their clothes were bloody, ravaged and reeking with the smell of the environment that moments ago besieged them. A blemished look appeared on Katherine's face as she watched the stretcher carrying Nick being wheeled past them. Neither she nor Sarah wanted to look at Nick's face, but were unable to tear their eyes away. As they watched the stretcher being loaded into the ambulance, Katherine and Sarah let out a sigh of relief as they slowly made their way to Detective Rice's car, with Ganeli leading and supporting them. Rice could not believe what had happened as he and his men looked around. The bloody sight of Katherine gave him chills.

Once seated inside the car, they gazed into the crowd. Unfamiliar faces were pressed like play dough against the car window trying to get a closer look at them. As they waited for Rice to drive away from the scene, each of them thought about the recent events in their own way.

Ganeli was relieved that he'd gotten there in time and was able to save them, though he knew it would take a while to repair the damage. He wanted to think of himself as a hero, but he knew the repercussion of his involvement would diminish his only moment of triumph.

Katherine was exhausted. She was not able to believe the cruel nightmare that she'd been living the past couple of days was finally over. Unable to understand how and why her life had become so entwined in this mishap, she looked at Sarah and though about Nick, a man who now seemed so different. Katherine wondered if things would have been different if she had told him the truth about his father. *What would all this mean?* She thought, as she tried to put Sarah's and her life back together. Her thoughts scrambled as she held Sarah close to her.

Sarah was confused and tired and did not quite understand everything that had happened. She found it difficult to comprehend why she had not been told the truth about Nick and why, if he was her father, he had tried to hurt her.

Rice started up the car and drove away. All were happy that their ordeal had finally ended, as they sat back and absorbed the tranquility inside the car. From afar, Katherine saw the Willis Avenue Bridge and the murky waters of the Harlem River. She thought about how she had almost lost Sarah, and felt comforted because she was safe. Katherine knew Sarah would have questions; questions she would have to be prepared to answer and silence would not be an option.

As the car distanced itself from the crowd, a statuesque man arrived on the scene. It was Riggins, and he wanted the list...